A BRAZEN CURIOSITY

LYNN MESSINA

potatoworks press
greenwich village

To Joyce, without whose careful copyediting I would have embarrassed myself again and again. (Tumbridge Wells!)

CHAPTER ONE

All through dinner Miss Beatrice Hyde-Clare imagined tossing food at Damien Matlock, Duke of Kesgrave. The projectiles varied depending on the course—fish patties with olive paste, stuffed tomatoes, veal cutlets, poached eggs, fillets of salmon, meringues with preserves—but the impulse remained steady. At one point, while he was correcting their host, Lord Skeffington, on the number of ships under Nelson's command during the Battle of the Nile, she envisioned hurling an entire plate of eels *à la tartare* at his head. The thought of him shaking parsley loose from his golden curls amused her greatly, and she smothered a grin at the image of bread crumbs affixed to his sternly set square jaw.

Everything about the duke was sternly set, from his broad shoulders shown to advantage in superfine cut so perfectly even Weston would stare to his opinions, frequently expressed with a faint sneer he didn't condescend to hide. His height was imposing—a few inches above six feet—and he looked down on his fellows with bored indifference, as if scrutinizing a particularly uninteresting colony of ants.

His attitude was hardly astonishing, given the way the beau monde bowed and scraped in his lordly presence. A man of his circumstance—handsome demeanor, elevated status, inordinately fat purse—was allowed any trespass, and Bea had little doubt that if he suddenly ran his host through with a sword, Skeffington would promptly apologize for bloodying the blade.

Truly, Bea had never met such an insufferable creature in the whole of her life, and it had taken but a few minutes in his presence for him to become the focus of her most ardent dislike.

Forty-eight hours later, it required all her self-control not to fling a spoonful of lemon ice in his direction.

'Twas an unusual experience for her, for, if anything, Beatrice Hyde-Clare was a mild-mannered young lady whose emotions rarely strayed outside the accepted boundaries. She lamented the death of her parents when she was barely out of leading strings, honored her aunt and uncle for taking her in and treating her with generosity if not kindness, and respected her cousins, whose youth and enthusiasm she sought to temper with her age and experience. She'd never taken an instant dislike to anyone before, not even to Miss Otley, a classic English beauty—pale skin, rosy cheeks, pouty lips and light-blue eyes defined by dark lashes—who had entered the drawing room two mornings before like a queen greeting her subjects. As the young woman, reputed to be an heiress of significant worth, made sniping comments about Bea's unmarried state at the ripe old age of six and twenty, her victim merely smiled warmly and complimented her on the sweeping confection she balanced on her head. Indeed, the towering achievement of millinery perfection, bedecked in feathers and swathed in silk, was far too grandiose to simply be called a *bonnet*. Bea, whose own collection of hats did not extend beyond practical mob caps, wondered aloud if there remained on the isle any ostriches with plumage left.

Delighted with the profuseness, Miss Otley assured her there were not.

Naturally, such extravagance appealed to Flora, who instantly offered herself up as factotum, volunteering to fetch and carry anything the young lady might require.

Bea was hardly surprised, for her cousin was only nineteen and easily impressed by displays of both wealth and confidence. Flora's brother, older and wiser by two years, found this sudden devotion to be laughable and made a series of cutting remarks about his sister's obsequiousness that put her on the defensive.

As the two started to bicker, Bea had thought, Oh, yes, it's going to be a delightful week in the country at the Skeffingtons', with Flora toadying, Russell mocking, and Kesgrave condescending.

When she'd agreed to accompany her aunt to her old school friend's house for a gathering in the Lake District, she'd anticipated a relatively quiet week of reading and long walks though the countryside in the cooling warmth of mid-September. She'd known her cousins' fondness for squabbling but had assumed Russell would be too busy fishing or shooting to tweak Flora's ego.

Although her reasoning was sound, it had failed to allow for the possibility that it might rain for three days straight. If she'd realized she would be at the mercy of unfavorable weather, she would have politely declined the invitation like her uncle, who claimed to have a prior commitment.

To be fair, Lakeview Hall was supremely comfortable, with its opulent Jacobean architecture and refined colonnades, and she had thoroughly enjoyed her tour of the manor, almost as much for Lady Skeffington's amusing stories about the various rooms as for the grandeur of the structure itself. And she could not have wished for more hospitable hosts, as his lordship was an amiable man of fifty-five years whose impressive height and intimidating black brows belied a kind heart, and her ladyship—only a few inches shorter and dauntingly poised—was charmingly self-deprecating and generous with both her time and her home.

But these advantages did not compensate for the weather, which seemed to be taunting the guests, as the skies had cleared that afternoon just long enough for the gentlemen to gather their gear, arrive at the lake, cast their rods and catch but a single fish among them before clouding up again and raining torrents. As the only bounty of the day belonged to Kesgrave, it appeared as if even Mother Nature was conspiring to confirm the duke's estimation of himself, a development that peeved Bea greatly.

Her refusal not to attend the house party, however, would not have carried any weight with Aunt Vera, whose sharply pointed chin, off-center nose and cloud-gray eyes gave her a perennially disapproving air. As the impoverished relation, Bea went where she was directed and did what she was told. Naturally, if she wanted freedom and independence, she was welcome to make her own way in the world.

Her aunt and uncle were fond of her, of course, in the way obligated by the familial bond, but they would never stand the expense of a separate establishment, and Bea would never expect them to. An unmarried woman of her advanced age was uncontestably a failure and did not deserve to be rewarded with comfort and quietude. Rather, she was duty-bound to make amends by offering herself as a companion to her aunt or governess to her cousins' children.

Bea knew both prospects to be unappealing, and yet the threat of such a future had not been enough to shake her free from the crippling shyness that had made her first season such a disaster. Like any miss fresh from the schoolroom, she had approached her social debut with a mix of anxiety and excitement. Having no illusions about her appearance—plain features, dull hair, slim build with unexpectedly sharp shoulders that her aunt sometimes described as ideal for fencing—she nevertheless believed the spray of freckles across her nose lent her otherwise ordinary face an appealing whimsy.

How wrong she had been!

It had taken only a few weeks for her to realize that her charming freckles were as drab as the rest of her.

Yes, drab.

That was the word most frequently applied to her during that debut season, first uttered by Miss Brougham, an insidious heiress whose vanity demanded sacrifices, and quickly adopted by the *ton*. Already prone to diffidence, she'd found herself entirely tongue-tied and incapable of speaking without a humiliating stammer. It didn't matter the quality of reply that was required of her: Benign observations befuddled her as much as bon mots.

Even now, years later, she was still stunned to realize the depth of her insipidness, for in her own head she was quite interesting: clever, decisive, adroit. The difference between who she perceived herself to be and who she actually was was vast, and if she had any fight left in her, she would resent how easily she'd succumbed to everyone's low expectations, including her own. Alas, she'd long ago used up whatever portion of willfulness she'd inherited from her parents, which was why she was sitting in Lady Skeffington's elegantly appointed dining room glaring daggers at the pompous Duke of Kesgrave and imagining coffee custard *à la religieuse* dripping down his handsome face.

She assumed she wasn't the only person in attendance who wished she was somewhere else. Lord Skeffington's son, Andrew—possessed of his father's ferocious brows and his mother's gentle green eyes, an attractive but disconcerting combination—had been tapping his fingers against the tablecloth from almost the moment they'd sat down, as if counting the seconds until he could leave the room. His friend Amersham, an earl whose soft features and distracted air hinted at a compliant nature, was also eager to retire, although he revealed his impatience in a more subtle way, every so often darting his eyes to the door.

By contrast, Lord and Lady Skeffington were delighted by the turn of the events, for they loved showing off their hospitality and the rain provided them with constant opportunities. Just that afternoon, they had taught the party how to play a new card game based loosely on baccarat that his lordship had devised and proposed the performance of a play that her ladyship had written.

Beatrice had cringed inwardly at the prospect of an amateurish production performed by the guests of the house party. Flora and Russell would be useless, for their voices froze up and their words became stilted whenever they tried to tell a lie. Their mother, though better suited to obfuscation and half-truths, had the disconcerting habit of chortling with discomfort whenever a gentleman gave her his complete attention. The ravishing Miss Otley seemed to possess just the right amount of drama, but Beatrice suspected she was too pleased with herself to ever consent to be someone else. It was unlikely that her parents would agree to it either, for the only reason Mrs. Otley had attended the event was to form a connection with the family. Her husband, a pinched-faced gentleman with a penchant for bright colors—tonight he sported an emerald-green waistcoat—and a hint of commerce beneath his fingernails, for he had made a vast fortune in the spice trade, was equally single-minded. The Skeffington heir would propose to their daughter if they had to stay in the soggy countryside for the next ten months.

Beatrice could hazard no guess about Mr. Skeffington's thespian talents, nor that of his friend's, but it struck her as implausible that either young man would willingly acquiesce to a theatrical presentation. That afternoon, they had forcefully pooh-poohed any suggestion that they play a ramshackle version of baccarat and had set up their own game in the study across the hall from the front parlor. After an interval, they were joined by his lordship's cousin Michael Barrington, Viscount Nuneaton, a dandy with exquisite taste and an affect of disinterest so finely honed Bea wondered if he knew he was in the Lake District at all. With his impeccable Bedford crop, high shirt points and satin breeches, he seemed rather convinced he was still in Mayfair, and the surprise of discovering he was not only in the wilds of Cumbria but also expected to participate in a performance there would be an exceedingly unwelcome one.

That left only the Duke of Kesgrave to assume multiple roles, a prospect that was very much beneath his dignity. Indeed, his contempt for the endeavor was so keenly felt, Beatrice was inclined to promote the project just to watch him suffer. She didn't doubt he would perform horribly in his role, and she delighted in the possibility of the company hurling rotten tomatoes at his head in disgust.

Beatrice was so diverted by the idea of sour tomato juice trickling into the duke's eyes, she didn't realize the meal was over until the ladies stood up.

The drawing room at Lakeview Hall was as opulent as the dining room, and Lady Skeffington gracefully presided over the tea service while accepting compliments on her elegant furniture.

"The sheen on this brocade is wonderful," Mrs. Otley said as she ran her fingers over the blue settee. Like her ladyship, she was in the middle of her fifth decade of life and rouged her cheeks in hopes of drawing attention away from the evidence. Unlike her esteemed host, she was barely five feet tall and a little plumper than was flattering to her round face and pale blue eyes. "And it's so silky to the touch, I'm in awe. I must also commend your table, as I recognize quality craftsmanship when I see it. Naturally, I will not embarrass you by asking its provenance, but I hope you know that I, at least, appreciate your willingness to spare no expense to turn a room out in style. So many people feel compelled to pinch their pennies."

Although Mrs. Otley did not appear to have a particular person in mind with her comment, Beatrice watched her aunt stiffen her shoulders at the implication that she didn't appreciate extravagant design.

As if a grave misunderstanding had taken place, Aunt Vera rushed in to assure their hostess that she, too, valued quality. Nevertheless, she didn't hesitate to add that she also held comfort in equal esteem. "It would never do to become so luxurious in my notions that I cannot enjoy my possessions. What is the purpose of having a lovely Axminster carpet if you never get to see it beneath the drugget?" she asked, tightening her lips as if such an injustice had just been perpetrated.

Mrs. Otley agreed and then launched into a catalog of all the beautiful rugs she'd seen debased by mud and rhubarb pie. "Sometimes, a well-placed drugget does not go amiss."

Nodding in accord, Aunt Vera suggested that perhaps the solution was to train one's servants better so that boots were properly scraped before entering the establishment and pie was appropriately served in the dining room or at the breakfast table, where it belonged.

Around and around the ladies went, agreeing and disagreeing with excessive cordiality, and Beatrice marveled that the two women considered themselves friends when they so assiduously vied for Lady Skeffington's approval. Had it been like this when they boarded together at Mrs. Crawford's School for Girls three decades ago or was it a more recent development? Perhaps it stemmed from the fact that Aunt Vera, who lived comfortably on the margins of society with characteristic humility, did not spend as much time with Lady Skeffington as her rival, who had made it vibrantly clear that the two women saw each other frequently in London.

Now Mrs. Otley was determined to draw the two families even closer with the marriage of her daughter to her ladyship's son. It made perfect sense, of course, for nothing was more natural than joining wealth and beauty with wealth and rank. That Aunt Vera's intention in accepting the invitation to Lakeview Hall had been exactly the same—the two new, entirely superfluous gowns she'd bought Flora for the visit stood as testament to her commitment—in no way mitigated her disgust at what she considered Mrs. Otley's blatant attempt to social climb. Her mother had been the daughter of an earl, which was considerably more impressive than the lowly baron who'd sired her school friend, and if anyone was going to secure a titled husband, it would be Flora, not Emily.

As far as Beatrice could tell, Mr. Skeffington, who had just entered into his four-and-twentieth year, was not aware of his prize status, for he seemed neither interested in the two young ladies nor afraid of them. Beatrice rather thought a little healthy fear would serve him well, as her Aunt Vera wasn't beyond a spot of thoughtful manipulation if it would bring about a consequence much to be desired. She didn't know to what level of infamy Mrs. Otley might sink, but given the competitive streak she'd demonstrated thus far, Beatrice imagined it would equal or exceed her aunt's.

Although their mothers sought to pit their daughters against each other, Flora and Emily refused to comply with their wishes. Flora, who was pretty in an understated way, with straight auburn hair, hazel eyes, even white teeth and a dowry that could be described as liberal if not lavish, was far too much in awe of Emily to do anything but admire her silently and wait to be addressed. At that very moment, she sat on the settee, across from the fire, in full anticipation of what the other girl would say next. When Miss Otley finally did say something, it was to confirm that the shade of blue in the room was as flattering to her complexion as she suspected.

"I have never seen a shade of blue more flattering," Flora said earnestly before realizing the comment gave credit for the felicitous arrangement to the wrong party. "I mean, I have never seen a complexion so willing to be flattered by blue as yours."

Beatrice, observing the exchange, rolled her eyes and decided it was the most inane thing she'd ever witnessed. If she were inclined to mischief, she would have tried to focus their attention on the duke, who would no doubt find their admiration extremely irksome.

No, she thought as another idea occurred to her. She should make the duke the target of Aunt Vera's and Mrs.

Otley's interest. Without question, he was a prize worthy of overturning thirty years of friendship to attain.

That would be far better than watching him pick quenelles of chicken with peas and fruit jelly out of his hair.

Beatrice, however, was not inclined to mischief, as she was a docile woman who had discovered by the age of seven that being dependent on the kindness of family was the same as being at their mercy. Her aunt and uncle, although indulgent with Flora and patient with Russell, expected immediate compliance from her, and being of a practical bent, she delivered it without complaint. Her ability to understand processes and to swiftly grasp the nature of problems made her an indispensable resource to all her relatives. If she sometimes resented their presumption, she was always grateful for the physical comforts they supplied. Her belly was always full and her bed was always soft and her clothes lagged behind the most fashionable trends by only a year or two, which struck her as reasonable.

If she wanted to, she could find things to be discontented about, for there was much injustice in the world, starting with her parents' tragic drowning in a boating accident when she was five, but she saw no value in picking over circumstances she couldn't change. It was simply easier to do what was required of her and then retreat into the privacy of her own thoughts, which she did now as Aunt Vera wrangled with her old friend and Flora worshipped her new one.

She would have preferred reading a book to examining her thoughts, but her evening gown did not have pockets for smuggling useful objects into dinner and the drawing room contained only fashion magazines. She knew there was a library on the first floor, across from the music room, for her ladyship had pointed it out when she'd shown them around the manor house soon after they arrived, but the pace of the tour had been too fast for browsing. Beatrice was moderately confident she could find it again and planned to do so at the earliest opportunity.

The gentlemen did not linger long over their port and

joined them in a jovial mood, enthusiastically discussing the next day's outing, for it seemed inconceivable to them that the rain could continue unabated.

"The wind is strong this evening," Amersham explained, "and will almost certainly shoo away the clouds."

Beatrice thought this observation revealed a deep misunderstanding of the way weather worked, but Lord Skeffington and his son agreed. Viscount Nuneaton speculated as to the ideal wind speed for scattering clouds, and Mr. Otley relayed the story of a river trip down the Ganges made unpleasant by strong gales.

The Duke of Kesgrave, who had refused to let even the most minor inaccuracy slip his notice during dinner that evening or tea that afternoon or breakfast that morning, said nothing. Rather than assume the infamously informed lord knew nothing about the elements, Beatrice attributed his silence to the distracted air he wore. His blue eyes, usually clear with purpose, appeared clouded with abstraction.

Maybe we're boring him, Beatrice thought with amusement. It would serve him right, for being such a tedious pedant for so much of the day.

It was surprising to her that a man of his rank felt compelled to offer corrections at all. If she were a duchess, she would be so busy relishing the privileges of her station, she wouldn't even notice other people. Indeed, she would spend her days doing all the things she enjoyed such as reading and playing the pianoforte and taking long walks and pestering the kitchen staff to make rout cakes and acquiring new skills, like perhaps learning how to drive a coach-and-four. She'd always admired an accomplished whipster's touch with horses and could only assume that exerting such control was thrilling. Sadly, her own experience was limited to a sedate gambol on whatever old nag was grazing half-heartedly near the Hyde-Clare stable.

Obviously, Kesgrave, at two-and thirty, was so accustomed to advantage he didn't notice it anymore, a development that further disgusted Beatrice.

Why was he even there? she thought in annoyance.

The other guests made sense, as Nuneaton was family and the Otleys hoped to become family. Amersham's presence was contrived to tether the Skeffington heir to his estate, for no young man almost in possession of his majority wanted to rusticate in the country without an ally. Aunt Vera's motives for bringing the lot of them to Cumbria were a combination of curiosity and avarice, and Beatrice didn't doubt that her aunt was as interested in seeing her old friend's country seat as she was in securing her fortune for Flora.

But there was no simple explanation to account for the duke's attendance, and it felt to Beatrice as if he had been invited with the express purpose of bedeviling her.

Naturally, such a conclusion was outlandish folly, for Beatrice Hyde-Clare did not rise to the level of person one sought to bedevil, a fact that had the unfortunate effect of bedeviling her even more. Although such testiness was absurd for a woman who had long resigned herself to being a nonentity, she couldn't quite smother it or her irritation with the duke and the rain.

No, she thought upon reconsideration, just the duke.

If she had a whole plate of saucisson de Lyon, she would fling rounds of sausage at him one at a time.

Not long after the gentlemen arrived, Lady Skeffington announced that she would retire, and Beatrice, grateful for the opportunity to end the evening, made her excuses as well. The uneventful day, with its interminable chatter and innumerable cups of tea, had exhausted her, and she expected to fall asleep as soon as her head hit the pillow.

And yet hours later, she was still awake.

After counting sheep, calculating complex mathematical equations in her head, and reviewing the plot of every Shakespeare play—comedies, tragedies *and* histories—Beatrice abandoned the effort. She climbed out of bed, lit a candle and considered her reading options, which were slight. The night before, she had finished a fascinating biography of Viscount Townshend, which had accomplished the seemingly impossible by making her want to farm turnips for the first time in her life. She'd also brought a novel with her, *The Vicar of Wakefield,* but was curiously uninterested in starting it.

Rather, she'd enjoyed the biography so much, she wanted another, preferably one that also addressed agricultural advances in Britain.

'Twas an arcane request, to be sure, but the extravagant library she'd seen, with its floor-to-ceiling shelves stuffed with books, would certainly be able to meet it. Pensive, she climbed out of bed, lit a candle and carried it to the clock to see the time. Almost two. It seemed inconceivable to her that she had been trying to fall asleep for three hours, but there was her proof.

Clearly, a dire solution was needed.

As she slipped on her dressing gown, she tried to figure out who might still be awake in the house and come upon her suddenly. Mr. Skeffington and his friend Amersham, perhaps, as they'd been up late the night before, drinking brandy and playing cards. Russell, who considered the older men to be out-and-outers, might be with them, although he was under strict orders from his father not to gamble. If they were still playing piquet, then they would be firmly ensconced in the drawing room again, which was on another floor.

She was unlikely to bump into any of the Otleys either because all three members of the family considered a good night's sleep to be essential to Emily's beauty. Her mother provided a detailed account of their philosophy at breakfast that morning to explain why she and her husband had risen so late.

"We keep neither town hours nor country hours but only Otley hours," she'd said as she dropped a third lump of sugar into her teacup.

That left only Nuneaton and Kesgrave, she thought as she opened her door and peered into the inky hallway with her candle, but all the single gentlemen were domiciled in another wing. The corridor was empty, of course, and the carpet pile seemed thick enough to muffle her footsteps. If anyone was still awake in his room, he would hear nothing.

Silently, she traversed the hallway to the staircase and scurried down the steps as quickly as possible in the darkness. At the bottom, she paused a moment to find her bearings. If she remembered the layout of the house correctly, she was at the north end of the hall and in close proximity to the music room, her ladyship's sewing room, and library. There were also bedchambers on the first floor, but they were on the south side.

Beatrice held her candle before her to provide as much light as possible in the murky blackness and took several steps into the corridor. Enveloped by the gloom, she tried to recall what the passage had looked like in the bright light of day. Cheerful, she'd thought, with seafoam molding and a landscape painting of the park to the east.

She heard a floorboard creak, and her heart jumped in terror before she realized she was the cause of the noise.

"For God's sake," she muttered under her breath, "the hallway is deserted. Stop behaving as if you've never wandered around a strange house in pitch-blackness before."

In truth, however, she never had. She'd wandered around Welldale House at night with a candle plenty of times, but there she knew every loose floorboard and crack in the wall.

This was different.

Even so, it wouldn't do to let her imagination get away from her. Nothing was hiding in the corner of the hallway except tufts of dust the parlor maids missed in their ministrations.

She remembered that the room was somewhere in the middle of the hallway, so she paused halfway, raised her candle and walked to the nearest door, which, when opened, revealed the imposing shadow of the Skeffingtons' magnificent pianoforte.

Excellent, she thought. I've found the music room.

That meant the library was across the hall.

Lifting her candle in the other direction, she noticed a door was already open and, stepping inside, quickly confirmed that she'd found the library. Weak light from the moon—perhaps the Earl of Amersham's wind theory was correct after all—entered the sprawling room through a series of high, arching windows and illuminated the bookshelves, which lined the walls of the central space. In the middle of the floor, a pair of settees faced each other across a walnut pedestal table buffed to a high shine. To the left of the entrance, stairs led to a mezzanine with freestanding shelves and a cozy reading nook so inviting, she'd wanted to curl up in its armchair the moment she'd set eyes on it.

The sumptuousness of the space thrilled her, for it far surpassed the library at Welldale, which was really just another room for Aunt Vera to use to serve tea. It had books, of course, including several important first editions, but it lacked the munificence of Lakeview Hall. Indeed, its collection, a tepid selection of literature from the past one hundred years, seemed stingy by comparison, a glass of water measured against the sea.

She felt confident she'd find exactly what she was looking for here.

Now, where were the biographies?

The first section she examined contained novels from the eighteenth century, and although she was an admirer of Samuel Richardson and Jonathan Swift, she walked briskly to the next shelf. She read the spines: *Paradise Lost...La Princesse de Clèves...Don Quixote....* Then John Donne, George Herbert, Robert Herrick, Ben Jonson, Henry King.

Realizing the main floor was devoted entirely to fiction and poetry, she climbed the stairs to the second level and browsed the shelves: geography, religion, history. The deeper she went into the stacks, the greater the darkness, for the shelves blocked the light of the moon. She held the candle up to read the section marker—Egyptology— turned the corner and tripped on something so hard it bruised the arch of her foot through her slipper.

She gasped in surprise, the swift breath of air extinguishing her light.

Perfect, she thought, and bent down to retrieve the offending item. It was cold, hard, metallic, long.

A candlestick?

Truly?

Who would be so careless as to leave a candlestick lying in the middle of the floor? She could hardly believe Lady Skeffington would employ maids so slapdash.

As she wrapped her fingers around the stem, she felt something sticky. Some sort of jelly, perhaps? She tried to get a better look at the substance in the dimness. It was futile, however, with her candle snuffed and the moonlight too weak to extend into the aisle.

Distracted by the odd familiarity of the stickiness— maybe elderberry jam—Beatrice strode to the end of the stack where the large windows let in an iridescent glow, faint but lustrous. Once free of the shelves, she turned the corner and there, in the full light of the moon, his blond curls shining like gold and dipping onto his forehead as he looked down, was the Duke of Kesgrave.

And he was standing over the slain body of Mr. Otley.

CHAPTER TWO

Don't scream. Don't scream. Don't scream.

Beatrice chanted the words silently to herself as, heart pounding like a dozen galloping horses, she stared at the dead man in the familiar emerald-green waistcoat. He was lying facedown, his nose pressed against the rug, the back of his head saturated with blood from the hole bashed into the back of his skull with a—

Oh, God.

The fingers holding the candlestick suddenly slackened in dawning horror, and she dropped the weapon that had ended the life of poor Mr. Otley. It landed on the floor with a thud, a loud, echoing, thumping clunk, she thought in dread, and the duke raised his head.

"You!" he gasped in shock.

Yes, me, she thought in terrified understanding, a witness to your villainy.

What would he do to her? Whack her on the head as he had the spice trader? Strangle her to death? Smother her with a book?

He could do anything he wanted, for he was almost a full head taller than she and finely muscled. All those afternoons sparring with Gentleman Jackson like a proper Corinthian had made him well suited to snuffing the life out of her.

What would he do with her body? Leave it in the library for one of the maids or footmen to discover? Bury it in the park? Throw it into the lake so that her family would never know what became of her? Would he forge a note in her hand announcing that she was leaving the Hyde-Clares forever and seeking her fortune on the Continent or in the Americas?

Would Aunt Vera believe such nonsense? Beatrice had certainly never demonstrated enough spirit in twenty years to make a tale like that plausible. The farthest she'd ever been on her own was the northern boundary of their Sussex estate and then only—

Run, you fool. Knock over shelves. Scream!

She knew she had to do something, but she remained there, frozen in fright, a willing lamb to the slaughter.

Goodbye, cruel world.

"Do not move an inch," Kesgrave ordered.

Oh, the irony. Beatrice could have laughed.

But her terror was so pervasive she couldn't manage even that measly response, she thought, disgusted by her own uselessness. Two decades under her aunt's thumb had made her docile, yes, but surely when her life was on the line she could muster the mettle to respond.

One word of protest, for God's sake!

And it was that sensation—a sense of sickening fear that the last emotion she would ever feel was loathing of her own insipid cowardice—that spurred her into action. She reached down quickly to retrieve the candlestick, held it at a threatening angle and said, "*You* don't move an inch."

How weak her voice sounded. If she were a murderous duke confronting her, she would cackle in delight before doing great damage to her person, and she raised the candlestick higher so that it gleamed in the moonlight.

"You will not kill me too," she said, her voice reassuringly firm, and in that moment she not only meant it, she also felt it. She would not die there, in a deserted library in a quiet corner of Cumbria in the dead of night.

But the duke didn't hear her, for he spoke at the exact same moment: "You're going to kill me too?"

Although his words made no sense at all, she was struck more by his tone, by the mix of amusement and incredulousness lacing it. Plainly, he didn't believe she was capable of wielding the instrument with the same effectiveness as he, a supposition that immediately made her bristle. His confidence was maddening. Why was he so sure? Because she was inferior in size and stature, a nonentity with no important acquaintances and few connections, and he was the large, commanding duke with every advantage one could possibly possess? Of all the conceited, smug, self-important notions in the—

And then she heard it: the meaning of his words, not just the tenor.

He'd said *too*.

What did he mean by that?

Who else had she killed?

She looked at the body of Mr. Otley, the blood still oozing over his ear, and then stared up at the duke with fresh horror.

He couldn't possibly think that she had...that she could...

"I didn't do it," she said.

Again, they spoke at the same time, for Kesgrave issued his own denial that sounded very much like hers.

Beatrice knew at once it was a trick. He was trying to throw her off balance in an attempt to disarm her and gain the upper hand. Did he think her an utter ninny to fall for a ploy as facile as that?

She tightened her grip on the candlestick.

Seeing the movement, Kesgrave smiled wryly and shook his head. "I understand your caution, Miss Hyde-Clare, for the situation is as damning for you as it is for me. I discovered the body, but you discovered the weapon. You have no more reason to believe in my innocence than I have to believe in yours, but I'm a rational creature and can look at all the evidence and logically conclude you aren't responsible for Otley's unfortunate condition." He spoke calmly and smoothly, as if determined not to upset the wild beasts in the Royal Menagerie. "I trust you are also a rational creature who will look at the evidence and likewise conclude that I'm not responsible either."

As she was neither a leopard nor a grizzly bear at the Tower of London, she took offense at his tone. "Evidence?" she asked, tilting her head.

"I'm the Duke of Kesgrave," he said simply.

Beatrice wanted to laugh, for the way he cited his rank as proof of his innocence was one of the most absurd things she'd ever heard. Imagine believing that your personage alone was confirmation of your fundamental decency. She didn't indulge the impulse, however, as levity was entirely inappropriate to the situation and she knew how the duke would interpret it—as an indication that she was a weak-willed female unable to bear up under the pressure of the situation. She felt certain his opinion of her was already low and genuinely doubted that he considered any person of her sex to be genuinely rational.

"I was getting a book," she said, providing an explanation for her presence in the darkened room. "After several hours of trying unsuccessfully to fall asleep, I came down here to find fresh reading material. I brought a novel with me, *The Vicar of Wakefield,* but didn't feel quite in the mood to read it, as the struggles of a family that has come down in the world did not suit my mood. I'd settled on a biography and felt certain a library as well stocked as this one would have exactly what I was looking for."

If the duke was annoyed that his importance wasn't enough to clear him of suspicion, he gave no hint as he said, "I too was seeking something to read."

The vagueness of his answer was hardly reassuring. She'd provided as many details as possible to give her account credence. "What or who in particular?"

"Sir Philip Sidney," he said promptly.

The speed of his response was comforting, but the substance made her heart leap in terror. "Poetry is on the first level," she said accusingly, "with novels and story collections."

"*The Defense of Poesy,*" he clarified. "Literary criticism is on this level, next to law texts and horticulture."

Beatrice wanted to take comfort in the specificity of his answer, for it was exactly what she'd been looking for, but she wasn't familiar enough with the layout of the library to confirm the accuracy of his statement. A clever murderer would speak with confidence regardless of fact.

Perceiving her wariness, he snapped, "My dear Miss Hyde-Clare, I've been patient with you because you've had a shock and your suspicions are justified, but you push my forbearance too far. What possible motive could I have had to commit this crime? I not only had no business with an overstepping nabob from Kent but also little interest or interaction. The insinuation that I'd bestir myself to extinguish his life when all I had to do was dampen his pretentions is as ridiculous as it is insulting. I'll thank you to acquit me of all nefarious deeds and focus on the larger matter of who is actually responsible for this monstrosity."

It was an excellent setdown—cutting and dismissive, with the right amount of irritability to imply even issuing it was beneath his dignity—and prior to discovering Mr. Otley's lifeless body, the prospect of being subjected to such ducal acerbity would have terrified her more than the possibility of being in the company of a murderer. But fear had made her brave, and with bravery came the revelation that she had nothing to lose. Other than life itself, she didn't have a single thing on the line, and if the Duke of Kesgrave wanted to make her the mockery of the season, then he was welcome to try. She doubted, however, that he could do more harm than Miss Brougham had done by calling her drab.

She raised her chin and said, "I'm sorry, your grace, if displaying concern for my safety is inconvenient for you. Naturally, your comfort must come before my peace of mind."

If Kesgrave had been taken aback to see her in the deserted library clutching the murder weapon in her hand, he was astounded to discover himself the target of such untempered sarcasm. How dare a mousy little charity case with few connections treat him with so little respect!

No, Beatrice thought, aghast at her own daring, he wouldn't know enough about her to be aware that her parents were long dead and she lived on her aunt and uncle's sufferance. All he would know was that he didn't need to know anything.

"Very well, Miss Hyde-Clare," he said with a sneer, "do tell me how I may put your mind at ease so that you no longer stare at me as if I'm moments away from wrapping my hands around your throat. I'm yours to instruct."

Oh, she very much doubted that.

Nevertheless, she considered the request and wondered what it would take to convince her entirely of his innocence. To be fair, she acknowledged it was exceedingly unlikely that he had been driven to murder by circumstance, for he had everything a gentleman required to be satisfied with life: status, wealth, a pleasing demeanor, the respect of his peers. But just because something was improbable did not mean it was impossible. Could Mr. Otley have uncovered secret information about the duke that required Kesgrave to neutralize the threat in the most extreme manner available to him? Yes, of course. Anyone with such a pitch-perfect sneer obviously had little respect for the comforts and concerns of others. Did Beatrice really believe that might have happened? No, she did not. If anything, she could imagine the duke brazening out the scandal, whatever it was, and making Mr. Otley the victim for his ill-advised tongue wagging.

Bea sighed heavily and felt some of the fear seep out of her.

But she kept her grip firm on the candlestick as she looked down at the horrifying sight of Mr. Otley's battered skull. No longer in terror for her own life, she felt the keen burden of sadness for the one taken in such a brutal fashion. She'd had little interaction with the man personally, save for an exchange over the tea tray the day before that was as pleasant as it was brief, but he was a beloved father and husband and respected gentleman, whose success in India was often spoken of in awed tones. He would be missed.

Aware of how deeply and profoundly his family would be affected by his loss, she decided there was no purpose in waking them up in the middle of the night to alert them to the tragedy. They would have the rest of their lives to mourn their loved one and deserved one final night of peaceful slumber.

But *someone* must be awoken to handle the matter in an official capacity. "I will inform our host of what has transpired while you remain here," she announced firmly, for she had no desire to wait in a deserted library in the middle of the night with a dead body, the killer perhaps only a bookshelf or two away. Although she did not relish the prospect of wandering the empty halls of the large manor house, it seemed like the lesser evil. "I'm sure Lord Skeffington will want to send someone for the constable immediately."

"No," he said.

"No?" she echoed, taken aback by the force of his refusal. Did he have the same concerns about staying behind as she or was his denial motivated by more disreputable reasons? Her suspicions, so recently assuaged, rose again.

"As much as I endeavor to please you in all things, Miss Hyde-Clare"—such exquisitely turned sarcasm!—"I cannot consent to your plan. Revealing that you and I spent time together in an empty room in the middle of the night would put you beyond the pale. I will not allow that to happen."

Aghast, Bea stared at him as if he were crazy. He seemed entirely in control of his faculties, but to spare a thought for the proprieties at a time like this indicated a mind in disarray. "What person of sense and understanding would consider our chance meeting beside a dead Mr. Otley a lovers' tryst?"

He stiffened his shoulders at her tone, as if offended at the implication that he wasn't a person of sense and understanding. Then he said with high-minded determination, "The situation is hardly auspicious for a budding romance, yes, but even the least accomplished gossip in London has created whole courtships out of less and I'm unwilling to subject you to that sort of speculation."

Beatrice couldn't believe they were debating decorum while the dead body of Mr. Otley cooled before their eyes. 'Twas pure insanity—and the Duke of Kesgrave had the temerity to call himself a rational man!

"I don't care about that," she said firmly.

"Well, I do," he announced.

Although it was hardly appropriate for the setting, Bea could not contain the laugh that welled up in her throat, and she giggled with genuine amusement at the stiff-necked duke's admission. Her instinct was to turn his attitude in on herself and take it as a measure of her own repugnance, but she recognized that it pertained to more than just plain-faced spinsters: Without ambiguity or moderation, he saw the world and all unmarried ladies within it as snares determined to entrap him.

Acutely aware of how improper her response was, she quieted her laughter and sought to quell his concerns. "I assure you, my lord duke, that short of your—how did you put it?—wrapping your hands around my throat, I can think of nothing less appealing than being leg-shackled to you for all of eternity. We would all be miserable, but most particularly your poor cook, who would never be able to keep up with the demand for edible projectiles."

Although no offer had been made and the duke himself had stated his intention of never making one, he stiffened his back at her rejection and said, "Excuse me?"

Beatrice admired the way he managed to sound so offended when he was the one who'd offered the insult. She'd been merely trying to assure him they were in agreement. "A private joke, your grace. You wouldn't understand. Now, let us return to the more important issue of how to proceed. To be clear, you would like me to toddle back to my room as if naught had happened and let you handle the matter from here. Do you plan on leaving the body alone whilst you seek out help or do you propose also returning to your chamber and allowing the upstairs maid to stumble across poor Mr. Otley in the morning?"

"Yes, do toddle, Miss Hyde-Clare," he said tersely, resolutely determined to conclude their business as quickly as humanly possible. "You may consider your obligation to Mr. Otley at an end. I will take care of it. How I do so is no more concern of yours."

Given that Beatrice had yet to determine what her obligation was to the deceased spice trader, she could not share the duke's confidence that it was indeed at an end. She knew justice for victims was not an easy thing to come by. The parish constable whom she was so eager to contact would no doubt be the same or similar to the one they had in Bexhill Downs: an older man of indifferent temperament who would rather toil in his workshop than uphold the office to which he had been elected. She didn't blame Mr. Smithson in the least, for being constable of the parish was a thankless job beset by acrimony and expectation, while blacksmithing provided him with solitude and a reliable income for his family. Even if he were inclined to investigate the crime, he had few resources to do so other than posting a reward for information that would lead to the apprehension of the perpetrator.

In this particular case, she actually was in possession of useful information, and withholding it from the constable seemed like an abdication of her obligation to Mr. Otley, not the fulfillment of it.

Her options, however, were limited, for Kesgrave would clearly not be swayed from his position. No matter how rational her argument, he would remain committed to preserving his reputation by insisting he had to preserve hers. She knew this because he was a man and a duke and a pedant who liked to correct his host when he misidentified the number of English ships at the Battle of the Nile, and his kind never compromised, certainly not with a woman.

No, women were merely that thing you shooed away when their presence became inconvenient, like an ant on your picnic blanket.

As unpalatable as she found his point of view, she resisted the urge to counter it with facts and reason. The Duke of Kesgrave seemed inured to any thought or opinion that was not his own. The smarter tactic, she decided, was to pander to his beliefs. If she was going to have to leave either way, she would rather do so possessing all he knew of the gruesome affair.

"You're right, your grace, of course you are. Thank you for relieving me of this burden," she said with sickening sycophancy. To her own ears, her excessive docility sounded faintly mocking, but the duke's expression, which remained placid, indicated he held no such suspicion. No doubt her obsequious tone was directly in line with the way he was accustomed to being addressed. She continued, "I don't know what I was thinking, insisting on being a part of such a horrific scene. No doubt I will have nightmares for a week. I will leave now and allow you to take care of Mr. Otley as you see fit. It's very fortunate you were here. I would be out of my mind with fear right now if I were alone. I'm sorry if I seemed less than grateful earlier."

Kesgrave manfully accepted her apology with a dip of his head. "Naturally, you were discombobulated by the unhappy turn of events. Nobody would expect you to remain clearheaded in the face of such tragedy."

"I'm so glad you were able to hold on to your composure," she simpered, head tilted down so he wouldn't be able to read the contempt in her eyes. Only a toplofty duke with a sky-high opinion of himself would readily believe a female could be so missish. She was offended on behalf of all womankind. "It must have been terrifying for you, too, to come upon Mr. Otley's body in the dark. It was in the dark, wasn't it? I don't see a candle in your hand."

As obvious as this question seemed to Beatrice, Kesgrave noticed nothing amiss and answered with sincerity. "It was dark, of course, as it is night and a single candle does not throw much light, as I'm sure you yourself noticed. But I actually did have a candle. I put it down when I discovered Mr. Otley. I saw a body in supine position in the bright moonlight and raced over to provide help. I knew at once that I was too late, for the wound to the skull was unmistakable. Before running over, I put the candle down on one of the shelves," he explained, looking around as if to point to the spot in question. Unable to find it, he furrowed his brow.

As he did not remark upon it further, Beatrice decided not to draw attention to the detail, but it seemed quite meaningful to her. Either he was lying about the candle, which again struck her as unlikely, or someone had removed it.

Not someone, she thought, as a sudden chill overtook her, *the killer.*

At once, her heart began to race as if she were running a great distance, and she ordered herself not to panic, for it was obvious what had happened. After striking Mr. Otley with the candlestick, the murderer ran forward, toward the aisle Bea had come through, dropping the candlestick in his haste to leave before Kesgrave could discover him. Then, while the duke was distracted by the body, he'd circled around the other end of the shelf to take the replacement candlestick his grace had thoughtfully supplied.

He's gone, she assured herself. He's long gone.

"I see my concern for your welfare was well justified, Miss Hyde-Clare, for you're too unsettled by the ghastliness of the situation to gather your thoughts," Kesgrave said as she stood there disturbed by the order of events. How close they had both come to being victims themselves. Just a few more seconds.... "Perhaps when you return to your room, you can request a sleeping draught to help you slumber."

Although he managed to inject his voice with an admirable amount of concern, she knew he wasn't genuinely worried about her welfare. He simply wanted her to be gone and was not above using whatever means were at his disposal to bring about her absence. But his attempt merely disgusted her further, for only a duke of overweening pomposity would assume one could arrange for any sort of draught, sleeping or otherwise, in another person's home at two in the morning. She couldn't imagine having the temerity to wake up the housekeeper and insist she bestir someone on her staff to make the potion. Nevertheless, Bea agreed readily with the duke's suggestion because it allowed her to linger a few minutes more.

"Indeed, yes, your grace," she said, feigning sudden breathlessness and pressing a hand against the bookshelf as if to steady herself. "I'm far more affected than I'd realized. Why, my head feels faint." She inhaled deeply and exhaled with equal fervor. "Pray, allow me a moment to collect myself. I seem to be having a delayed reaction to the vileness of the situation. My head is spinning and my stomach feels queasy. I will endeavor to compose myself as quickly as possible."

If he was impatient for her to be gone, his response did not reveal it, for her frailty was perfectly in line with his expectations of how a female should behave in the situation. "Of course, my dear, of course. You must take as long as you need. I would insist you sit down, but there isn't a chair handy."

"I will be all right in a moment," she insisted as she continued to consider the matter of candlesticks. Kesgrave's was gone, but Mr. Otley's appeared to have fallen with him, for there was one about four feet away from his left hand. Did the force of the blow cause him to throw the candlestick a goodly distance or had it landed near his hand and then rolled? "Your calm is commendable. I wonder how you can sustain it, having chanced upon such a disturbing scene. Mr. Otley was dead, you say, when you found him? I can't imagine having the strength and constitution to get close enough to him to confirm his status. Did you have to move him around to do so or is this exactly the way you found him?"

"Like you, I recognized him at once from his waist-coat, so I did not have to adjust his position to ascertain his identity. I simply checked his wrist for his pulse, which was absent," he explained. "I was fairly certain where matters stood before doing so, but I'm nothing if not thorough."

Beatrice nodded and filed away the information for later, although she freely admitted to herself that she had no idea what she would do with it. She was acting as if she intended to find and identify the villain who had brutally ended Mr. Otley's life. It was a laudable goal, no doubt, but one that was as impossible as it was impractical. She was no Bow Street Runner to investigate a crime or apprehend a perpetrator. She wasn't even an indifferent constable conscripted to discharge a public duty. She was merely an aging spinster with a sleep difficulty seeking respite in an entertaining biography. To presume to know anything about the inspective process would be pure impertinence.

And yet she couldn't help but feel that the duke's missing candlestick was an important piece of evidence that she should pursue further.

But how would one do that?

"You're looking quite dreadful, Miss Hyde-Clare," Kesgrave said with what appeared to be sincere concern. "You're far too pale for my comfort. I fear you have been much more adversely affected by this incident than I'd originally supposed."

Given that her spell of faintness was feigned, Beatrice perceived in this statement the duke's true feelings about her appearance and knew that he would consider a lady with her meager attributes to be dreadful looking in even the most auspicious of circumstances. To everyone's dismay, including her own, her skin was frightfully pale. The word Aunt Vera used was *wan*. "Do pinch your cheeks, dear, so you don't look so wan," she'd say. Or, "You were always such a wan child."

Beatrice did not appreciate the description, as it implied not just a pallid complexion but a feeble character, which she didn't believe was an entirely fair assessment. Being an orphan required her to depend on the generosity of others, a condition that hardly encouraged strong-minded behavior. When she complied with her relatives' requests, she wasn't being wan, she was being sensible. Too many opinions and she would have been sent to the village to work as a scullery maid for one of the families.

"I must insist you return to your room at once," the duke continued. "As I said, I will handle matters from here. It will be very disagreeable, I assure you, and thoroughly unsuitable for someone with a delicate constitution like yours."

She immediately agreed to his suggestion but stayed firmly rooted to the spot, her eyes focused on the grim sight of Mr. Otley's wound. How did one create such a hole in another person's skull? Could it be done with one single, forceful strike or did it require repeated blows?

Contemplating the effort made her knees weak.

And the blood! There was so much of it, coating the back of his head and soiling the rug. Speckles of it even dotted the wall.

Was that useful information? Bea wondered. If the blood had also spread to the assailant's clothing, perhaps discovering who did it was as simple as locating his dirty laundry.

As reasonable as the idea was, she knew it would not be so easy, for she doubted the constable had the authority to search every wardrobe and closet in the manor. Lord Skeffington would have to grant it, and what host would allow his guests' privacy to be invaded in such an intrusive manner? Even if his lordship did, men like Kesgrave and Nuneaton would not calmly accept the insult.

Poor Mr. Otley, she thought, forever denied justice because men were too arrogant to subject themselves to suspicion.

Beatrice wondered if it was very difficult to remove blood from one's clothing, for she knew very little of the process. Indeed, all she really knew was that her own garments regularly returned to her without the marks and blemishes she'd caused with her clumsiness or inattention. Could washing out blood be as effortless as eliminating, for example, a mud stain?

While she silently pondered the problem of laundry, she considered the fact that Mr. Otley had been attacked from behind. That struck her as significant, for it indicated that he either did not fear his killer or didn't realize he was present. Perhaps he'd arranged the meeting in advance. Perhaps he was discovered unsuspecting by the villain.

The fact that he was still sporting his evening clothes implied he'd yet to retire for the evening. The duke's outfit suggested the same thing, but his cravat, which had been artfully arranged in a no-nonsense Mail Coach earlier, was gone, revealing the broad column of his neck. He, at least, had made an effort to relax—a sign, Beatrice thought, that supported his story about seeking reading material.

"Yes, I shall return to my room posthaste, for I'm utterly exhausted," she said with an exaggerated yawn. Then she looked at Kesgrave. "You must be tired as well, as I know you gentlemen like to play your cards well into the night. Did the party break up only a little while ago?"

"I cannot say, Miss Hyde-Clare, as I did not make up one of its number," he said stiffly. "Neither the company nor the game interested me so I returned to my chamber to read quietly. Even so, I'm not at all fatigued and can handle matters with the utmost competence—as I've observed several times now. As someone who has been on the verge of leaving for fifteen minutes, you seem remarkably inclined to linger. As that is the case, I must ask that you hurry along, if not for your sake then for my own. It would never do for someone to discover us here, dressed as we are. We would both be hopelessly compromised."

His fear of being dragooned into marriage was so intense, she felt a perverse desire to dawdle indefinitely. It was only the body of poor Mr. Otley that prevented her from teasing him further, for the recently slain gentleman deserved more respect than to be a prop in her campaign to increase the Duke of Kesgrave's discomfort.

"Your impatience is justified," she easily admitted, "for I have been appallingly weak in my ability to handle this affair with composure. Every time I think my head has stopped spinning, it starts whirling again and I feel as though I'm about to faint. But you're right. I must think of you, not myself. My presence here doesn't aid you in any way, and I apologize for not making myself scarce in a more timely fashion. I will do so now. But first I must retrieve my candle. This wing of the house is far too dark for me to navigate without light."

Although Beatrice knew her words would not put the duke to blush, she thought showing overblown concern for his concern for himself would at least make him cringe. But his egotism was far too entrenched for him to notice anything amiss. He expected self-effacement as his due.

Poor dead Mr. Otley undoubtedly deserved better, but if she'd had any foodstuff—a teacake, a piece of toast, a single raisin from a scone—in her hand at that moment, she would have hurled it at him with all the force in her body.

What an insufferable human being!

As appalled as she was with his attitude, she smiled sweetly and waited for him to fetch her candle. She hadn't made the request outright, but a proper gentleman would eagerly offer. Seconds ticked by. After several dozen, the duke perceived the subtle hint and brushed past her to look for her candleholder. As soon as his back was turned, she jumped forward and leaned down to get a better view of the body. She was most interested in the soles of Mr. Otley's boots, for she thought she'd noticed a clump of mud clustered there. If so, it would mean that prior to his death, he had been outside. Naturally, it was not unheard of for a man to step outside to smoke a cigar or even to finish a glass of port in the cool night air. But that was what terraces, balconies and patios were for. One did not go stomping among the roses for a moment of quiet repose.

Was that—

No, she thought, pressing closer. The dark spot near the heel of his boot was just a patch of black leather sewn in to hide a hole or an imperfection, not mud as she'd hoped.

"What are you doing?" Kesgrave asked, his tone an intimidating mix of shock, outrage and disapproval.

Damn. She'd assumed it would take him longer to find the candle. She wasn't even sure where she'd left it.

Think quickly, she ordered herself, clutching the candlestick in her hand.

The candlestick!

Beatrice placed the instrument next to Mr. Otley's hip and rose to her feet. "I thought it was best to leave the candlestick with the body, where the moonlight is bright, as much of the room is dark. I didn't want you to lose track of it as you did your own."

She'd meant to prick his ego with her remark and was delighted to see him stiffen at the criticism. She waited for him to explain in detail how the missing implement was not in fact missing, but instead he nodded in agreement. "Good thinking. It would never do for you to inadvertently bring it back to your room."

The thought of sleeping with a bloody candlestick on her bedside table horrified her, and yet without the grisly instrument she felt oddly vulnerable. She still had to return to her room via the deserted corridors of Lakeview while a murderer wandered the halls. What easy prey she would be.

No, he's gone, she told herself firmly. He's gone and has no reason to return.

Kesgrave held out her candleholder, which he had kindly relit.

"Thank you," she said, grasping it firmly with both hands. It had neither the size nor the heft of the candlestick used to snuff out the life of Mr. Otley, but it felt like some measure of protection, if only against the dark.

The duke nodded.

Beatrice still did not feel entirely right leaving Mr.

Otley in Kesgrave's care, which seemed indifferent at best, but she had run out of excuses to delay her departure and nothing more would happen until she was gone. Presumably, his grace would wait a short interval to ensure her removal, then wake up a footman, who would in turn rouse Lord Skeffington. She could only imagine the horror with which his lordship would greet the news that one of his guests had been viciously slain. He and his wife prided themselves on being consummate hosts and yet somehow they had fallen short on the requirements, for no house party that contained a murdered corpse could be described as a complete success. Indeed, it would properly be categorized as a failure.

She did not exactly feel bad for them, as the dead nabob deserved the lion's share of her pity, but she knew well the sensation of having your plans not quite come to fruition as expected and sympathized with their pending disappointment.

Although Beatrice didn't know what in particular the moment called for, she felt some salutation must be offered and after reviewing and rejecting several options, settled on bidding Kesgrave a good night. She wanted to arrange an interview for later in the afternoon to discuss how events unfolded in her absence, but she could not imagine the supercilious lord agreeing to hold a consultation with a female.

With reluctance, she left the library and returned to her room, a journey that took far less time now that she was confident of the route and somewhat terrified for her life. Once inside her chamber, she felt a curious light-headedness and she put down her candle as she sat on the edge of the bed. It was not fear that undermined her composure, but a growing understanding of the full horrors of the past hour. How brazen she had been, snuggling closer to look at the corpse, her mind calm as she examined the mark at the bottom of his boot and her nerves unruffled as she appraised the splatter of blood on the wall. And the way she had spoken to the duke, brashly and boldly, her thoughts clearly articulated without stammer or hesitation. She'd felt none of the intimidation, uncertainty or awe she usually experienced when in society.

A murder scene was hardly society, she scornfully reminded herself, but that just made her behavior all the more remarkable, for surely the former was more likely to overwhelm the equanimity of an awkward young lady.

But now that she was restored to the safety of her room, the recollection of her conduct frightened her, for she had no idea where the audacity came from. Her courage in inspecting the body or addressing the duke had no precedent, and it deserted her now that the moment had passed. The Beatrice Hyde-Clare who had stood in the darkened library seemed like an entirely different woman from her, a stranger with some of her mannerisms, and she could not imagine her ever returning. Indeed, she did not know if she wanted her to, for drawing that much attention to herself could only result in disaster.

And this thought, too, was part of her increasing dismay, for a man had been ruthlessly bashed over the head until he died and all she could think of was its effect on her. Poor Mr. Otley, relegated to the role of a secondary character in the drama of his own death.

It was insupportable, really, and ashamed at the monstrosity of her vanity, she thought again of Miss Otley in all her bright plumage. The beautiful girl would be inconsolable when she learned of the events of that evening, as would her mother.

Bea resolved to be a compassionate and reassuring presence in the morning.

Having decided on a course of action, she slid off her slippers and climbed into bed. Sleep, however, remained elusive, and rather than devote another three hours in useless pursuit, she relit her candle and submitted without complaint to *The Vicar of Wakefield.*

An hour later, just as Sophia was falling off her horse into a stream, her eyelids finally fluttered closed and she was asleep.

CHAPTER THREE

As Beatrice's late-night sojourn to the library had to be kept secret to spare the Duke of Kesgrave's blushes, neither her aunt nor her cousin had any patience with her exhaustion the following day. When she failed to appear at breakfast by half past eight, they both arrived at her door to challenge her lethargy and prod her awake.

They were, it turned out, eager to inform her of what had transpired in the library, for everyone else in the breakfast room had already been apprised of the situation.

"It's a tragedy, of course," Aunt Vera said, sitting at the foot of the bed, her eyes gleaming with impatience. She was not a gossip in the traditional sense, as she did not care to chronicle the comings and goings of well-known members of the *ton,* for she found it presumptuous to speculate about her betters, but like anyone in society, she relished a good story and this one, unfolding beneath her very nose, had an irresistible immediacy.

"A great tragedy," Flora agreed, also settling herself comfortably on the bed.

Bea reluctantly crossed her legs to make space for the pair and marveled at her relatives' morbid excitement. She judged neither of them harshly, for she herself had behaved in a similarly uncharacteristic fashion only hours before. Death was a particularly discombobulating addition to a house party and made people behave in unusual ways. She knew under the fascination her aunt was desperately sad for both Mr. Otley's murder and Mrs. Otley's loss.

"I can scarcely believe such a thing happened while I was tucked in my bed," her aunt added, her tone laced now with grief and confusion, "entirely unaware of the very great tragedy transpiring while I slept dreamlessly."

Flora reached out a comforting hand to her mother. "You mustn't blame yourself. I'm sure there was little you could do. The die was cast long before we entered the picture."

Being in full possession of the facts, Bea found these remarks to be both horrifying and humorous. Certainly, Aunt Vera was a determined matriarch who ruled Welldale House and the Hyde-Clares with frank austerity, but even she could not dissuade a murderer from his purpose. At best, she could harangue him with tips on how to more decorously comply with the demands of the guest-host relationship. For one thing, resist the impulse to sully thine host's library with a corpse and blood.

Aunt Vera closed her eyes, sighed deeply and squeezed the proffered hand. "Thank you for saying that, my love. I know it's true, and yet I must learn to live with the regret. My dear, dear friend does not deserve this and would that I could have spared her this pain."

Flora, who expected nothing less from her mother, nodded her head sympathetically. "Yes, we all feel that way."

As the two women consoled each other, postponing an explanation of what had actually occurred, Bea struggled to remain patient. Without the benefit of a proper night's sleep—or even an improper one—she found herself still deeply unsettled by the murder and uneasy with her own response. If only she had been allowed more than a few hours of rest, she would have a firmer grasp on her emotions.

A cup of tea would help, she thought, casting a long-ing glance at the door. If they were at home, she would have put on a dressing gown, slipped out of the room and gone in search of a pot herself, but being a guest of the Skeffingtons required she don more proper attire before presenting herself in the breakfast room. And proper attire meant proper grooming and that required the assistance of a maid, which her aunt would inevitably notice. There would be no sneaking out of the room unseen and return-ing with the soothing hot beverage.

"If he'd just given us some indication of what lay ahead, we might have known enough to be alarmed," Aunt Vera continued, her tone turning critical, as if irritated at the spice trader for not alerting her to his pending murder.

It was a spectacularly self-absorbed moment, even for Aunt Vera.

"Perhaps he himself did not know until it was too late," Flora pointed out reasonably. "I believe suicide can often be an act of spontaneity."

Perhaps he did not know? Bea thought with wry amusement. One did not write "submit to murder" on one's calendar and then quietly watch the date approach. It simply happened while one was—

Wait a moment: Did Flora just say *suicide*?

Astonished, Bea stared at her cousin. "*What?*"

Sparing her daughter an irritated glance for uninten-tionally disclosing the development she herself had meant to reveal slowly for maximum effect, Aunt Vera nodded vigorously and rushed to share the remaining details. "Yes, Mr. Otley took his own life last night in the library. It's quite the most shocking thing that's ever happened."

"Mr. Otley took his own life?" Bea repeated aghast and confused. She recalled the scene: the candlestick, the dented skull, the blood, the nose pressed against the rug. "But that's impossible."

"There, there, my dear," Aunt Vera said, plainly de-lighted with her reaction. "We are all having a difficult time reconciling what happened. Why, just last night, he and I were saying how delightful it would be for the two families to visit Vauxhall Gardens together in the spring, and now he's gone, taken from this world by his own hand."

Even if one put aside the troubling question of how Mr. Otley could bash himself in the head hard enough to cause a fatal injury, there still was the matter of the candlestick being ten feet away from the body and down the adjacent aisle. No man, she didn't care how skilled he was at tossing darts or lawn bowls, could throw an object around a bend. To believe it for even a second was pure madness. How could the constable concoct such an absurd story?

"The Duke of Kesgrave was the one who found the body," Flora said. "Apparently, it was a dreadful scene. The poor man."

"The duke!" Bea exclaimed. Of course it was he who had arranged the scene to make it appear as if Mr. Otley had killed himself. No wonder he wanted her gone! He couldn't manipulate events to suit himself with her standing right next to him.

Did that mean Kesgrave was the killer? Had she been duped by an autocratic air and an attitude of condescension?

"Yes, the duke," Aunt Vera said, her perverse pleasure at being the bearer of bad news easily overcoming her despair at the bad news itself. "He discovered Mr. Otley when he went to the library to get a book. By all accounts, the sight was beyond terrifying. There was blood."

"A tremendous amount, apparently," Flora added, "for the duke insisted that it wasn't seemly for Mrs. Otley and her daughter to see him until Skeffington's staff had an opportunity to clean him up. Can you imagine? I would think any man who had decided to leave his wife and child to the vagaries of fate would have the decency to choose a more pristine method. Poison, perhaps. Like that Greek philosopher. Socrates, yes? He took a potion that allowed for a very dignified death. I believe he held court until the end."

"Hemlock," Aunt Vera said with approval.

"I would advise all suicidal men to seek hemlock," Flora said.

"A laudable suggestion," her mother affirmed. "Or perhaps an extra dose of laudanum. There are several ways of ending one's life that don't necessitate a full scrubbing by servants before your loved ones can pay their respects."

Bea looked at her relatives as if they had gone mad, for she couldn't believe they were taking the poor dead man to task for killing himself improperly.

But he didn't kill himself!

Mr. Otley was the victim of a cruel attack.

Was the Duke of Kesgrave the one who had wielded the weapon?

Truly, she had no idea. Last night, in the library, such a thing had seemed wildly implausible, and yet she could think of no explanation for why he would tell such a blatant lie other than to protect himself. Making Mr. Otley's untimely death a suicide ensured that the constable would investigate no further. The only person who would benefit from such a turn would be the perpetrator.

The reasoning was sound, and yet she couldn't help but feel that lying to slither out of blame wasn't the way the arrogant duke would free himself of suspicion. Rather, he would stand on his consequence and dare anyone to point a finger. She imagined nobody would, certainly not the village blacksmith whose concern for justice was second to feeding his family.

"All the talk of blood has made Mrs. Otley quite frantic in her grief," Aunt Vera said. "The poor woman doesn't know what to do with herself, roaming the drawing room from end to end and whimpering from time to time. Helen and I have tried insisting that she retire to her room to mourn in private, for the whimpering, although understandable, is quite distressing to one's nerves. She sounds like a cat whose tail is trapped under the leg of a rocking chair, which, at a time like this, is the last thing one wants to think of. But she refuses to go. She says she finds the presence of other people comforting, but there are more things to consider—such as the comfort of those other people. I swear, my nerves are stretched quite as far as they can go."

And yet her eyes glittered with excitement, Bea noted, for a nabob succeeding in ending his own life was quite the most dramatic thing that had ever happened in her aunt's vicinity. Previously, her most oft-told tale was the time she suddenly found herself in the path of a notoriously high-in-the-instep dandy whose cutting remarks were so effective he frequently left his victims stunned for days. Fortunately for her, a goldfinch fluttered its wings, drawing the dandy's attention with its loveliness, and in that brief moment of distraction, Uncle Horace pulled his wife aside, as if out of the way of a rampaging horse.

"Despite my own trials, I'm determined to be as consoling as possible," her aunt said with withering graciousness. "We must be strong for Amelia and her daughter."

"Especially for Miss Otley," Flora said, her tone as admiring as ever as she spoke of the ravishing young lady whose esteem she sought. "This is a setback from which she might never recover. And with Mr. Skeffington on the verge of proposing too! Naturally, that cannot happen now. The stigma of aligning oneself with a family whose patriarch had done himself in is far too great. She will have to remain buried in the country or"—here she gasped—"retire to a nunnery. In either case, her perfection would be wasted on the unworthy."

Bea thought it was foolish to cast the Skeffington heir's pronounced indifference in such an optimistic light, but her aunt agreed readily with her daughter's assessment before emphasizing that God appreciated beauty in all its forms. Flora conceded the point in theory but remained firm in the belief that her idol deserved an admirer with more rigorous standards.

Although Bea thought both her relatives were inclined to extravagant exaggeration, on this topic their respective assessments were accurate. Suicide wasn't a matter that the church or the state took lightly, and the family would suffer far greater consequences as the victim of self-murder than actual murder, something she'd been too shocked to consider when she first heard of the duke's lie. But now that she was able to consider the stark implications—burial at a crossroads rather than on consecrated ground; surrender of his property to the Crown—she knew she could not remain silent. Mr. Otley had suffered enough injustice without compounding the wrongdoing by depriving him of the ability to care for his family upon his death.

No, the Duke of Kesgrave would simply have to admit the truth.

She would make him.

Naturally, she erupted into laughter the moment she had the thought, for there was nothing she could do to make the gentleman speak if he didn't want to. He wasn't a pliable sapling she could bend to her will, but an impervious oak tree. Every decision he had made since attaining his majority had no doubt been done to please himself and please himself only. She would have to devise a plan that was a little more complicated than her simply asking him to do the moralistic thing. She would need to be devious.

It was some indication of her exhaustion that she had quite forgotten the presence of her aunt and cousin, for she was quite surprised to find herself the target of their disapproving gazes.

"Really, Beatrice," Aunt Vera tsked, "I'd expect you to show more sensitivity in the face of such a very great tragedy. A man's life is lost as well as his family's standing and wealth. I'm sure your levity is the even greater insult."

Ah, there was the hypocrisy she was used to!

"You're right, aunt," she said, composing herself at the rebuke, which she felt was well earned. "I apologize for the display of levity. I fear your news is so distressing, it has undermined my ability to respond appropriately."

"I expected it would," Aunt Vera said with a glimmer of pride. To have the honor of delivering such distressing tidings was a rare opportunity. "You were always a sensitive child, more prone to tears than to laughter."

That was true, yes. As a young girl who had become an orphan over the course of one very long afternoon, she'd frequently been morose and difficult to tease out of her moods, which were sullen and serious. But her reaction to Mr. Otley's death was considerably more complicated than a decades-old tendency toward sadness, a fact she could not explain to her relatives. Instead, she kept her eyes focused on the bedcovers and wondered aloud if it was too late to get breakfast.

As far as hints went, it was too subtle for her aunt and cousin, for rather than jump up and insist she get dressed right away, they entered into a ten-minute discussion on the topic, with each insisting their hosts were too thoughtful to remove a single plate from the sideboard before each and every guest had partaken. Although their opinions aligned perfectly on the matter, mother and daughter vigorously exchanged ideas as if they were in robust disagreement.

Knowing her presence was incidental to the conversation, Bea considered closing her eyes and going back to sleep. It was only the thought of the lecture on rudeness that her aunt would subject her to that kept her awake—even though waking someone up to talk at her for forty-five minutes was arguably the greater social transgression.

Inevitably, Aunt Vera and Flora, having reached a consensus on their consensus, turned their attention to Beatrice and chastised her for remaining in bed at the advanced hour of nine-thirty. Knowing it was futile to protest, she apologized for her laziness and rang the bell for her maid, grateful when her family left her to her own devices.

Now all she had to do was get her hands on a cup of strongly brewed tea and come up with a plan to maneuver the Duke of Kesgrave into confessing the truth about Mr. Otley's demise, and everything would be well.

CHAPTER FOUR

By the time Beatrice finished her second cup of tea, she was forced to admit that a self-inflicted death did not spoil the mood of a house party as stridently as one would expect. Tones were hushed, of course, and appropriately somber, but the young men seemed incapable of keeping admiration entirely out of their voices as they discussed the method by which Mr. Otley had ended his life.

"With a candlestick," Amersham observed, shaking his head with wonder as he leaned forward in the armchair. The company had gathered in the well-appointed drawing room after breakfast, ostensibly to relax for a few minutes before the events of the day began but in actuality to gossip. The room was large and well-appointed, with tufted settees, oversize bergères, ornate moldings and imperious ancestors masterfully recorded in oil. "Made of gold, of course, and of considerable heft, but still only a device for lighting one's way. That is to say, it's not a knife, which is more of what one would expect."

"I would have aimed for my forehead," Mr. Skeffington said, inflecting a practical note, "and spared myself the contortions of reaching behind my back."

"I cannot believe a man of Otley's age was agile

44

enough for what you're proposing. I say he took the northern route, carrying the candlestick over his head to strike himself on the back of his skull," his friend said and demonstrated the technique by tapping the area with a spoon.

"Head wounds are the most unpleasant in terms of blood and bleeding," Russell said decisively, before crediting the information to a friend's father who had fought on the Peninsula. His mother, sitting across from him, frowned at the comment, but Bea couldn't tell if she disapproved of the ill-advised topic or resented the fact that as a woman she could not offer her opinion on the benefits of an extra dose of laudanum without appearing unduly macabre. She hoped it was the former, as the conversation was highly distasteful. "Which is why I would never choose the candlestick method. It seems boorish to leave a mess behind when I'm already leaving a mess behind."

Amersham and Mr. Skeffington cackled at this sally, which made Russell, who was unaccustomed to an appreciative audience, blush slightly, while Viscount Nuneaton rustled his newspaper in disgust and muttered, "Ignorant puppies."

He lowered *The Times,* and Bea waited for the older man to issue a stinging rebuke for their disrespectful treatment of poor dead Mr. Otley, whose widow and daughter were upstairs resting—hopefully sleeping—after a tragically difficult morning.

"The pistol is widely accepted as the traditional weapon for honorably discharging one's obligations," he explained. "Anything else is indulgent and inappropriate."

Although the viscount spoke with the authority of his years, which gave him a decade on the other young men, Mr. Skeffington didn't hesitate to contradict him. "Falling on one's sword is also a time-honored tradition. Isn't that how Brutus ended it? Plutarch tells the tale of Brutus asking a friend to help him hold his sword so he may stab himself and when Volumnius refuses, he grasps the hilt with two hands and falls on it."

"Andrew!" his mother exclaimed, entering the room

just in time to hear her son's ghoulish description. "Given your grades and the reports I received from your tutors, I'd assumed your education was a complete waste of time. I'm astonished to discover you've learned something after all."

Mr. Skeffington straightened his shoulders in offense. "Your shock is insulting, Mama. I scored consistently high marks on my mathematical exams, as you well know. Literature, I will admit, was not my strong suit, but I'm capable of recalling some details."

Amersham, who had been sent down from Oxford with his friend at least three times, added, "'Twas inevitable he would eventually manage to absorb a bare minimum of information. Even a stopped clock is correct two times a day."

The comment drew soft chuckles of amusement from several of the room's occupants, including its target and his mother.

Knowing how greatly unsettling death could be, Bea tried to be patient with their humor, which she knew to be of the gallows variety. Nevertheless, she found it grievously distressing to listen to them chatter so frivolously about a man whose life had been taken from him in such a brutal manner only hours before. Weighing the relative merits of the way he'd chosen to kill himself! It was an outrage, and every inch of her longed to scream at the top of her lungs until they all shrunk in fear of her.

Naturally, she did not, for she'd never raised her voice in the presence of company in her entire life. Once, when she was a child newly settled with the Sussex Hyde-Clares, she'd shrieked at her aunt for daring to throw away the worn glove she carried with her everywhere. Yes, it was stained and torn, as her aunt claimed, but she was wrong when she said it served no purpose. It was Bea's mother's glove—a lone, threadbare memento that hadn't been sold off to pay for Bea's upkeep—and the purpose it served was to provide comfort.

How cold Aunt Vera had gotten, listening to a child of six wail as if she'd just cut off her arm with a dull ax rather than merely tossed away what she considered to be a tattered rag. Bea's punishment, immediate and harsh, was made worse by a frigid lecture on the importance of not letting one's affection for one's husband's niece corrupt one's good judgment.

It was the last time Bea had shouted.

Although the urge to scream was so strong she felt as if she would shake from it, she sat immobile on the settee, her expression as serene as a spring morning.

Sitting several feet away from her, also silent, was the Duke of Kesgrave, placidly drinking a cup of tea while perusing the *London Daily Gazette*. His pose was one of complete indifference, almost as if he were alone in the room or at his club. For all he knew, the company could have been discussing the weather.

It was infuriating.

His depraved apathy to Mr. Otley's suffering and the consequences of the lies he'd told was quite the most maddening thing Bea had ever seen in her life. It was somehow more enraging than her aunt's destruction of her mother's glove, for Aunt Vera could not have known the depth of the knife she was twisting. But Kesgrave understood every aspect of his action. He knew exactly what his selfish decision exposed the Otleys to and he didn't care.

Unable to contain her fury, for, like her grief over the glove, it came from a deep and wild place, she spoke with a rage so tightly suppressed you would never know it was there. "What do you think, your grace?"

Next to her on the settee, her aunt gasped in horror, for not only was it remarkably out of character for Bea to speak a cogent sentence in public, it was also outrageously bold of her to initiate conversation with a duke. The Hyde-Clares, as a rule, did not approve of audaciously addressing those more favorably situated in Debrett's than they. They preferred a more subtle approach such as staring in wonder at their betters out of the corner of their eyes.

For more than two decades, Bea had complied unfailingly with her relatives' founding principle, and now suddenly she was talking to a duke. She didn't even have the decency to start slowly, with a knight or a baron, but shot straight to the top rung of the social ladder.

Thank goodness Prinny wasn't in the room.

If Kesgrave found her interest as impertinent as her aunt did, he didn't reveal it as he lowered the corner of the broadsheet to look at her over the edge of the paper. It was a smooth move—just a flick of his wrist—and she resented even that small act because she knew for him everything was so easy to manipulate.

"About what?" he asked mildly.

"About why Mr. Otley would kill himself," she said plainly.

"It would be rude to speculate," he said.

Bea knew she should leave the matter there, for the duke's tone was as firm as it was polite and the rapid beating of her heart made her highly aware of how fragile her cogency was. It had been easy in the early-morning hours to respond impertinently because the horror of the situation overwhelmed her natural reticence, but now she was in a drawing room surrounded by titled gentlemen and her family. It was precisely this milieu that had cowed her time and time again.

And yet she didn't feel herself shrinking in embarrassment or discomfort. The notion that he would take refuge in civility when he had defamed an innocent man for his own, unknown ends further stoked her ire. "Ordinarily, I would agree, as it is the height of discourtesy for people to dissect the matter for their amusement without thought of the poor man's suffering. But your situation is different, as you were the one who found him."

That Bea had just insulted their hosts' son and half their guests did not escape anyone's notice, least of all Aunt Vera, who glared at her angrily.

Too deep into the discussion to worry about her aunt's censure, Bea continued, "Although I can't conceive what an experience like that must have been like for you, having that ghastly image seared forever in your memory, I believe it created a bond between you and the victim. Given that bond, I don't believe that speculation would be rude. Rather, it would be an act of respect."

During this long discourse, Flora turned red and Russell coughed awkwardly. He might have even muttered, "I say, Bea." But Kesgrave kept his steady gaze focused on her and twisted his mouth into a sardonic smile.

Unable to bear the humiliation, her aunt rushed through an apology on her niece's behalf, explaining that she was a sheltered girl who hadn't seen much of the world and was unquestionably unsettled by the morbid turn of events. "As we all are," she added with an anxious glance around the room. "I trust it goes without saying, your grace, that nobody would like to hear your thoughts. Indeed, I can think of nothing I'd like to hear less than your thoughts on any matter." Her satisfaction with this speech, which, Aunt Vera felt, rang with the esteem and deference she hoped to convey, lasted only as long as it took for her to replay it in her head. "I...mean...that is, your grace, I would *love* nothing more than to, um, hear the words you wish to speak. But I have no desire to hear the words you don't wish to speak. Please do keep those to yourself." Then, fearing that her last statement sounded a little too much like a command, she sputtered out an additional clarification. "But, of course, only if you *wish* to keep them to yourself. I leave the matter up to you, your grace, as you know best what you wish to say. Or not to say."

The duke's expression remained wryly amused as he dipped his head at the mortified woman in appreciation of her consideration. "Thank you, madam, for that spirited defense of free will. I agree that we should all speak only when we wish."

To be in the presence of such graciousness—how well he deserved his elevated spot in Debrett's!—made Aunt Vera a little light-headed, and all she could manage in response was a faint titter that sounded like something between a giggle and a hiccup. She colored slightly at the further humiliation but brazened it out with an unwaveringly bright smile.

"As for the other matter," Kesgrave said, the newspaper still perched in front of his nose as if he meant to return to the exact place where he left off at any moment. "If I had to speculate—and to satisfy Miss Hyde-Clare, it appears I must—I would hazard a guess that the motive was financial. After all, money is the root of all evil."

Bea wasn't at all surprised that the duke quoted scripture to support his own purpose. That was what the devil always did. "Actually, Timothy chapter six, verse ten, says the *love* of money is the root of all evil."

Aunt Vera chortled painfully. "Really, Bea, let's do his grace the courtesy of interpreting the Bible as he sees fit. Nobody likes a pedant."

Again, Kesgrave took the opportunity to cozy up to her relative. "Thank you, Mrs. Hyde-Clare. It's a pleasure to be in the presence of a like-minded soul. Some people can be such sticklers for detail."

Naturally, it was beyond all things galling to be called a stickler for detail by a man who could list by name every single English ship that had engaged in the Battle of the Nile and did not hesitate to do so, however irrelevant it was to the substance of his dinner conversation. But Beatrice held her tongue, for she knew it would be futile to antagonize the duke further. He was obviously not going to confess the truth in the Skeffingtons' crowded drawing room, and to lay an accusation against him would be to open herself up to ridicule or worse. She wouldn't put it past the man to claim she was unbalanced or cocked in the head if it would advance his objective. A few more lavish compliments directed at her susceptible aunt, and he could have her signing the papers to commit her dear niece to Bedlam.

No, the only way to have a frank conversation with Kesgrave was to get him alone, which in the current situation presented a significant challenge. In a crowded London ballroom, one could usually arrange a tête-à-tête with a gentleman, for it was easy to hide among the multitudes, but the feat was harder to accomplish at a small country house party. Now that the rain had stopped, the men would be off hunting, shooting or fishing for most of the day, while the women demurely sewed samplers in the parlor and gossiped over tea. Although Beatrice genuinely enjoyed working with a needle and thread, as she counted it one of her particular skills, she resented the forced inclusion. Unless she cried off with a headache, she would be obliged to participate in the activity. It left little opportunity for her to sneak off and confront Kesgrave. Dinner provided its own logistical challenges, for it was unlikely an illustrious guest such as the duke would be seated next to her, and even if he was, the two could not conduct a private conversation without everyone at the table noticing and wondering at its meaning.

Kesgrave would never consent to that. Why would he? It provided him with no advantage. The only way to achieve her goal was to force his hand.

How to do that exactly occupied her thoughts for the rest of the afternoon. Soon after the men went to the lake to try their hand at catching brown trout, the remaining Otleys appeared to accept the comfort of their friends and to discuss what was to be done next. Mrs. Otley, her skin disconcertingly red in places and deathly pale in others, felt they should depart immediately for Kent.

Lady Skeffington reached over to clutch her school friend's hand and insisted that she not make any rash decisions on her account. "Of course, if you feel you must rush back to begin sorting through all the unpleasant details, then you must. But Skeffington and I are not eager to see you off. Indeed, we are grateful for the opportunity to provide solace during such a distressing time. The details, such as they are, will still be there in a day or two when you're feeling stronger."

It was, Bea thought, a lovely speech, for it was delivered with sincerity and warmth, and Mrs. Otley promptly welled up again. Her daughter, whose complexion was as pale as her mother's but without the disagreeable splotchiness, thanked their hostess for her offer and said that they would take it under consideration.

"We are not accustomed, you see, to making decisions on our own," she said, "without the input of my father."

Mrs. Otley attested to this fact with a soggy nod, which surprised Bea, who had formed the opinion that it was quite the other way around. During the short time she had known the family, she'd observed Miss Otley's mother acting as the decisive one. In contrast, Mr. Otley appeared to have cultivated an air of bemused subordination, as if not quite sure why an instruction must be followed, only confident that it should.

"Papa always knew what was best for us," Miss Otley added softly. "That is why this situation is so difficult. The way he has chosen to deal with the latest setback does not seem to be what is best for Mama and me. Rather, it feels calculated to be the worst, which is confusing, as it makes me wonder if he gave any thought to us at all."

Indeed, her tone reflected her confusion, for it was more baffled than distraught, as if the turn of events presented a great mystery that could never be solved. At once, Bea found herself in sympathy with the young beauty, for her perplexity was the product of the Duke of Kesgrave's machinations, not her father's actions.

She deserved to know the truth.

With that in mind, Bea said, "What setback?"

Miss Otley looked at her blankly while Flora drew her brows together crossly, as if annoyed that her cousin would dare presume to address the object of her adoration. Neither mother nor daughter protested the question, however, and Bea decided to press forward. "You described your father as suffering a 'latest setback.' What do you mean by that?"

"Oh, dear," Aunt Vera said nervously, the recollection of the mortifying scene with Kesgrave still fresh in her memory, untempered, it seemed, by the bond she and the duke had formed over Bea's rudeness. "As we discovered earlier, my niece's sensibilities have been strongly undermined by Mr. Otley's...Mr. Otley's"—she couldn't bring herself to use an accurate description and a figurative one eluded her—"predicament...yes, his predicament." She all but smiled in triumph as she stumbled across the right word. "And isn't quite herself at the moment. She needs rest. She's tired. Flora and I woke her up from a sound sleep this morning to tell her the ne—" She abruptly halted her speech as she realized what she was about to say and changed course with an agility that surprised her niece. "To tell her the new day had arrived. Yes, we thought it was time she greeted the new day. But I see now that we did her a grave disservice, for sleep is important for one to deal with the...predicaments...life presents. Please, dear, do run upstairs now to take that much-needed nap. I promise you, your presence will not be missed."

Flora echoed her mother's concern for Bea's welfare, pointing out the dark shadows under her eyes as proof of her exhaustion. "It would not be so pronounced, except your ashen complexion makes the contrast particularly stark."

Although Bea thanked her relatives for their concern—which, to be fair, appeared to be sincere, as they could not conceive of any other explanation for why their silent relation was suddenly talking so much or so pointedly—she did not heed their advice. Instead, she addressed her question directly to the grieving widow. "Did your husband have many setbacks? And was the latest particularly egregious?"

Aunt Vera moaned as if in pain and lay her head against the back of the settee. But Mrs. Otley, who had the greater reason to protest Bea's curiosity, answered without complaining. In fact, she seemed grateful for the opportunity to talk about something that had been causing her distress for a while. "Hibiscus shrubs. With the East India

Company always expanding its influence, Mr. Otley decided to diversify our interests and invested a large portion of our capital in planting hibiscus fields. It was a sensible decision, as our land is well suited to the crop and the hibiscus tea trade with China is thriving. The locals are doing very well with it, and he felt confident the strong Chinese market indicated that the tea would soon find popularity in England. Truly, I cannot fault his logic, for it was solid. Very solid indeed. The tea is such a pretty color, I don't know what hostess would resist serving it. I will send you a tin, Helen, and you will see."

Lady Skeffington dipped her head in gratitude and said kindly, "I would like that very much, my dear. Thank you."

Taking a deep breath, Mrs. Otley continued, "As sensible as my husband's decision was, he could not account for the cruel vagaries of an indifferent universe. Alas, we received notice just a few weeks ago that a very great tragedy had destroyed our entire crop. A fire, you see. It razed everything. It's all gone. All our hibiscus shrubs and all our money. We have been miserable."

With each word she spoke, the widow's composure deserted her a little more until she was openly weeping into a handkerchief on the settee. Deeply distressed, her daughter wrapped her arm around her and murmured words of solace as she, too, began to cry. Flora darted her cousin an angry look, as if Bea were the cause of her friend's anguish, not an unfortunate lightning strike or a careless worker who failed to properly extinguish his candle and caused the conflagration.

"And you said nothing before now, Amelia?" Lady Skeffington asked in amazement as she leaned over and grabbed her friend's hand in comfort. "How you must have suffered, my dear. I'm sure it's always distressing to lose a significant amount of money. Fortunately, Skeffington doesn't invest in the 'Change, but I do get violently cross when he loses large sums at the hazard table. Given Thomas's prior successes, however, I'm sure the situation isn't quite as dire as all that. Oh, I do wish you had said something."

"It was such a cheerful party," Mrs. Otley explained with a sad smile, "and I did not want to ruin the mood."

Aunt Vera, having decided it was her niece who had ruined the mood, rather than Mr. Otley's corpse, reiterated her demand that Bea take a nap posthaste. "You look even more tired now than you did five minutes ago. If for no other reason than concern for my peace of mind, you really must retire to your bedchamber at once or risk falling asleep during dinner."

A protest rose to Bea's lips but she immediately smothered it, for she could perceive no disadvantage in agreeing with her aunt. It was unlikely the other woman would allow her to press the Otleys for more information, and she did not want to sit in the drawing room and engage in meaningless chatter. It seemed her aunt was doing her a favor by giving her an excuse to leave. "You're right, Aunt Vera," she said, not above pandering a little, for she knew how much her aunt enjoyed having her opinions affirmed. "I'm more tired than I realized. A rest before dinner would be just the thing."

Aunt Vera softened immediately. "You'll feel better after a nap, I'm sure."

Bea thanked her for her concern and took leave of the company, fully intending to spend the time quietly scheming in her room. She still needed to devise a way to get the duke alone, so she could figure out what game he was playing. He was an autocrat, to be sure, but she didn't think he would condemn a man's immortal soul out of whimsy and selfishness. There had to be a point to the lie, and she was determined to discover it.

As Bea climbed the steps, she noticed how quiet the top floors were. Downstairs, the servants buzzed with activity, fetching tea, changing the table linens, refreshing the flower vases. Up here, however, she felt quite alone, and as she walked down the corridor toward her bedchamber, she wondered what was the chance someone else would retire before it was time to change for dinner. It seemed unlikely, as Lady Skeffington had just ordered a fresh pot of tea and the ladies were comfortably engrossed in their sewing. If she silently slipped into the deceased man's rooms to look around, who would notice?

She couldn't.

Of course she couldn't.

Poor Mr. Otley had already suffered enough indignities without her adding invasion of privacy to the list. But, she reasoned, much of that disrespect was the product of the duke's actions. The fact that her purpose was to unravel the knot of lies Kesgrave had told and to help the victim's family meant her looking through Otley's things was actually an act of kindness. Her intentions were honorable and sincere.

Even as she told herself she would not do it, for the thought of being caught was so distressing it made her knees week, Beatrice approached the room she knew to be Mr. Otley's and turned the knob. She opened the door, slipped inside, closed it swiftly and paused to marvel at her audacity. She had never done anything so bold as to sneak into a dead man's room.

Daylight lit the chamber, making it easy for her to take stock of her surroundings, which were, for the most part, neat and organized. The bed was made, and Otley's things were still tucked away in the clothespress. By comparison, her room was a mess, with her books stacked on the end table and her various pins and hair ribbons scattered on the vanity. Mr. Otley had only one tome next to his bed, and discreetly, as if trying to hide her movements from an unseen observer, she opened it to examine its contents. She kept the book on the table, at arm's length, because she thought it made her actions seem more benign, then realized how ridiculous it was to pretend she wasn't prying. Her presence alone was all the information anyone needed to condemn her.

Bea picked up the book and looked through it

properly. Too small to be a ledger, it contained details about various business transactions and sundry daily dealings. There were some numbers and calculations, but it was mostly made up of notations about things he needed to arrange or matters to be settled. The comments varied. Yesterday, for example, he jotted a reminder to contact his agent in London to increase his stake in mining stocks. The day before, he observed how well Skeffington's butler, Crawley, discharged his duties and indicated he would compensate him for his competence with a thoughtful gratuity before departing.

She flipped farther back. Six months ago, he ran through a series of calculations to figure out how much money the household could save by using rushlights instead of candles. He must have decided the economy was not worth it, for dated a few weeks later was a note in the margin: "They stink to high heaven! Worse than a cheroot! Loathsome things, both."

Although her experience as both a sneak and an investigator was limited, she recognized the chronicle as an important source of information and debated reading the whole thing now or taking it with her. Both options had their risks, for if she lingered too long, she would almost certainly be discovered, and if she removed it from the room, his wife would most likely notice its disappearance.

The only viable option was to skim as many pages as she could as quickly as she could. Investments, lists of items for purchase, reminders about upcoming engagements, more grumbling about the unpleasantness of tobacco—the diary covered a wide variety of topics and went back almost two years.

When she was done, she carefully replaced the journal on the night table and turned her attention to the chest of drawers in the dressing room, with its neatly folded shirts, cravats and trousers. It felt particularly invasive to poke through a man's garments, and she looked over her shoulder several times to confirm that nobody could see her.

You're being ridiculous, she thought, sliding back the shelf of the clothespress and opening the top drawer, which was filled with more sundry items. She didn't know what she hoped to find. Perhaps a letter tucked under a waistcoat from an enemy swearing to avenge an old injury: "My dear Mr. Otley, how dare you call my team of grays 'adequate'? Watch your back, sir, for I promise you shall rue the day!"

Sadly, the only thing under the cerulean-blue waistcoat was a half-finished cheroot.

Smothering an annoyed sigh, she looked in the sitting room but found little of interest: a couple of newspapers, a pair of silk slippers, some stock reports on mining companies, an issue of *La Belle Assemblée*. Presumably, the magazine belonged to Mrs. Otley, whose room connected with her husband's through the sitting room.

Bea stared at the door that led to the adjacent bedchamber thoughtfully for almost a full minute before deciding she did not have the effrontery to inspect the room of a grieving widow who was only a few floors below. 'Twas a gross invasion of privacy and a risky venture as well. She'd managed to pass—she glanced at the wall clock—forty-seven minutes in Otley's rooms without anyone being the wiser, and leaving now was the smartest way to ensure that her luck held. She would return to her own room, digest the information she'd discovered that afternoon and figure out a strategy for confronting the Duke of Kesgrave.

Now for the risky aspect of the endeavor, she thought as she pressed her ear against the door. It wouldn't do for anyone to see her sneaking *out* of Mr. Otley's room. Hearing nothing in the corridor, she opened the door just a crack and listened again, her eyes closed as she tried to detect the sound of slippers on the carpeted floor. Still nothing.

Convinced that the passage was clear of fellow guests and servants, she opened the door wider and slipped into the hallway. She wanted to run to her room, but fearing that might look suspicious to the unexpected passerby, settled for walking as quickly as she could. By the time she passed over her own threshold, she was out of breath—from anxiety or exertion, she couldn't say.

Her heart rate had only just returned to its normal speed when a knock sounded on her door and Aunt Vera strode in to discuss her expectations of her niece's behavior during dinner.

"I trust you have had an appropriately reviving nap," she said, although all evidence pointed to the contrary, such as a perfectly made bed that had not been touched. "Your conduct, as you know, has been unacceptable to both me and your uncle, who, though not physically present, is here enough in spirit to be mortified by how his brother's daughter has comported herself. You were raised to know your place and not to question your betters. Naturally, I'm sympathetic to the fact that we have all found ourselves in a situation that's highly irregular, for it's an act of inconsideration that trumps even your own recent behavior to kill oneself in someone else's house and can only speak to the depths of Mr. Otley's despair. If there's one thing in the world that should be confined to the privacy of one's own home, it's suicide. But even if Mr. Otley transgressed first, that does not excuse you."

Beatrice, who had sat down at the escritoire to organize her thoughts—another indication for the observant bystander that she had yet to take a nap—kept her eyes down so that her aunt would not see her amusement. How decidedly unfair of Kesgrave to expose poor Mr. Otley to the severity of her aunt's disapproval.

"Given that Amelia and her daughter will be in attendance, dinner will be a less formal affair than last night," Aunt Vera continued. "Even so, you're not to speak. You will sit at the table with your customary silence and the proper expression on your face. A smile isn't suitable to the solemnity of the circumstance, but nor do I want to see your features twisted into a scowl. Do contrive to come up with something appropriately benign. You may, of course, respond if someone makes a comment directly to you, although I do not anticipate such a development. But you will offer no unsolicited opinions. Indeed, when at all possible, you will confine your answer to a single word such as yes, no or maybe." Her aunt, well aware that these lectures to her niece ordinarily went the other way, wherein she chastised her for not being fulsome enough in her replies, shook her head in exasperation. "That you cannot see how your waywardness is adding to the strain under which I'm already suffering is deeply disappointing. I'd expect occasional obliviousness from Flora or Russell, for they are still young, but not you, my dear. You've always appeared to have such a solid grasp of understanding."

Although her aunt was far from the ideal guardian for a young orphaned girl, frequently chafing at the idea that her emotional resources had to be divided among three children, rather than just her own wonderful offspring, she'd done the best she could with her limited faculties. In twenty years, Bea had never resented her for her inability to be a better person and she did not resent her now. "I'm sorry for the distress I've caused you and promise to do better."

Aunt Vera smiled in relief. "Thank you, my dear. I must own, I'm especially anxious because I saw his grace in the hallway as the men returned from their fishing expedition and he asked if there was anything to be done about your outspokenness. I assured him of your habitual reticence, so it will be a great relief to have it restored. Now, before I go change for dinner, let's practice your appropriately benign expression."

Discovering that the duke sought to silence her through her aunt, Bea sneered.

"No, that's not quite right," Aunt Vera said. "It's a touch too feral. Recall that you are in the dining room at a country estate, not a cockpit. Let's try again."

Bea's second and third attempts weren't much better, but her fourth showed improvement and by the time she'd hit a baker's dozen, her aunt was delighted with her progress.

"Ah, yes, perfect," she said enthusiastically. "That's the

bland, easy-to-overlook young lady your uncle and I know and kindly tolerate. Now just hold that expression through dinner and all will be well." Bea agreed to this request with a nod, but the head movement altered her appearance just enough to alarm her aunt. "Buh-buh. I said hold it. Perhaps you should watch yourself in the mirror until Annie comes up to help you dress. She's with Flora now and should be with you in forty-five minutes to an hour."

"All right," Bea said because there was no point in arguing with such an unreasonable request.

Aunt Vera, sincerely grateful to have an obedient niece, patted her gently on the cheek and said fondly, "We'll show that duke what true maidenly reserve looks like."

Again, Bea agreed, but as soon as her aunt left, her expression turned stormy as she imagined the smug satisfaction Kesgrave must have felt at her aunt's eager assurances. Nothing must give him greater pleasure than watching lesser mortals genuflect before him. The amount of control he exerted over people, over the situation, over everything that had happened at Lakeview Hall in the past four-and-twenty hours, infuriated her. He'd muted Mr. Otley's brutal and violent end by turning his death into a self-inflicted wound, and now he sought to mute her by manipulating her aunt.

It was intolerable, and she could not let it stand.

The Duke of Kesgrave might be used to controlling everything in his orbit, but he could not control her. She wasn't hopeful for his approval or impressed by his stature or infatuated with his money or intimidated by his bearing. Indeed, he'd been the one last night to cower, so terrified at the thought of being compelled by circumstance to marry a plain-faced nobody. If poor Mr. Otley hadn't been lying there with his brain cracked open and his blood splattered on the curtains, it would have been funny—although it was precisely the fact that Mr. Otley *was* lying there with his brain cracked open and his blood splattered on the curtains that would have made it funny. She still couldn't conceive of anyone making scandal broth from such incongruous ingredients.

But the important thing, she realized, was that Kesgrave could. A dozen years dodging the machinations of matchmaking mamas and aspiring duchesses had put him on high alert. Everywhere he looked, he saw the jaws of the parson's mousetrap threatening to snap shut. Although she couldn't believe there were quite as many people out to ensnare him as he imagined, she was grateful for his distrust, for it provided her with the advantage she needed to get answers.

For the second time that afternoon, she listened at the door for fellow houseguests, then stepped into the empty hallway. Kesgrave's rooms were on the other side of the building, at the far end of the east wing of the elegant residence. She knew his location for the same reason she knew where the Otleys were situated—because her aunt made it her business to know who was staying where so she could compare the relative levels of comfort, style and convenience. The Yellow Room, to which Mrs. Hyde-Clare had been assigned, was more spacious than Mrs. Otley's Blue Room but was twice as far from the staircase. The Hunting Room, which Kesgrave was given, was in the older part of the house, which was more elegant in its details but prone to draughts.

At the end of the passage, Bea turned right, traipsed down the stairs and immediately felt the air temperature drop a few degrees. It was indeed cooler in this section.

Although she had a story mapped out should someone require her to explain her presence—a button lost when Lady Skeffington had led them on the grand tour of the house—she was relieved to find the corridor empty. Knowing that could change at any moment, she scurried down the hallway to Kesgrave's door and opened it slowly, fearful that his valet was already within.

It took her only a moment to confirm that the room was vacant.

Perfect, she thought, slipping inside.

Fortunately, Aunt Vera was not with her to see how much late-afternoon sunlight the Hunting Room afforded its guest or the expansive view of the lake from its windows.

Her aunt's view, like her niece's, was impeded by great oak trees with sprawling branches.

The room was large and comfortable, and having successfully completed a secret perusal of Mr. Otley's belongings, Bea was tempted to look through Kesgrave's as well. She resisted the urge, however, as her position was precarious enough without adding snooping to her sins. She was there for one purpose and one purpose only: to press Kesgrave for the reason he lied about the spice trader's death and to threaten ruination if he resisted providing satisfactory answers.

And yet, despite her firm resolve, she couldn't resist peering at the stack of books at his bedside. He'd claimed to be in the library looking for a specific book. Was it among these titles....

Ah, yes, there it was: *The Defense of Poesy.*

Her initial response was relief, for it meant that the duke had spoken the truth last night when he said he had come to the library in search of the book. At least that much of his story was accurate. The emotion was quickly superseded by horror, however, for what kind of monster had the presence of mind to look for a book after discovering a dead body? And when did he find the opportunity to retrieve it? Before alerting Skeffington to the scene in his library? After watching the constable examine the body? *During* its removal? Did it really matter? Wasn't one moment as horrendous as the other?

At once another notion occurred to her: Perhaps it was Kesgrave's own copy and the reason the title sprang so easily to mind was he already had it on hand. If that was the case, then the duke had lied about why he was in the library.

Why lie?

There was only one answer: The Duke of Kesgrave wielded the candlestick. He was the one who struck Mr. Otley on the head until his skull caved in and he ceased to live.

"I see you're prying again, Miss. Hyde-Clare, despite my insistence that you leave matters alone," said a voice disconcertingly close to her shoulder. "Now, what in the world are we going to do with you?"

CHAPTER FIVE

To say that every muscle in Beatrice Hyde-Clare's body froze would be to wildly understate the case, for it felt as if all her bones and even her skin had turned to stone at the sound of the duke's voice. She was like a statue in a garden—vulnerable, exposed, powerless to defend itself against the elements that threatened it.

If Kesgrave had a candlestick in his hand, he could bash her over the head with it and she would submit without a word.

Was this what it had been like for Otley? Did he, too, find terror so debilitating that he barely put up a fight when his life was about to end?

No, no, she thought, recalling the chilling scene in the library. Mr. Otley had no idea what was coming until it was too late—if he ever knew at all—and he certainly did not stand as still as a marble sculpture of a Roman statesman and wait for his executioner to strike the fatal blow.

She tried to remember her plan for coming to his rooms, but fear made her thoughts fuzzy and all she could do was think of death and statuary.

And her aunt.

With what agony Aunt Vera would greet the news

that her niece, usually so docile and yet suddenly so recalci-
trant, had been found prying in the Duke of Kesgrave's
rooms. The egregious invasion of privacy would be secondary to the gross betrayal of her particular request to
leave his grace alone.

She would get the tongue-lashing of her life.

But, no, she would get nothing and her aunt would
never know of the violation, for if the duke was the killer he
would dispose of her body without anyone being the wiser.

Without a murmur of complaint, she would disappear
from her family's life.

The thought of dying with the same reticence with
which she'd lived horrified Beatrice, and at once she recalled her scheme to compromise him.

"I will scream," she said softly, her voice barely a
whisper. How feeble it sounded to her own ears—as if she
were almost asking permission to speak. Determinedly, she
turned around and forced herself to confront him face-to-
face as she said with more vigor, "I will scream."

"Naturally, Miss Hyde-Clare," Kesgrave said, his expression as amused as his tone. "I'd expect nothing less from
so middling a young lady. Do you write your own material or
are you following one of Mrs. Radcliffe's scripts?"

It was a scathing remark, to be sure, for it cut to the
heart of who she was: unimpressive, ordinary, prosaic, banal. But it also revealed his failure to understand the threat
she posed, as it was precisely her mediocrity that presented
the greatest risk.

"I will scream," she announced again, pleased by the
strength and smoothness of her voice. There was nothing
like reaffirming one's true inconsequentiality to make a
young lady feel calm in the face of danger. "I will scream
and someone will come running, for at this hour the house
is filled with guests changing for dinner and servants helping them. I will scream and you will find yourself compromised beyond all hope and forced to marry me. Think
of it, your grace, leg-shackled to middling Beatrice Hyde-

Clare for the rest of your life: bland looks, insipid conversation, dull children. Surely, you have something better in mind for yourself—a diamond of the first water, a paragon of elegance and intelligence: clever, obedient, poised, virtuous, capable of conversing with equal graciousness with a king and a chimney sweep."

Bea didn't think such a creature of perfection actually existed—and if she did, she would certainly be insufferable—but she wholeheartedly believed that the duke lived in expectation of meeting his womanly ideal only a day or two after deciding to set up his nursery. No doubt he thought women came made to order like topcoats and boots.

"Take a step toward me, and I will scream," she said, examining his face for an indication of how he felt and finding nothing but mild good humor, "and the glorious tableau you've always imagined for yourself—the beautiful wife and the cherubic children as lovely as porcelain figurines on the mantle above the fireplace—will vanish into the air like smoke."

Inconceivably, he smiled. "I'm not sure the description of *middling* is apt, Miss Hyde-Clare, as you have me sufficiently cowed, a feat nobody else has ever managed to accomplish. Please do tell me how you would like to proceed, so that I may readily comply and avoid the fate so chilling that even the great Horace Walpole never conceived it."

Although the teasing note in his voice belied his words, she was grateful that her threat was daunting enough to make him at least feign apprehension. "Let's sit down and have a chat."

The duke pointed to two wingback chairs next to the bay window overlooking the lake, which seemed to glimmer with gold in the late-afternoon sun. "If these do not satisfy your requirements, there are a pair of Egyptian-style klismos chairs in the dressing room. They're a trifle ostentatious for my comfort, but they might suit your middling taste."

The unabashed mockery in his tone was distracting,

but she refused to let herself be provoked by his taunts. "Those chairs are fine, thank you."

Kesgrave, determined to display yet more contempt, bowed slightly before walking across the room to the window. He indicated the chair on the left, as if seeking her permission to claim it, and Bea, seeing no difference between the two pieces of furniture, nodded impatiently. As soon as she did, she wondered if she'd thoughtlessly given him an unknown advantage.

She told herself to stop being absurd. Both chairs were exactly the same, and he could not have anticipated her presence by, for example, securing a knife underneath the cushion of one.

And yet she worried that she'd fallen into a trap by agreeing to sit down, even though it was she who'd made the suggestion.

Although she was no devotee of the Gothic, she'd read enough to know that no heroine ever benefited from indulging a fanciful imagination. Bea took a deep breath and focused on discovering whether or not the Duke of Kesgrave was a merciless killer. She began by putting the question directly to him. "Did you murder Mr. Otley?"

Kesgrave heaved a theatrical sigh and shook his head with exaggerated disappointment, as if playing to the farthest row at Drury Lane. "Did I say *middling*, Miss Hyde-Clare? Let me revise my assessment of your character, for your least appealing trait as a potential wife is your utter lack of trust. It would be wearying unto death to be bracketed with a young lady who was always suspecting me of one gross depravity or another. No, I did not murder Mr. Otley. Did we not address this matter sufficiently last night? I acquitted you of any wrongdoing, and you returned the courtesy by acquitting me. Do let the record show that I remain convinced of your innocence even though I discovered you in my rooms inspecting my belongings in my absence, an act that most people would consider to be highly suspicious at the very least."

She ignored his nonsensical preening. "Explain the book."

The question, a seeming non sequitur, genuinely confused him, and for the first time since he'd found her in his room, he looked surprised. "What book?"

"*The Defense of Poesy,*" she said, "which is on your bedside table. If you recall, you cited it last night as the reason you were in the library. Its presence here strikes me as problematic, as I cannot believe that even you would be so ghoulish as to remember to select reading material from the library after the victim's bloody body had been removed."

The duke dipped his head. "Thank you, Miss Hyde-Clare. I believe that's the first compliment you've ever paid me."

"Unmistakably, the book was already in your possession," she pointed out, "which means you lied about why you were in the library."

"Yet again, I must take issue with my own use of the word *middling,*" he said, "for your intelligence is quite above average."

Unlike with the matter of the chairs, Bea could clearly see the trick at work, for his method was hardly subtle. "I'm not sure about that, but I'm certainly smart enough to recognize when someone is attempting to distract me from the truth with empty flattery."

"Is that what I'm doing?" he asked thoughtfully. "I'm not quite convinced."

"Despite what you believe, I'm not a pliable schoolgirl in the first blush of youth to have her head turned by the first handsome man to flirt with her," she said dampeningly.

"And that's the second," he said.

Suspicious and irritated, she narrowed her eyes. "Second what?"

"Compliment."

A scream of frustration rose in her throat at his seemingly endless ability to thwart serious conversation, and she ruthlessly swallowed the sound. Despite her threats, she had no more desire to be discovered than he did, and his valet was sure to come by soon to help him prepare for dinner. "Your grace, this conversation will go much faster if you stop trying to charm me. It's a waste of my time and yours, as my susceptibility to Spanish coin is so remarkably low it might as well be nonexistent."

"A sincere compliment is not Spanish coin," he insisted.

"Then please do me the sincere compliment of answering my question," she said, unswayed by the note of pained offense he'd injected into his words.

"I would be happy to, except you haven't asked a question," he said. "I assure you, Miss Hyde-Clare, I have a very good memory and can recall even the most minute detail of any subject."

"You don't have to tell me that," she muttered under her breath as she resisted the urge to roll her eyes. "HMS *Majestic,* HMS *Goliath,* HMS *Audacious.*"

"HMS *Goliath,* HMS *Audacious,* HMS *Majestic,*" he immediately corrected with pointed emphasis. "If you're going to list the British ships that fought in the Battle of the Nile, then you should do so in their order of appearance. It's a sign of respect, you see, as well as maritime tradition."

Beatrice didn't have to observe the expression on the duke's face to know he was teasing her again. Kesgrave had the most inappropriate sense of humor of any person she'd ever met, which was a baffling discovery to make, for there had been nothing in his preening displays of pedantry during their stay that suggested frivolity. She could not conceive what his game was now save a desire to put off her questioning indefinitely with nonsensical blather. She would not allow it to happen, of course, for the situation was far too serious for his antics.

"Duly noted. Very well, your grace, here is my query: If you weren't in the library to get *The Defense of Poesy,* and we both know you weren't, why were you there?" she asked. "That's the topic currently under discussion, and I'll thank you not to go off on a tangent again, as I will not leave this room until I'm satisfied with all your answers."

"Make no mistake, Miss Hyde-Clare, your satisfaction is my single biggest concern," he said.

His blue eyes sparkled with humor—oh, indeed, they did, bright and cheerful, with a sense of knowingness and wonder—and Beatrice decided he would make a very fine murderer. There was something about him that was intolerable, a perfection that was inhuman, and she could easily imagine such physical beauty seeking out corruption as an antidote to its own flawlessness. It was too simplistic, she thought, how one always seemed to expect an ugly person to perform ugly deeds.

"The library, your grace," she said calmly.

"You're correct, I did not go there to borrow a book," he confirmed.

"Then why did you?"

He paused as if to give his answer great consideration before responding, and something about him appeared to change. It wasn't the expression in his eyes, which remained amused, or his face, she decided. It was his bearing, as if his shoulders were straining under something unexpectedly heavy. When he spoke now, it was without levity or irreverence. "I was following Otley."

As startling as this revelation was—and it was quite shocking to discover that Kesgrave had entered the story long before she—Beatrice kept her features still and showed no reaction. She didn't even ask why, preferring to let the weight of the silence press for an explanation.

The silence stretched into minutes as the duke regarded her thoughtfully, which Beatrice decided was a promising development. If he intended to fob her off with more banter and half-truths, he would do so without hesitation. But making the decision to treat her like a genuine ally took time and consideration. She was willing to wait however long it took—provided it didn't take quite so long that his valet returned and ended their interview entirely.

Was it a stalling tactic?

Naturally, she couldn't dismiss the prospect entirely, but she thought it was unlikely, as he had already demonstrated how effectively he could delay intelligent conversation with ridiculous prattle. He didn't need to lapse into dumbness to put her off.

No, the duke was paying her the compliment of taking her seriously.

At last, he said, "My attendance at this party is at the behest of a friend who has suffered financially in his dealings with Otley."

Beatrice nodded and recalled Mrs. Otley's lament in the drawing room. "The hibiscus scheme?"

If he was surprised that she knew anything about the dead man's fiscal arrangements, he didn't reveal it. "Yes, my friend invested heavily in Otley's hibiscus crop in India, for Otley's plan to sell to the Chinese market had been a sound one and my friend agreed with Otley's belief that the tea market would soon expand to England as well. Furthermore, Otley had a sterling reputation as a successful spice trader in the region, and there was no reason to believe this enterprise would not prosper as well as his others. Naturally, my friend understood the risks involved in the investment and accepted them, as he would with any business venture."

Appreciating his friend's astute comprehension of the situation, Beatrice asked, "Then what appears to be the problem?"

"A fire," he said.

"Yes," she replied with another firm nod, "Mrs. Otley mentioned it destroyed the entire crop and quite devastated the family's coffers."

"That is indeed the story my friend was told," he said with a cynical twist of the lips.

"Is it so difficult to believe?" she wondered. "If I were to invest in a hibiscus crop in India, I would expect it certainly to be destroyed by a large conflagration raging out of control. It's the reason why I would never put my money into a hibiscus crop."

Although his demeanor remained serious, his eyes brightened at the notion that it was an aversion to risk that kept an impoverished unmarried woman of six and twenty from investing in shares. "Precisely," he said. "Tell me, what do you know about the weather in India?"

"Very little," she admitted, suddenly aware of the failure of her education to include the climates of distant countries she never intended to visit. For all the narrowness of her provincial life, she had a remarkably wide breadth of knowledge about the world, from the Arctic explorations of the ancient Greeks in 325 B.C. to dog-breeding methods of the American Indians. And yet now, when the moment had finally arrived to impress someone with her vast repertoire of arcana, she had nothing to add. Her eclectic reading tastes proved not eclectic enough. "I understand from various gentlemen who have traveled there that it's quite hot."

"It is, yes," he said. "According to the information my friend received, the fire that devastated the crop occurred in May. May, however, is monsoon season in the southern region, which means it rains almost constantly. You perceive the problem, I trust?"

She did, of course, for she wasn't a daft parsnip with no understanding of the natural world. Immediately, she could see the difficulties it would present to burn down an entire field of soggy bushes. "If your friend doesn't believe a fire ruined the crop, what does he believe happened?"

"That is not clear, which is why he asked me to look into it," Kesgrave explained. "Since I started investigating three weeks ago, I've discovered two dozen other gentlemen who bought into the hibiscus scheme, as, given Otley's prior successes, many investors were interested in supporting his next venture. Calculating the number of shares sold, I can only conclude the crop's failure was the best possible outcome for Otley. Otherwise, he would have had to pay out more money in dividends than he'd earned in profits."

As he explained the simple math, Bea pictured Otley's diary, which she'd read only two hours before, with its scribbled reminder to increase his stake in a copper-mining company in Cornwall. He'd made the notation just the day before, an indication that the fire hadn't been quite as financially devastating as his wife had indicated. Evidently, he still had enough funds to invest in reliable enterprises if he wanted to. Did Mrs. Otley not know the truth of her family's situation, or was she keeping up the appearance of insolvency even in the aftermath of her husband's horrible death? If it was the latter, then Beatrice's estimation of her increased tenfold. She couldn't imagine having the presence of mind to maintain a facade in the wake of tragedy.

Unless…

No, she assured herself, unable to complete the thought. Mrs. Otley wasn't the one who had killed her husband. For one thing, she wasn't tall enough to strike him on the top of the head, for he had towered over his wife by almost a foot. Even if she had a convenient stepstool to increase her height, Bea doubted the woman would be able to wield the candlestick with enough force to damage his skull so egregiously. At best, she would be capable of creating a very large bump. And why would she make his death a public spectacle when all she had to do was slip a little too much laudanum into his drink in the privacy of their own home?

"You may share what you're thinking," Kesgrave said.

Surprised, Beatrice drew her brows together and looked at him curiously. "Excuse me?"

"I cannot help but conclude from the look on your face that you have thoughts on Otley's death," he explained, his blue eyes once again wryly amused, "and I want to assure you that you may share them with me without fear of mockery or disbelief. In my experience, even the most outlandish theories have value."

Bea needed little persuading to hold her tongue, for she couldn't decide if the duke's story was true or a tale meant to lead her away from the truth, but his attempt to reassure her convinced her to remain silent. Even if he did indeed have experience with outlandish theories, then she had a hard time believing he'd take a woman he barely knew into his confidence.

He was more likely playing a very deep game.

"No thoughts," she said with a breezy smile. "Just surprise and disbelief that a man of Otley's excellent reputation might be guilty of some devious financial dealings. It's so difficult to know whom to trust. Your friend is lucky to have you to help him sort it out. And how very impressive that you can attend any house party in the kingdom you choose. How did you contrive an invitation to this one?"

Although she'd meant the comment to be sarcastic, for she truly found nothing less remarkable than a duke shouldering his way into any gathering he wished, Kesgrave answered sincerely. "I merely mentioned to Nuneaton how much I enjoyed fishing, and he managed the rest. As you can imagine, having a duke present lends a certain prestige to any proceeding. I'm not disinclined to take advantage of that fact when it suits my needs."

Presumably, he intended the remark to be sardonic, as well, for he had to know how impossible it was for an observer to imagine him denying himself anything that suited his needs, a consequence that made him at once more and less likable. She respected the fact that he was honest about his methods and aware enough of himself to acknowledge them, but his sense of entitlement was infuriating. He would deny himself nothing and neither would anyone else. Examining his countenance, which wasn't so much smug as satisfied, she felt an overwhelming urge to hurl raw vegetation at his head. Oh, to have a basket of strawberries or a parcel of apples!

Determined not to be diverted from her purpose, she

pushed aside all thoughts of assailing him with fruit and focused her attention on the original issue. "If you followed Mr. Otley into the library, then you must have seen the man who attacked him."

Kesgrave shook his head. "I did not. Contrary to what I said last night, I did in fact stay up playing cards, and when the game broke up, I tried to follow Mr. Otley. As I was leaving the drawing room, however, our host called me into his study to commend me on making the only catch of the day."

Although the baron's congratulations had frustrated what could have been a very simple solution to a complex problem, Bea relished the idea of Kesgrave being derailed by his own overweening skill. "Hoisted by your own gurnard."

The duke smiled at her witticism but couldn't resist explaining that the gurnard, which came in a variety of species, including the gray gurnard, the tub gurnard, and the red gurnard, was a fish that inhabited the Atlantic Ocean, not the lakes of Cumbria. "Here, you are likely to find char and trout."

Although Bea wasn't surprised by either the fact that he had the information readily at hand or felt compelled to share it, she'd expected a lecture on the more obvious point that fish, unlike a petard, typically lacked a mechanism for exploding. 'Twas far too easy to imagine him explaining with painstaking specificity the absence of gunpowder in the aquatic animals' physical composition. "Your attention to detail is humbling, your grace. It must be difficult to know so much and have so few occasions to demonstrate it."

She was being facetious, of course, as he spared himself no opportunity to bestow his knowledge on unsuspecting bystanders. The target of her teasing either chose to ignore the undercurrent of her observation or failed to detect it, for he accepted her praise with an appreciative nod. "By the time I extricated myself from conversation with Skeffington, who can be verbose when in his cups,

Otley had disappeared. It required several discreet inquiries of the staff to fathom his whereabouts. Although I can't know for sure if he had a planned assignation in the library, I'm inclined to think he did not, as I have discovered no evidence that he was working with an associate. My investigation indicates that he was the sole author and beneficiary of the hibiscus scheme."

"Then he was in the library for the same reason I was—to find a book to lull him to sleep?" she asked, the prospect sounding doubtful to her own ears if not Kesgrave's. It would be absurd to think she knew Mr. Otley well enough to make judgments about the extent of his literacy, and yet she felt certain it was limited to materials that furthered his interests. She recalled the stock reports she'd seen buried under his wife's magazine in the sitting room. There had been no novels or treatises among the assortment.

"I presume so," Kesgrave said, and Bea wondered what information he was withholding. Although she found his refusal to share everything frustrating, it was hardly startling. If their circumstances had been reversed, she'd be equally hesitant to reveal everything. "You know the rest, of course, for you came upon the scene a mere minute after me and I've already explained to you how it was. I arrived in the library to find Otley's supine form and his head grievously wounded. I ascertained immediately that he hadn't survived his wounds and had just resolved to look for his assailant when you appeared from behind a shelf of books and gasped in horror."

Had she gasped in horror? Bea couldn't remember.

"And that, Miss Hyde-Clare, is really all I know about the matter. Naturally, I do not blame you for having your qualms about me"—and yet the surliness of his tone did just that—"as the situation is quite out of the bounds of the ordinary, with many elements that one could describe as suspicious, but you are far too intelligent to indulge in wild speculation." Ah, there was that Spanish coin again, as if all he had to do to raise himself above the muck was flatter her ego. Was anyone desperate enough for praise that they would succumb to such blatant manipulation? "If you think upon it, you will realize it's slightly too absurd to suppose I had anything to do with Mr. Otley's barbarous and untimely death. Now I trust you will return to your own room and allow me to dress for dinner. The hour grows late, and I'm sure your family will soon wonder where you are. It would never do for *them* to speculate wildly."

Bea smothered the laugh that rose in her throat, for there was no amount of evidence one could present to any of her relatives that would persuade them that their mousy poor relation had been closeted in a bedchamber with any duke, let alone one so high in the instep as Kesgrave. It was simply too incredible a notion to believe an exalted member of the aristocracy had standards so low.

Despite her amusement, she kept her face placid and addressed the issue that had brought her to his rooms in the first place. "I will leave you to the ministrations of your valet just as soon as you explain why you convinced the constable that Otley's barbarous and untimely death was caused by his own hand, a conclusion so contrary to fact that I can only imagine the man is a senile old fool who recently lost his spectacles."

Kesgrave sighed, as if genuinely disappointed by her inability to simply take his essential goodness on faith. If a duke's goodness cannot be assumed based on his standing in the social order, then what was the point of having a duchy? Bea settled in for another lecture and was only partially surprised when he redoubled his efforts to flatter away her concerns. "Come now, Miss Hyde-Clare, we both know you're far too clever not to have known at once what I hope to achieve by issuing the false report. I'll thank you not to insult your intelligence in my presence!"

Bea opened her mouth to protest and immediately closed it again when she realized renouncing her own shrewdness was perhaps not the best way to respond. Instead, she paused to consider the question as if it were a riddle, leaning back in her chair and staring out at the sparkling lake stocked with char and trout. She found Kesgrave's ready admission unsettling, for she'd expected him to affect confusion to deflect the charge. With Mr. Otley tucked under a sheet in the wine cellar and the floor of the library scrubbed clean, she had no proof that her version of events was more correct than his, and if the duke had stuck to his outrageous lie, she would have had no recourse but to abandon the field. Her threat to compromise him, which had borne surprising fruit, had merely been a bluff all along. If he'd held his ground, she would have slunk out of his room no more enlightened than when she'd arrived.

But to own the falsehood without equivocating implied he wasn't just playing a deeper game than she, he was playing a different one.

Or perhaps she was crediting him with too much cunning and his object was much more simple: He hoped to confuse her. She'd assumed his purpose in praising her so much was to turn her head, but it was just as likely he thought compliments were so absent from her daily existence that a spate of them would confound her into silence.

She was certainly quiet now.

True, but she was still there, in his bedchamber, demanding answers.

Although Bea distrusted the duke's motives, she didn't believe he actually wanted the murderer to go free. He cared far too much for order—in the listing of naval ships, in the cataloging of local fish—to allow a moral trespass such as homicide to go unpunished. The idea of a villain escaping justice would offend him on a deeply personal level.

Realizing that, she understood at once what he hoped to accomplish with his lie about Otley's death and discovered she wasn't outraged by it at all. Indeed, she was impressed with the practicality of the solution.

"Your plan is to lull the murderer into a false sense of

security by letting him think he got away with his crime," she observed with determined calm, for she didn't want Kesgrave to know how much she admired his reasoning. "It has the added benefit of keeping everyone exactly where they are, for if the guests suspected a murderer roamed among them, they would leave the country post-haste and return to their homes. Now we have the time and leisure to investigate properly."

"We?" he asked, his eyebrow quirking.

Bea blinked innocently. "I mean 'you,' your grace. Now *you* have the time to investigate properly and I have the time to embroider a sampler in Lady Skeffington's very comfortable drawing room. I cannot thank you enough for ensuring I have ample opportunity to do so."

Although she said all the right words with the correct mix of sincerity and eagerness, he narrowed his eyes skeptically. "This is a dangerous matter, Miss Hyde-Clare, not some lark for you to indulge your ill-advised sense of humor."

Having never been credited with a sense of humor before, she was delighted to discover he considered hers to be ill-advised. She hoped by the end of their stay he would promote it to utterly foolish. "Of course, your grace," she said placatingly. "I would never deem it anything else."

For some reason, he found her quick agreement less than reassuring. "I'm serious," he said sternly. "You will not pursue it."

Beatrice laughed as she stood up, for she had several things to do before changing for dinner, including launching a full-scale investigation into Mr. Otley's death. "Now you are the one being frightfully suspicious, and I must agree it's an unpleasant experience indeed when someone will not take you at your word. I hope you will accept my apologies for my earlier mistreatment of you. You are un-doubtedly a very fine upstanding duke, and I wish you all success with your very dangerous pursuit."

"Miss Hyde-Clare!" he said, his shoulders stiff as he stood before her to impede her progress.

"No need to say it, your grace," she insisted as she brushed past him toward the door. "I know you wish me success with my embroidery as well. I will admit to you since there's no one else present to witness my humiliation that my skill doesn't quite match my enthusiasm. But every day is a chance to improve."

"I know what you're up to."

Her hand on the doorknob, Bea turned to look at the duke, his handsome features pulled into a scowl, and raised a finger to her lips to shush him. "Remember, if anyone discovers I was here, you will be ruined. Think of your incandescent future with your Incomparable wife and those impossibly perfect children."

While the Duke of Kesgrave stared at her with bewildered horror, she opened the door a sliver, peered through the crack, confirmed that the corridor was unoccupied and slipped silently out of his room.

She had a murderer to find.

CHAPTER SIX

The corridor did not remain empty for long.

As soon as Bea closed Kesgrave's door behind her, she heard the rumble of male voices—Mr. Skeffington and Lord Amersham!—and although she had prepared a practical explanation for why she was in that part of the house, it eluded her in the panic of being caught outside the duke's rooms. Heart racing, she looked around wildly for a place to hide and threw herself behind the first viable object she spotted: a voluminous fern in the corner near the staircase.

She landed with a thud, bumping her head first against the wall and then the planter as she settled into her hideaway. Pulling a frond out of her mouth, she cursed the ridiculousness of the situation: hiding behind a potted plant!

Perhaps she *had* read too many of Mrs. Radcliffe's Gothic novels after all.

Nevertheless, she appreciated the coverage the fern provided, for crouched behind the large ceramic planter, she was almost entirely shielded from view. Only a careful inspection of the corner would reveal her presence, and fortunately the gentlemen were too distracted by their conversation to look behind them.

She listened carefully as they strode past her and down the hall.

"...why you must continue to fixate on the matter," Amersham said. "It was a sound investment, and sound investments sometimes go awry. That is all anyone need know. Although I do remind you, nobody need know, especially your parents. If you must talk incessantly about something we did recently, let's discuss your excellent day of angling."

"I caught one fish," Mr. Skeffington said sulkily as they arrived at his door. "That hardly constitutes an excellent day."

"Well, it seems very impressive to me. If you remember, I caught nothing at all despite my enthusiasm," Amersham pointed out reasonably.

"That is because you don't know how to tie a fly properly, as you were born and bred in..."

Mr. Skeffington's reply was cut off as the two gentlemen disappeared into his room and closed the door.

Bea extricated herself from the fern as smoothly as she could manage, and as she walked back to her section of the house at a clipped pace, she considered the information she'd overheard. It was possible, of course, that Mr. Skeffington and Amersham were discussing an investment in an enterprise wholly unrelated to Mr. Otley—coal mining, for example, or the construction of a canal—but there was something about the way the earl had said, "That is all anyone need know" that was quite specific. He emphasized the word *need*, indicating that there was much more to the story than he was willing to tell.

Was that elided information the fact that the two young men had been swindled by an old friend of the family?

Had they figured out that the hibiscus investment was a fraudulent scheme?

Bea recalled her own ignorance about the weather in India, despite her wide breadth of knowledge, and found it difficult to believe the two callow youths, who had both been sent down from Oxford several times, were better read than she.

Ah, but this wasn't an exam on *The Iliad*. It was an investment opportunity involving what might be a significant amount of money. Indisputably, before sinking funds into hibiscus plants in a foreign country, one investigated the venture thoroughly.

Mr. Skeffington's own mother's dismal view of his education, however, argued for the opposing view, and deciding that neither man would have done his due diligence, she settled on the two dupes as her first viable suspects. She thought it was unlikely either could handle the swipe to his vanity with equanimity and imagined how the scene in the library would have played out. Seeking a moment alone with Mr. Otley to discuss their concerns, they would have been angered by his denials or made irate by his confirmation and struck without thinking.

The bash on the head with the candlestick would have been as impulsive as it was vicious.

As theories went, Bea thought it had much to recommend it. Young men were not known for restraining their passions, and even a personage of advanced years would react with spontaneous fury upon discovering he had been tricked by a man his parents trusted. It would account for the oddity of the murder weapon, as a knife or pistol was far more common for disposing of one's enemies.

If the event had indeed occurred without preparation, then the perpetrator would have had no plan for how to dispose of the damning evidence after the crime. Thinking of the blood that dotted the wall, Bea wondered what a young man of Skeffington's or Amersham's ilk and breeding would do with clothes that had been contaminated by his vile deed. Would it occur to him to discard them immediately so that nobody could trace the crime back to him or would he simply leave them for the valet to dispose of, as per his usual habit?

Bea felt her heart pound in excitement as she realized her original supposition had validity: Finding the murderer could be as straightforward as locating the gentlemen's pile of soiled clothes. All she needed was an opportunity to sneak into their rooms and look around.

Tonight was out, obviously, for Mr. Skeffington and Amersham would soon be changing for dinner and she could not be certain when they would return in the evening. The risk of being caught was too great, but if the weather held, tomorrow would present plenty of opportunities. Both men would participate in whatever activity Skeffington arranged, be it fishing or hunting or shooting.

Delighted to have a course of action so cleanly mapped out, Bea smiled brightly as she turned into the hallway that contained her bedchamber and found herself unexpectedly face-to-face with Miss Otley.

The daughter of the victim!

Surely, she had additional information Bea would find useful in her quest to attain justice for her father.

Knowing that the right approach would be vital in getting the beautiful young lady to share personal information, Bea nodded solemnly and said, "Miss Otley, if you will allow, I would like to give you something I think will help you greatly during your time of anguish."

The other girl opened her large blue eyes wide as she contemplated Bea with surprise. "Indeed, Miss Hyde-Clare?"

Given the slimness of their acquaintance, Bea was startled to discover the young lady even knew her name. With no indication to the contrary, she'd naturally assumed Miss Otley thought of her as "plain female of no import No. 2." The fact that there wasn't another woman in attendance at the party who could fit the description did little to improve Bea's place in the hierarchy.

"Yes, only I need a moment to retrieve it. Do wait here," she said, running to her room to hunt through her top drawer. She tossed several items to the floor and pushed the remaining clothes to the side. She knew it was there somewhere...

Aha!

Grabbing the article, she dashed outside to discover Miss Otley had not stayed in the hall, per her request.

No matter.

She knocked on her door, and as soon as the other girl opened it, she held up a plain cloth bonnet festooned indifferently with a thin gray ribbon. "A mob cap," Bea said, holding it up triumphantly.

Miss Otley stared blankly. "A mob cap?"

"A mob cap," Bea repeated with a firm nod as she entered the room. "Since the moment we met, I have envied and admired your impressive assortment of beautiful bonnets with outlandish, cheerful feathers, which show your beauty to great effect, and realized you must be lacking in appropriately forlorn mob caps."

"A mob cap," Miss Otley echoed wretchedly, her expression so dire, Bea felt as if she were consigning her to a corset of the sturdiest whalebone rather than a slip of linen that rested lightly on one's head.

"It's yours to keep," Bea offered.

Although the item was too banal and unwanted to be regarded as a gift, Miss Otley's breeding ensured that she thanked her visitor for bestowing it. "You're too kind."

"It's the least I could do," Bea said, looking around the room, which was as lavishly decorated as hers, with deep, rich colors and handsome furniture. "I find that a good mob cap always makes me feel better."

Miss Otley nodded, as if this statement made sense, for she was too tired not to be agreeable, but then the substance of the comment struck her and she opened her eyes as wide as saucers in surprise. "Really? How?"

"They're warm and cozy," Bea explained. "I thought given the unfortunate circumstance, you would appreciate a little warmth and coziness. I can only imagine how difficult this is for you. I barely knew my own father, for I was only five when he died, and yet I still miss him every day. It must be so much harder when he is a cherished and familiar figure in your life."

"Thank you, yes, it is quite difficult. It's as if someone"—she blanched as she recalled who that person actually was—"ripped a large hole in the middle of my life. It's unbearable how everything is familiar but nothing is the same."

Given Bea's assessment of Miss Otley as a pretty peagoose, she was surprised by the astute articulation of her feelings. "You're lucky to have your mother. She seems like a dependable woman in a time of crisis," Bea said, recalling how sternly the matron had ordered her husband about. "She's had so much to contend with recently, including your father's misfortunes in India. Imagine, a fire destroying your entire investment. Even before this terrible and tragic turn, she was bearing up under an oppressive weight. I hope you will tell me if there's anything I or my family can do to help."

"You are very kind and I will keep your offer in mind. But you mustn't listen too closely to what my mother says. She has a way of increasing the intensity of her suffering to earn the sympathy of others. Although it was a setback, to be sure, the destruction of the hibiscus crop has not been the great devastation she described. We are certainly not miserable," she said firmly, then her face clouded with sadness as she considered the substance of her words. Her fingers wrapped around the mob cap as she found some consolation in fiddling with it. "That is, we *were* not miserable. Our lives had hardly been affected by the fire."

Bea found her experience difficult to reconcile with her mother's discouraging description of events. "I'm happy to hear you haven't suffered, my dear, but I wonder how your father managed it."

Miss Otley's eye brightened as her face took on a calculating look. "I wondered the exact same thing, especially as Mama's concern over the hibiscus shrubs was minor compared with her apprehension over the loss of Papa's other crop of a few months before."

At once Bea recalled the Incomparable's words in the drawing room: *the latest setback.*

"On that occasion," the girl continued, "Mama was wild with concern, and she and Papa did not calmly discuss the matter over breakfast like they did last month with the fire. Indeed, they tried to hide it from me because they didn't want me to worry. Anxiety can have a disastrous effect on one's appearance, as you must know. But I overheard them whispering about it one morning. Mama was telling him that he had to figure out something immediately or the tradesmen would come pounding on the door—the *front* door, you understand—at any moment. Her tone was quite frantic, but Papa, bless him, remained calm and assured her he had the matter well in hand. And of course he did, for I never had to miss a single fitting at Madame Babineaux's. If his business disappointment had curtailed our ability to buy the latest French styles, then I could understand Mama's distress, for what is the point of being in London if not to turn yourself out in the height of fashion. But our credit was always good with the modiste, so the only conclusion I can draw is Mama was overreacting. She does like to do that, I'm afraid. Nobody can enact a Cheltenham tragedy in the drawing room with the same fervor as my mother."

As skewed as the other girl's perspective was, Bea acknowledged the validity of measuring the world in increments of fashionable gowns. It was only when a calamity affected something you held dear that it took on the patina of reality. "And what had happened to the crop on that occasion? Was it another fire?"

"A rival company," she said. "One was larger and had more influence in the region. It simply swooped in and claimed our fields for its own. It was a very sordid display of brute force. I don't wonder why they refused to tell me anything about it."

Miss Otley was curiously knowledgeable for a woman in whom her parents refused to confide, Bea thought. "How did you discover the truth?"

"I searched their things," she explained simply, "and

discovered correspondence from Mr. Wilson, my father's agent in India, discussing what had happened. I could find no letter that mentioned the fire that destroyed the hibiscus plants, which is how I know it's not quite the huge calamity my mother claims it to be. Despite my appearance, I'm quite a sensible young lady, Miss Hyde-Clare, and I'm prepared to sink into the doldrums if the fire has made us wretchedly poor. But the truth is, I simply don't know if that's the case and it's been very confusing. I cannot tell you how dreadfully disheartening it is not to know whether you are able to buy the new ostrich hat with the pink plume you saw in Madame Chevalier's shop window." Her tone, which had turned mournful at the mention of the hat, dissolved into despondency as she realized the answer was finally clear in the wake of her father's actions. She began to weep quietly as her fingers twisted the mob cap so tightly Bea feared the sturdy linen would tear. "Perhaps Papa found it disheartening as well, and that is why he did this awful, terrible thing to us. Perhaps he grew tired of waiting for fate to knock him down once and for all, and he decided to do it himself. How cruel of him not to consider me. I'm far too beautiful to sink into despair. My eyes are supposed to sparkle with merriment and gaiety as I contemplate my noble husband, not simmer with misery as I consider the lowly country squire to whom I've been tethered to settle a debt. He will have dirty boots and use rushlights in the parlor. Just think of it: *rushlights*."

The prospect of such a dim future was more than the girl could endure, and she dissolved into a deluge of tears, which she sought to stem with the mob cap. The bonnet, of course, was an inadequate substitute for a handkerchief, and Beatrice quickly surveyed the room for a more appropriate item. Spotting a cluster of accessories on top of the chest of drawers, she rifled through the articles—gloves, hairpins, a bracelet, a letter from...hmm, was the Mr. Wilson on the return address her father's agent in India?—and found what she was looking for. She picked up the cloth square while discreetly sliding the letter into her pocket.

Beatrice handed the weeping Miss Otley the handkerchief and wrapped a comforting arm around her shoulder. "There, there, all will be well, I promise," she said soothingly as she lamented her inability to provide anything more substantial than empty platitudes. She appreciated the practical aspects of Kesgrave's manipulations, but it struck her as cruel beyond imagining to allow the poor girl to think she was penniless as well as fatherless.

Miss Otley dabbed delicately at her tears with the handkerchief, her beauty heightened further by the hint of fragility, and took several calming breaths as she struggled to restrain her emotions. After a few minutes, she regained her composure and apologized for the outburst in a voice deepened by sorrow. "Even in these trying times, I know it's unseemly for one to lose control, and I must beg your forgiveness."

Although Bea didn't doubt for a moment the girl's sincerity, her words could not have been more precisely calculated to make Bea feel like a splotch of mud on the bottom of a gentleman's boot, for she had come to her room with the express purpose of poking and prying. Her goal had not been to make her cry, of course, but she'd known how unlikely it was that she would gain information without waterworks. "You must not apologize for being human," she said sternly. "Nobody could suffer as you have and not break down. I'm surprised you didn't do it sooner. Here, let's rest for a moment before we change for dinner. We still have a few minutes before we must summon the maid. I must confess, Miss Otley, that I greatly envy how beautifully you cry. Whenever I cry, my skin turns blotchy—overly pale in some places and violently red in others. Yours simply took on an ethereal quality as the tears ran down your cheeks."

Miss Otley perked up at once and agreed that her complexion was particularly well-suited to tragedy. "My eyes, as well, for they become luminescent in grief, not at all bloodshot, which I know is the more common reaction," she said before launching into a list of other ways her beauty had always set her apart.

Grateful for the opportunity to offer silent consolation, Bea listened dutifully as Miss Otley…Emily, as she insisted on being called…bemoaned the many hardships that came with physical perfection. 'Twas a constant struggle to get anyone to take her seriously, a grievance whose validity Bea was forced to concede, as she herself was having a difficult time taking the girl seriously at that very moment. Nevertheless, she listened intently and nodded understandingly and kept her brows pulled together in an expression of sympathetic concern. She even murmured, "You poor dear" a few times—and meant it, for it was clear the young woman's life had been shaped almost solely by her appearance, a prospect that seemed quite depressing to Bea.

A knock on the door brought their tête-à-tête to an end, and Beatrice excused herself when she saw it was Mrs. Otley, who wanted to check on her daughter's progress. Her lips tightened in stern disapproval when she saw that none had been made. She was further annoyed when Emily thanked Bea for the mob cap. "It's quite the most marvelous one I've ever seen."

Bea dipped her head and returned to her room to sift through the information she'd gathered before changing for dinner. Emily's description of events seemed to align with Kesgrave's claim that the deceased had lied to his investors. The fact that the Incomparable had been unable to find a letter detailing the destruction of the hibiscus crop indicated that no such devastation had occurred. The fire was merely a fiction that allowed Otley to not only pocket the funds his investors had sunk into his new enterprise but also keep all the profit from the sale of the tea for himself. If the hibiscus plants themselves ceased to exist, then the obligation to pay dividends on the earnings derived from them likewise vanished.

Was it possible for a man to tell a falsehood so flagrant and get away with it? Did not the acres of thriving hibiscus plants belie the story for everyone to see?

Ah, but this is India, Bea reminded herself.

Confirming the report would be virtually impossible, for it would have to rely on firsthand accounts and those could not be attained easily. Kesgrave's friend, for example, would have to hire an agent in London, send him around the Cape of Good Hope to India, trust he could find the exact location of Mr. Otley's hibiscus plants and wait for him to send a report back. The trip from London to Bombay took at least four months, which meant investigating a claim might consume almost an entire year, by which time anything could have happened, including a fire that actually wiped out the entire crop.

Bea didn't doubt that Otley's business ventures—both his hibiscus shrubs and his swindle—continued to thrive. No wonder Madame Babineaux's bills were paid with customary haste.

But his earlier business, the spice trade upon which he had built his name, seemed to have suffered a genuine setback if Emily's description of both her mother's behavior and Mr. Wilson's letters was to be believed. The loss of the lucrative trade to a competitor had created a fiscal crisis that the immoral hibiscus scheme fixed.

Satisfied with that explanation, Bea retrieved the envelope she'd pilfered from the top of Miss Otley's chest of drawers and withdrew the letter.

My dearest, sweetest love,

I write to you with an eagerness that cannot be contained, for I have news, good news—indeed the best news. It's the news I have been hoping these many months to hear, for this trade is rough as are the forces that move within it. I'm desolate knowing it will still take several months to make itself known to you. At long last, the obligation that has kept me here in this arid place, this parched wasteland, with its relentless oppressive sun beaming down week after week after week, is at an end. No longer at night, when I'm unable to sleep because the intense heat has penetrated my skin and invaded my bones, will I have to picture your beautiful form, as dewy and fresh as an English morning. For you will be beside me or near me, in the verdant countryside. John Company can have this godforsaken field if it wants it so badly, I cannot care anymore. Now, finally, with the end of my exile in sight, we can begin to lay the groundwork for our future. I need only await my official release before booking passage home. Will we ever be together as husband and wife? I cannot say, for so much stands in our way. But I have been enterprising during my sojourn in this barren land and wily in my dealings with the Chinese. I leave in much better straits than when I arrived! And I hope I'm not descending into triteness when I say our love will make us rich. My darling, how happy I am that our long separation—only sixteen months and yet it feels like sixteen lifetimes—is almost at an end.

> Yr ever obedient servant,
> Charles

Stunned by the contents of the letter, Bea read it again and again to make sure she wasn't creating a love affair from a few heartfelt words. But no, it was clearly on the page: Mr. Otley's associate was enamored of his daughter.

Did Emily return his regard?

Considering the young lady's opinion of herself and her belief in the vital necessity of new hats with pink plumes, it seemed unlikely she would develop a tendre for a man of limited financial means. He had managed to make a decent sum of money while abroad, but even according to his own report, they would not be rich.

It was possible, Bea conceded, that Mr. Wilson had overestimated the warmth of Emily's feelings. Some men remained determined in their affection regardless of the encouragement they may or may not get from the object of their affection.

That could be the case here, certainly, but sincere indifference could not account for the letter's condition, which was well-worn. The grooves where it had been opened and read many times and smeared in places by teardrops indicated it was a cherished possession, as did the fact that Emily carried it with her when she traveled.

Bea looked at the date again and noted the letter had been written in late December. Had Mr. Wilson left India and reclaimed his love, as he'd intended, or had he stayed and cultivated the new hibiscus crop, as he must have been instructed? Given that his current employer was his prospective father-in-law, she imagined he'd remained to do his bidding. It would not further his suit to precipitously desert his employer in his time of need. Indeed, retaining Mr. Otley's goodwill would increase his chances of becoming a partner in the business after the marriage, which would be the best arrangement for all involved.

Had Mr. Otley known of the relationship? Would he have embraced Mr. Wilson as a prospective son-in-law?

Considering that the purpose of their visit to Lakeview Hall was to establish a connection with the Skeffingtons, the answer was a resounding no. The Otleys had higher expectations for their beautiful offspring and would never have welcomed the pretentions of an upstart former employee.

Would Emily's passionate pleas for her own happiness have swayed her father? Bea very much doubted it, for a man who valued social status and wealth so highly would find no benefit in surrendering his glittering prize of a daughter to a man who could advance neither. Skeffington's barony went back two centuries, which had to be especially appealing for Otley, who could not evade the faint whiff of trade that followed him around.

While Bea submitted to the ministrations of her maid, Annie, she tried to imagine how the scene between Emily and her father could have unfolded in the library. She pictured Mr. Otley chastising his daughter for not working hard enough to engage the affections of Mr. Skeffington, and Miss Otley announcing that she would have nothing to do with the excessively bright future her parents were bent on arranging. Instead, she would live humbly but happily with Mr. Wilson.

Bea knew there was no way either of the young lady's parents would respond with equanimity to such news. They were in awe of her beauty, yes, but only in so much as they were overwhelmed by its massive appeal on the open market. If Bea could understand all that after only a few days, then perhaps Miss Otley knew it too, and acting out of rage at their treating her like a commodity to be sold to the highest bidder, raised the candlestick and struck her father over the head.

There were several problems with her theory, as it failed to account for why the pair would choose to meet at such an infelicitous hour in a deserted portion of the home when either of their rooms would have done. But other factors fit, such as the daughter's motivation for confronting her father and her height, which put her a little below eye level with her father. Without question, she was tall enough to wield the implement effectively.

Would she have?

Could she have?

Bea had no idea.

Answering those questions would require another conversation with Emily, and Bea wondered how she would bring up the topic of Mr. Wilson without seeming to pry. Could she forthrightly ask her about him—in the context of her father's business, of course, as that was the way Emily herself had mentioned him in the first place? Or would that be too jarring? If Emily was as besotted with her father's agent as his letter implied, she would no doubt welcome the opportunity to talk about him to a sympathetic listener.

The bigger challenge, Bea decided a half hour later as she joined the subdued group in the drawing room, would be arranging another private chat with Miss Otley, who did not make a practice of seeking out intrusive spinsters. Bea didn't blame her, for Flora's attentions were far more flattering than her interrogations, and Russell's admiration, sparked by the young beauty's heightened fragility, was more gratifying.

Her surprise was therefore acute when she entered the room and Emily called out for her to sit next to her on the settee. "Look, dear, I saved you a seat," she said, indicating the cushion next to her, which was indeed empty.

At once, the hum of conversation in the room stopped, and it was impossible to say who was more stunned by the development: Flora, Aunt Vera, Russell, Mrs. Otley or Beatrice.

Smothering the urge to tell her aunt to shut her mouth before a fly flew in, Bea walked across the well-appointed room, with its blue-gray furnishings, and claimed her position next to Emily. She bid her new friend good evening and then greeted the other guests present with a dip of her head that was at once audacious and shy. The expression on Viscount Nuneaton's face was most amusing, for she could swear he was trying to figure out if he'd ever seen her before. Perhaps a new guest had arrived?

Although Bea had little experience in the role of confidante, she had a firm sense of how to perform it and she took Emily's hand with a reassuring grip. "I'm delighted to see you are looking well, my dear," she said in a low voice. "I trust you're feeling better."

Emily confirmed her spirits were much improved from her episode earlier just as Flora declared that the poor thing was too drained by recent events to make unnecessary conversation and Russell announced that the lovely dear was about to tell him about her childhood home.

The siblings stared daggers at each other as their cousin sat down.

"How sweet you both are to be concerned, but I'm delighted to make room for Beatrice," Emily said, further devastating her admirers by revealing her previous interest wasn't a mistake or an anomaly. "We just had a lovely conversation in my room, and I'm eager for it to continue."

The idea of a tête-à-tête behind closed doors so disheartened Flora that her face fell and she stuttered, "You...you d-did?"

"Your cousin brought me this mob cap," she added, pointing to the hat she wore on her head. "It was lovely of her to realize that I might wish for something ugly and plain to suit my mood."

"It was?" Flora asked wretchedly. "I don't have any mob caps, but I have a bonnet with a broken plume, which is just as ugly, if not exactly plain. I would be honored if you chose to wear it tomorrow on our walk to the folly."

Overhearing the comment, Mrs. Otley announced that she couldn't be sure she and her daughter would remain long enough in the day to embark on the planned outing. "We must pack our things and go to our home and meet with our solicitor and..."

Here, the widow trailed off because she either didn't know what came next or couldn't bear to contemplate it, and again her hosts insisted that she not feel compelled to rush off and confront the future.

Emily, aware of the compliment Flora had paid her in offering her the defective bonnet, promised to keep the item in mind but said it was far too early to consider what she would wear the next day. "Life is too unreliable to plan one's hats in advance."

Flora agreed with this observation and promptly enumerated all of the issues she was incapable of resolving beforehand. The list was comprehensive and, Bea thought, rather accurate, but the notion that her cousin avoided making decisions as a matter of precaution rather than indecisiveness struck her as a bit of a revision of history.

The conversation in the rest of the room resumed, but Bea could feel several people examining her with curiosity. Aunt Vera, for one, was trying to figure out why her niece had sought out the other young lady to give her the mob cap, as she had never made such a genial or charitable effort before. If she'd only been an outgoing child, they could have unloaded her onto another family years ago. Alas, Bea was shy and reticent, displaying a strident discomfort that was oddly infectious, as typically gregarious people suddenly became tongue-tied in her awkward presence.

Uncle Horace insisted that it was Bea's features—button nose, beady eyes, narrow lips—that unsettled people, for they made her seem perpetually steeped in remorse. She looked as if she was always on the verge of apologizing for herself.

Nuneaton was watching her too, trying, Bea thought with cynical amusement, to determine when she'd joined the party. Perhaps that afternoon, while the gentlemen had been fishing in the lake? It seemed the most likely, and yet how ghoulish to arrive at a house only hours after it had suffered a self-murder. If she was so bent on travel, then she could have stayed with some friends in Tunbridge Wells.

Although highly entertained, Bea kept her expression mild as she imagined the viscount's thoughts.

"What color I feel like wearing often depends on the weather," Emily said, "for it's impossible to wear green when it is gray outside."

"Oh, yes, indeed," Flora said with deep satisfaction, as if she'd had this exact thought many times in her lifetime but never before had the opportunity to express it. "And to wear pink when it is snowing is beyond supportable."

Bea, who had been looking at Nuneaton out of the corner of her eye, tilted her head toward Emily to see if she would respond to Flora's comment with equal fervor. Alas, Miss Otley did not hold this conviction and insisted that rose was the ideal shade to don on a winter's day, for it matched the color one's cheeks turned from the chill and bluster. Flora squeaked lightly in distress, then rallied with the insistence that if her cheeks flushed as becomingly as Miss Otley's, she would wear pink all the time.

While Bea listened to the girls' entertaining chatter and discreetly observed Nuneaton, she studiously avoided Kesgrave's gaze. Even without peeking under her eyelashes to confirm it, she knew he was staring at her with more interest than was appropriate to the setting. If he didn't divert his attention elsewhere soon, the viscount would begin to wonder if his toplofty friend had lowered his standards to consider a mousy spinster, and her aunt would chastise her for browbeating the poor duke—even though she hadn't said a word in his direction.

Affecting indifference was more challenging than she would have liked, for she could feel the prickle of his attention on the back of her neck and her body positively itched with the desire to face him head on. After her informative exchange with Emily, the advantage was hers, and the duke knew it. Moreover, he knew that she knew it. He'd warned her off investigating the murder as if he had any say over her actions, and she had openly defied him— because, despite his very great opinion of himself, he did *not* have say over her actions. Even her aunt, who had the most claim to the right of influence, would concede that the best she could do with Bea was point her strongly in the correct direction. A grown woman of six and twenty could not be bear-led like a child.

Bea maintained her pose of apathy for a full fifteen minutes, but when the butler announced that dinner was ready, her self-control flagged just long enough for her to turn her head toward Kesgrave. She'd expected his attention to be diverted in the bustle of transferring to the dining room, but his brilliant blue gaze remained firmly fixed on her.

Meeting it, she felt her heart tumble in her chest with anticipation, for it seemed as if some challenge had been issued and accepted. He must have sensed it too, for his head dipped as if in solemn acknowledgment and then his lips quirked with faint humor. The air hummed with awareness, and Bea, unsettled by the strange intensity of the moment, resolved not to be the one who looked away first. Kesgrave appeared to be equally reluctant to end the encounter and would probably be staring at her still if their hostess hadn't claimed his attention. He dropped his head nearer to Lady Skeffington's to listen more closely, and watching them together, Bea felt oddly bereft. It was a ridiculous response, of course, and all she needed to do to shake free of the unsettling sensation was recall the letter from Mr. Wilson tucked in her pocket.

Advantage Beatrice.

Dinner was a restrained affair, with Lord Skeffington directing the conversation to harmless topics such as that afternoon's fishing expedition, and Kesgrave obligingly accepted the opportunity to lecture the company on how to tie flies, as he considered himself something of a master of the art. Sadly, the other gentlemen shared his view as well, and Bea could not decide whose gushing was designed to inflate his self-esteem more, Russell's or Amersham's.

"I have never seen anything like your minnow," Amersham said. "A thing of beauty in green and white silk and a tail and fins made from feathers."

"It's true, your grace," Russell insisted. "Your minnow is perfection."

Accustomed to such flattery, for Kesgrave was a sportsman of some note, he accepted their praise with a simple nod, as he unmistakably considered it his due. Bea found his superiority so insufferable, she could not hold back her speech despite making a firm resolution before dinner to say nothing untoward that might upset her aunt during the meal. "Since the duke is such an authority, perhaps he would consider leading a seminar so that others may acquire his skill."

The possibility of learning how to tie a fly at the knee

of a master appealed to Russell so much, he said, "Oh, I say, your grace, that would be bang-up decent of you."

Kesgrave didn't respond right away because he was too busy aiming a look of annoyance at Bea. Before he could extricate himself from the situation, Aunt Vera, who couldn't decide where to direct her ire—niece or son—blushed hotly and began to offer excuses.

"Don't be silly, Russell...I mean, Bea...I mean, children," she said, her tone hardened by embarrassment. "His grace is far too important a man to lead instruction like a...like a lowly governess. His responsibilities are manifold, and to suggest he take half a day away from them to instruct anyone on how to tie a fly is preposterous."

Although Bea considered her aunt's feelings to be of utmost importance, she simply could not resist goading Kesgrave. "Ah, but an expert like the duke would require no more than an hour to impart his knowledge."

At this pronouncement, the red in Aunt Vera's cheeks deepened into an impossibly bright shade of purple, making her face resemble an overlarge beet. She tried to laugh off her mortification, but all she could produce was a soft squeal like an injured pig.

"Mrs. Hyde-Clare is correct to express concern over how I distribute my time, as there never do seem to be enough hours in a day for me to accomplish all that I require," Kesgrave said with a kind smile at his defender. "It's a great comfort to know you are looking out for my best interests."

Aunt Vera simpered at the praise. "My niece is young and naïve and does not understand what it means to be a person of your stature, your grace."

Kesgrave's look of amusement indicated he believed Bea to be neither young nor naïve, but he gave this observation his full approval. "I trust you will enlighten her on the matter, as it shouldn't take above half a day for you to impart *your* knowledge."

The duke's remark was only a suggestion, with none

of the obligations of an agreement or a pact, but Aunt Vera took it as if a decree from royalty and said, "Oh, yes, your grace, yes, I will do that posthaste. The session will start promptly at ten tomorrow morning. My daughter, Flora, will join us as well, for she is also young, though lacking the naiveté of her older cousin." Ignoring her daughter's cry of outrage at the prospect of being punished for Bea's crimes, Aunt Vera turned to her hostess and proposed she attend as a guest lecturer as well. "Your elevated position in society offers you insights to which I'm not privy."

Although setting up a schoolroom in the front parlor was not on the approved list of country-house-party activities, Lady Skeffington agreed to lend her authority to the proceedings and proposed an assortment of tea cakes as an appropriate refreshment.

Kesgrave applauded the addition of snacks and recommended the inclusion of biscuits as a treat. Then he complimented Aunt Vera on how quickly she'd taken charge of the situation. "I'm so inspired by you, my dear, that I'm also going to offer a session tomorrow at eleven a.m., for the gentlemen, of course, to learn how to improve their flies. As you so astutely observed, I'm too busy to lead the course myself, but Harris, my valet, shares my skill with silk and feathers and will provide instruction in my method for anyone who is interested."

Russell and Amersham tripped over each other in their rush to accept the gracious offer while Mr. Skeffington, whose curiosity was also keen, tilted his head and said he would be delighted to look in on such an event. Even Lord Skeffington, who had been tying his own flies since in leading strings, resolved to put off his usual morning ride to attend. Only Nuneaton professed himself too enamored of leisure to try to improve himself before noon.

"Excellent," the duke said with satisfaction before turning to Bea to preen in his triumph. "Thank you, Miss Hyde-Clare, for arranging such an enlightening and productive morning for all of us."

His gratitude was echoed by several others at the table, including her aunt, whose earlier humiliation had been forgotten in her eagerness to lecture her niece on proper behavior.

As difficult as it was for Bea to swallow, she had to concede the round to Kesgrave, who had smoothly outmaneuvered her at her own game. Meeting his smug gaze was somewhat harder, for he fairly radiated satisfaction, but she made herself do it. Looking away implied weakness.

Besides, she reminded herself as she twisted her lips into a smile, he might have won this round, but she still had the letter.

The advantage remained hers, and when Mr. Skeffington sat down next to her in the drawing room after the gentlemen had indulged in port, she perceived an opportunity to strengthen her superior position.

Opportunity, yes, but she had no idea how to make the most of it. She couldn't very well turn to him with a bright smile and say, "Tell me, Mr. Skeffington, have you invested in any hibiscus shrubs lately and were you handsomely rewarded for your efforts?"

He and Amersham liked to gamble at the card table, which was similar to investing in a faraway land, as both endeavors required luck and the potential to lose great sums. Perhaps she could start with a comment about piquet and deftly maneuver the conversation to India and crops.

Unable to stop herself, Bea laughed at the idea of her deftly maneuvering any conversation, for if she had the skill of polite drawing room chatter, she would have been married long ago.

"Is something amusing?" Mr. Skeffington said, turning to look at her with confusion.

Bea felt a hot flush begin to overtake her cheeks. "Not at all. I was just thinking of...of poor Mr. Otley." No, that would never do. "I mean...that is to say, I'm very saddened by his passing and saddened that I didn't get to know him better." It was far from a smooth recovery but perhaps she had stumbled into the opportunity for which she had been hoping. "Not like you did, to have business dealings with him or to learn about the spice trade in India."

As soon as she uttered the words *business dealings,* Mr. Skeffington stiffened, coldly excused himself and stood up.

Yes, Bea thought, watching him stride across the room, that interaction pretty much summed up her entire career on the Marriage Mart.

She was undaunted, however, for his response confirmed all that she'd surmised about his relationship with the dead man. Mr. Skeffington had invested in Mr. Otley's hibiscus scheme and knew he had been played for a fool.

Satisfied, she looked up and found Kesgrave watching her with an amused glint in his blue eyes. He had witnessed her exchange with the young man and no doubt thought her humiliated by his eagerness to get away from her.

Not at all, she thought, nodding at the duke and grinning widely. Not at all.

CHAPTER SEVEN

As Vera Hyde-Clare had not been trained in the latest peda-
gogical methods, she knew little about holding her students' attention and merely recited a seemingly endless list
of social dictates while standing at the front of the room.
If she had thought to engage her students using the Socrat-
ic approach, Bea would have been forced to pay attention
and Flora would not have been able to embroider a frond
motif on the edge of a handkerchief as a bereavement gift
for Miss Otley.

While Aunt Vera explained the many guidelines governing the use of calling cards—paper quality, style of en-
graving, ideal hour of delivery—Bea considered everything
she knew about Mr. Otley's business ventures in India. It
seemed obvious to her that his unfortunate end was relat-
ed to either the swindle of his investors or to his daughter's love affair with his associate. In order to get a better
sense of the cause, she would need to gather a comprehensive list of his investors and quiz Emily on her relationship
with Mr. Wilson. She'd been thwarted in her attempts at
the latter the night before when Mrs. Otley insisted they
both retire immediately following dinner in order to be
well-rested for the challenges ahead. Having discussed the

matter thoroughly with Lady Skeffington, the widow had decided they would take one more day to bask in the comfort of friends and depart the day after.

"It is such a bittersweet consolation to be among friends," she'd said upon announcing her decision. "To be sure, there's nothing to be gained from hiding here, but I'm in no rush to expose my husband's disgrace to the world."

Her reluctance made sense to everyone, as they all knew what desecration awaited the self-murderer outside the confines of the wine cellar, but only Bea felt the depth of the injustice.

"A calling card is not to be elaborately decorated, as ornamentation is considered to be in bad taste," Aunt Vera said in a tone curiously devoid of inflection, as if reading from an unfamiliar script. "A case for carrying one's cards is a necessity and can be made from the following materials, all of which are appropriate: sterling silver, Morocco leather, vermeil."

As the lecture dragged on, Bea thought about Mr. Wilson—or Charles, as he had signed his letter—and wondered what kind of future he could reasonably hope to share with Emily. Although she'd imagined the young beauty chafing at the expectations of her parents, she didn't actually believe the Incomparable, with her finely wrought plumed hats, would gamely enjoy a humble existence. How passionately she had railed against the indignity of rushlights! For such a woman, poverty would be even more restrictive than social-climbing parents. Mr. Wilson had claimed, however, to have done well while serving in the arid clime of India. Had he squirreled away enough money to satisfy Miss Otley and what hope did he have of supplementing his funds after he returned to England?

"A calling card should be engraved in a plain script, as its purpose is to present its holder in a straightforward manner. A card that is difficult to read connotes a person who is difficult to read, which is unwelcome for several reasons that I will catalog in the next section," Aunt Vera explained.

"As for the size of the script, it must be neither too large nor too small. A person who favors either extreme is a person who favors extremity, which is not a desirable trait in a caller. Indeed, extremity is the enemy of refinement."

Bea smiled at her aunt's pronouncement, for it seemed to sum up her relation perfectly. Aunt Vera did not like to live her life on the edge, preferring to remain in the middle, where it was comfortable. Too hot would never do but neither would too cold. It was the same with everything: not too hard, not too soft, not too wet, not too dry, not too—

At once, Bea froze as a detail from Mr. Wilson's letter struck her as being incongruent with already established facts. Mrs. Otley had said that her husband had settled on hibiscus plants because their land was well-suited to the crop, and Kesgrave had insisted that May was monsoon season in the southern region. Taken together, those two pieces of information meant that an amiable climate for growing hibiscus was a wet one.

Yet Mr. Wilson had complained about the excessively dry conditions of his location. His letter was dated December, so it was quite possible that area could be arid in winter and soggy in spring.

But was it likely?

Bea had no idea.

Once again, she was forced to lament the oversight in her education that had left her ignorant of the weather conditions in India. What she did know, having just finished an account of Viscount Townshend and the agricultural advances he ushered in, was that most crops were very particular about their growing environment. The mineral content of the soil, the air temperature and the amount of moisture they got had to be just right.

There was only one way to rectify the gap in her knowledge, and she stood up to search the library, for a collection that immense had to contain at least one book with relevant data about the country's climate.

At the front of the room, her aunt broke off her sentence and raised an eyebrow. "Going somewhere, my dear?"

Devil it! In her enthusiasm, she'd forgotten entirely the interminable lecture on manners her aunt was conducting.

"I...uh...thought you were done," she stammered.

It was a terrible excuse, which her aunt pooh-poohed. "I was going to discuss the etiquette that governs dancing cards next," she said with a moue of disapproval, "but we will digress first to the proper way for a lady to excuse herself from company, as that's the lesson of which we are sorely in dire need."

Bea slunk back down into her seat with a heavy sigh as her cousin grinned.

Aunt Vera spoke for another forty-five minutes before inviting Lady Skeffington to the front of the room to share her wisdom. Their host glided to the fireplace, curtsied slightly and thanked everyone for coming—to the seminar on manners or to the house party, Bea could not tell.

"During my years in society, I've learned that only one thing matters," she said with a cheerful smile. "Consider the comfort of others to be of paramount importance, and everything else will fall into place."

Her speech was so succinct and to the point, Aunt Vera could not grasp that it was over. She kept looking at Lady Skeffington with an air of expectation, and Lady Skeffington kept staring back with an air of finality.

As the impasse drew into its second minute, Beatrice stood up and said, "Thank you, my lady, for that very elucidating and profound advice. I know I will follow it all the days of my life. Now, if you'll excuse me, I need to visit the"—it was on the tip of her tongue to mention the library but feared that would reveal too much—"privy. Yes, I had quite a lot of tea."

"Bea!" her aunt exclaimed, appalled at this display of outrageous behavior. "We just talked about this. Ladies do not admit to any biological functions."

"Yes, Bea," Flora said, smirking. "Weren't you listening? It was in the section on hygiene."

"Of course, I remember," Bea lied smoothly. "The hygiene section was a favorite. I do particularly love disavowing my own physiological processes."

While Aunt Vera smiled appreciatively at the compliment, Bea walked toward the entrance, her steps measured and even. As soon as she crossed the threshold, she picked up her skirts and started to run down the hallway. She turned left, then right, then raced up the staircase and through another corridor until she arrived at the library. When she reached the doorway, she came to a sudden stop, surprised to find herself hesitant to return to the room where the murder had taken place.

Her reluctance was reasonable, she knew, for Mr. Otley's death had presented a grisly sight and there was the very real possibility that the killer had still been on the scene when she'd arrived. The prospect that he had seen her clearly, that he was among the guests at Lakeview Hall, unsettled her deeply, and being back in the library somehow made those feelings stronger. But as rational as her fear was, she had no patience for it. The library was empty now and presented no threat, and she had to believe she was made of sterner stuff than to let the memory of something awful curtail her movements.

She took two steps into the room, paused cautiously, as if to survey her immediate environs and confirm she was alone, then dashed up the stairs. Although the organization of the library was still a mystery to her, it was much easier to find the correct section in the bright light of day, and she quickly selected the two books that seemed the most promising: *The Almanac of the World* and *Book of Fascinating Facts* and *Travels in India: My Journey Through a Strange, Difficult and Wonderful Land,* a travelogue by the wife of the attaché to the sixth governor-general of Fort William.

With the two reference books in hand, she returned to her room, eager to find out what she could about the climate of India and the horticultural requirements of hibiscus shrubs. She had plenty of time for research, as her presence wasn't required for another two hours, when the ladies would accompany their hostess on a stroll to a folly that sat on the southern edge of the property. She thought the proposed walk was an excellent idea, for there were few things she enjoyed more than an amble through beautiful countryside and the activity would present several opportunities for private conversation with Emily. She would learn the details of her relationship with Mr. Wilson and discover if the young lady had anything to do with the death of her father.

She would do all this while the duke, who always thought he was the cleverest person in the room, wasted the day fishing for trout.

Delighted by the prospect, she settled in to read.

Bea began with the almanac, which proved to be almost immediately helpful, for after only twenty minutes of useful consultation with its index she knew that hibiscus grew only in soil that was moist year-round. Wherever Mr. Wilson was stationed, it was certainly not in the path of the monsoons. That meant that Mr. Otley not only never had a devastating fire, he never had a hibiscus crop either. The investment scheme, from top to bottom, had been an invention. She was sure of it.

The hibiscus shrubs might never have existed, but Mr. Wilson had been overseeing some crop that was taken over by John Company.

What plants prospered in the arid regions of India?

She returned to the almanac and resumed reading.

Ah, there is it, she thought: tobacco, cotton, wheat, barley, poppy and indica.

Thinking of Mr. Wilson's mention of China, she put down *The Almanac of the World and Book of Fascinating Facts* and opened the travelogue to figure out which of those crops would be of the most interest to the Chinese. Mrs. Barlow had not been thoughtful enough to include an index, but perusal of several chapters revealed China's deep and complicated history with opium, which Jiaqing, emperor of the Qing dynasty, outlawed at the turn of the century. The East India Company, the joint-stock firm that all but owned India and ruled it with an army large enough to rival the British force, relied too heavily to give up the lucrative trade just because it was now illegal. It had worked too hard and too brutally to corner the market on poppy production to simply abandon the monopoly. Instead, it created a large and successful smuggling operation.

Although the brutality of the East India Company's practices horrified Bea, Mrs. Barlow wrote about them with clear admiration, for she believed it was within its rights to seize the fields of local farmers and prohibit private cultivation.

It was this detail that convinced Bea that Mr. Otley's venture, however it might have started three decades ago, was most recently steeped in opium production. It could have been the cultivation of tea, of course, or even cotton, but Mr. Wilson specifically mentioned John Company, which was the informal name of the East India Company. It was too much of a coincidence that the setback described by Emily and her lover was exactly in line with the British firm's well-known behavior.

And yet somehow Mr. Otley, whose business dealings in the country preceded the opium ban, had managed to evade John Company's notice for years. Inevitably, it had been only a matter of time before the company took over his field and drove him out of business. Given how well established the spice trader's reputation was, Bea could only surmise that he used clever tactics to either elude its attention or soothe its concerns.

No wonder Mrs. Otley was so frantic when word of the seizure reached them. It was no simple thing to find another source of income, certainly not one that would support the family in the habit to which they had become accustomed. That would explain why they began to practice minor economies such as replacing expensive candles with rushlights and buying inferior-quality boots.

Mr. and Mrs. Otley must have realized quickly that these reductions in expenditures were too small to make a difference. Something drastic had to be done.

Enter hibiscus.

His sterling reputation intact, Mr. Otley probably had no trouble finding investors eager to reap his success. With the funds they provided, he had enough money to invest in reliable ventures like copper mines in Cornwall.

How much had Skeffington and Amersham lost? A few hundred pounds, perhaps? Possibly more?

Did the exact sum matter or was the true damage to their vanity?

Having discovered all she could from books, Bea consulted the clock and decided she had more than enough time left to search the young men's rooms for evidence. It was only two, and the walk to the folly was scheduled to begin at three.

Bea looked out the window to see if Skeffington and Amersham were still fishing. Frustratingly, she couldn't tell because the view was blocked by a large oak tree. Determined to not let the bucolic wonders of Cumbria stand in the way of justice for Mr. Otley, she opened the pane, confirmed the sturdiness of the branch outside and climbed out to get an unimpeded look at the lake.

Ah, yes, there they were, she thought, noting the figures in the distance. She counted their numbers, and feeling confident she could search the young men's rooms without discovery, climbed back inside and exited her bedchamber.

Bea started with Amersham's rooms because they were on her right as she entered the hallway. Mindful of the time—she still had to change into a walking dress before heading out to the folly—she rifled through his drawers quickly, carelessly tossing aside articles of clothing in her haste. She didn't worry about making a mess because Amersham's drawers and cabinets were already wildly disorganized, and she marveled that a man could employ a valet who so closely shared his habits. In less than ten minutes, she had searched very corner of his room and had uncovered no evidence of blood or bloody clothes.

Very well, she thought, closing the door to the dressing room, onto the next suspect.

As soon as she stepped into Mr. Skeffington's bedchamber, Bea could see that she would have to be scrupulous in her search, for the room was meticulously neat. The surfaces were bare except for a few essential items such as a candlestick next to the bed and a box of cheroots on the clothespress.

She sighed deeply and decided to start in the dressing room, as the first thing she wanted to inspect was the laundry. Before she could take a single step in that direction, she heard a floorboard creak and her heart flipped over in her chest.

Was somebody there?

Not Skeffington, she knew for sure, because she had confirmed his whereabouts. His valet, perhaps, ironing his cravats for his dinner clothes? Or maybe the upstairs maid putting away some freshly laundered shirts?

The creak sounded again and Bea called herself a fool for even wondering who was in the dressing room. It didn't matter who found her snooping around, only that she would be found.

Before she could scurry out of the bedchamber, she heard the door to the dressing room open and, terrified she was about to be caught in a position she couldn't possibly explain, she dropped to her knees next to the bed, bumping the bedside table in her mad scamper and knocking over the candlestick, which landed with a ringing thud.

Mortified, Bea looked up to confront her discoverer and found herself staring into the glinting eyes of the Duke of Kesgrave.

CHAPTER EIGHT

To say that Beatrice would rather it have been the maid or valet wasn't entirely accurate, but some part of her wished she was scrambling at that very moment to make convincing excuses to a servant rather than flinching under the duke's withering amusement.

"Ah, Miss Hyde-Clare, as enthusiastic as ever, I see," he said wryly. "I trust you are uncovering an incredibly vital piece of information under Mr. Skeffington's bed."

Knowing the mockery was well-deserved, Bea patted the letter from Mr. Wilson, which was tucked into her pocket, and reminded herself that she wasn't wholly without her competencies. "I am uncovering incredibly vital information, yes," she said, ignoring the hand he offered to help her to her feet. Instead she gave him the candlestick, which he returned to the bedside table.

Almost immediately after, however, he picked the implement up again, carried it over to the window, where the light was better, and examined it with intense concentration. He held it up to his nose for an even closer inspection, and Bea, who had initially found this behavior strange, grasped what he was doing.

Hoping to strike a note of being only a little bit smug,

she said, "Incredibly vital information such as the whereabouts of your candlestick, which disappeared from the library the other night."

"What?" he asked, raising his head to stare at her. "No."

'Twas an even more unconvincing lie than whatever nonsensical story Bea would have told to the maid or valet. "Tell me, your grace, how can you be sure?"

He considered her for a moment, several seconds of extended silence during which he debated the relative merits of holding to his fiction, a consideration that amused Bea in its futility, for she would not be pawned off. He must have realized this as well, for he decided to answer her simple question with a treatise on the candlestick's style, weight, material, design and authorship. He spoke for so many uninteresting minutes on the particular nicks and imperfections he'd noted during his limited use of the implement, she'd almost missed it when he mentioned blood on the fluting.

She stiffened in surprise and tried to grab the candlestick to get a better look, but Kesgrave held firm.

"Here, you see," he said, bending his head close to hers as he pointed to one area in particular, "the smudge. If I had to guess, I would say the blood transferred itself from the murderer's hand to the candlestick."

He was right, of course. Just above the petal motif on the flared base was a dark red mark that, in the circumstance, could only be blood.

The finding would indicate that Mr. Skeffington was indeed their killer.

Bea held the thought for a moment to see how satisfying it felt to have discovered the conclusive piece of evidence sitting on the bedside table in clear sight. After a moment, she shook her head and murmured, "No, not at all."

Kesgrave lifted his eyes, curious and blue, and Bea was suddenly aware of how very close they were too each other. She took a step back, cleared her throat self-consciously and explained, "This is meant to be clear, incontrovertible proof that Mr. Skeffington is the culprit, but it's too simplistic to believe a guilty man of four and twenty would have left a damning piece of evidence next to his bedside. There are other suspects with more-convincing motives and perhaps one was wily enough to place it here to give the appearance of guilt."

Slowly, the duke put down the candlestick on the clothespress and regarded Beatrice thoughtfully for long, drawn-out moments. If she'd thought standing so close to him was uncomfortable, it was nothing compared with the way he made her feel now, as if she were a butterfly under glass. She resolved not to flinch while he tried to identify her genus and species, or, as she conceded was more likely, come up with a believable lie to get her to stop investigating Mr. Otley's death as he'd already requested.

Finally, he said, "I'll scream."

Now it was Bea's turn to stare as if trying to figure out what rare and strange creature he was, for his announcement defied all reason. What benefit could he derive from bringing the house down around their ears? He was a duke, and she was a lowly orphan with a plain face and few prospects. Did he not understand the particulars of the situation? He'd previously impressed her as a clever man, but perhaps the pressure of trying to find a murderer had caused his brain to fail in a significantly debilitating way.

"Refuse to tell me everything you know about Otley's death," he continued in the same mild tone, "and I will scream. Everyone will come running and you will find yourself compromised beyond all hope and forced to marry me. Think of it, Miss Hyde-Clare, leg-shackled to a pedantic, know-everything duke for the rest of your life: tiresome conversation, plodding children, endless lists of British warships day and night. Surely, you have something better in mind for yourself—a cottage in the country, spirited debate with like-minded fellows, every book ever written at your fingertips and time enough to read them."

Although the duke's description of the future he

thought she wanted for herself showed surprising insight into the way her brain worked, for, "Yes, please, fortune, do bestow all of that on me," was the first thing that flitted through her mind, it also demonstrated a remarkable ignorance of the economic realities of the world. As an impoverished relation dependent on the generosity of her family, she couldn't simply insist they provide her with an establishment of her own, a few reliable old retainers and a well-stocked library. Rather, she would spend the rest of her life in service either to her aunt, as a companion in her dotage, or her cousins, as a nanny for their children.

Indeed, the only way for her to achieve the situation he described was to let him scream. No doubt the coins in his purse at that very moment were enough to provide her with a modest living for the rest of her life.

The unintended irony of Kesgrave's threat made Beatrice smile, and she decided to call his bluff just for the pleasure of watching him scramble.

"No need to put yourself out, your grace, I'm happy to scream for the both of us," she said and inhaled deeply.

Given all she knew about Kesgrave, she expected him to turn white with fear and press a panicked hand against her mouth, but he merely smiled.

The toplofty duke was calling her bluff of calling his bluff.

Beatrice couldn't help but admire the cool-headed response, and for the first time since meeting him five days ago, she found herself feeling grudging respect for the gentleman. Perhaps he wasn't quite the preening bag of wind he presented to the world.

"I must congratulate you, Kesgrave, on not flinching when confronted with a fate worse than death. A lesser man would have tackled me to the ground to forestall the promised scream."

He bowed his head in acknowledgment. "I'm delighted to discover you think there are men lesser than me, as your treatment would indicate that I'm in fact the bottom of the barrel. Tell me, Miss Hyde-Clare, why do you find my knowledge to be so objectionable? Would it be better if I pretended not to know things? Is ignorance suddenly in fashion?"

"I'm surprised you have to ask, your grace," she said. "Isn't ignorance always in fashion for ladies?"

Although she'd proffered the question lightly, almost teasingly, the duke took genuine offense at the charge, straightening his shoulders and asking with forceful indignation, "Do you dare imply that I expect less from women than I do from men?"

She'd indeed been implying that very thing, but taking his outrage into consideration and his consistently condescending behavior, she was forced to concede the injustice of the charge. Kesgrave thought himself superior to everyone—women, men, children, horses, strange long-necked animals on the savannah in Africa. A general disgust of the world wasn't a character trait she usually found admirable, but somehow a duke of his standing not holding his sex in higher esteem felt like a commendably broad-minded point of view.

"I do, your grace, or, rather, I did," she admitted honestly. "But I would like to withdraw the remark, as you're correct to object. You expect nothing from anybody across all realms and strata, and disdain that consistent deserves my respect."

She thought her comments would elicit another outburst, but the duke's lips twitched and he said, "That's all I ever wanted."

He was being facetious, of course, for there could not be anything of less value to a duke than an orphaned spinster's good opinion, and yet he spoke with enough sincerity to give her pause.

The pause, she realized with unsettling clarity, was regret that her respect would never be something he sought.

Hoping to diminish the feeling of foolishness such a revelation imposed, she directed her thoughts back to the information for which he had asked. Her immediate impulse was to deny the request simply because he made it, but recognizing her own perversity she held her tongue and examined her reasons in investigating Mr. Otley's death. Originally, she had been motivated by resentment at Kesgrave's treatment of the victim—claiming he killed himself when he had been brutally murdered. Was there anything more unjust? As soon as she figured out the duke's purpose in telling the lie, however, that motivation had been removed. She knew he was looking into the incident and wouldn't rest until the perpetrator was apprehended. So why did she still persist with her own investigation? Was it only to spite Kesgrave, who had pricked her ego by insisting she desist and annoyed her with his pedantry and arrogance?

If her primary goal was justice for Mr. Otley—and she sincerely believed it was—then she could not let her self-regard stand in the way. Working with the duke, rather than against him, was the only practical solution.

Taking the sensible approach, however, did not mean denying herself pleasure altogether. "May I say, your grace, how refreshing your willingness is to admit without shame or embarrassment that you're unable to finish a task on your own. Many men of my acquaintance"—this statement was a flat-out lie, as Bea had no men in her acquaintance— "would sooner give up membership to their club for a full year than admit they need help."

Kesgrave ignored her attempts at incitement and remained stubbornly focused on the topic. "All that you know, Miss Hyde-Clare?"

Bea was not the sort of woman who continued to dance after the orchestra had stopped playing. "Through investigation, discernment and research, I have discovered the following things: Mr. Otley was heavily invested in poppies and most likely made his fortune smuggling opium into China. His operation was taken over late last year by the East India Company, which left him destitute and without a source of future income. The hibiscus shrubs never existed. They were merely an invention to fleece investors, including

Mr. Skeffington and Amersham, who appear to be aware of the fact that they were gulled. His daughter, Emily, is conducting a love affair with his managing agent in India, a man named Charles Wilson. I found this letter"—she pulled it out of her pocket and handed it to him—"to that effect in her bedroom yesterday prior to dinner."

Although he unfolded the letter, he did not look at it because he was too busy staring at her in astonishment, for he plainly had no idea she could manage to gather so much information in so little time. He'd known, of course, that she'd been poking around, for he himself had found her in his own rooms examining the books on his bedside table. But he hadn't believed she'd uncovered anything of consequence through her efforts. He'd assumed she'd merely coaxed some useful gossip from a young lady only a year or two removed from the schoolroom.

As Miss Beatrice Hyde-Clare had had few occasions to impress anyone in her lifetime, save her parents, whose delight at her minor accomplishments as a five-year-old were barely a vague memory, it was an intoxicating sensation and well worth the humiliation of their meeting.

It was also deeply unsettling, for she knew how dangerous it was to desire his approval.

The Duke of Kesgrave could not be that important to her.

Unable to bear the thoughts that had emerged during the brief silence, she said, "Now it's your turn, you grace, to share what you've discovered. Since we've already established that you consider women to be no more or less trivial than men, I trust we are equals in this investigation. To be entirely frank, I don't believe you can solve the mystery without my input because, although I'm not as ostentatious with my knowledge as you, I'm just as clever."

Bea wasn't sure if she meant the boastful speech to be provoking or not, as her overriding concern in speaking was to distract herself, but now that the sentiment had been expressed, she didn't think the duke could resist the bait.

And yet somehow he did. "I'm investigating Otley's hibiscus scheme on behalf of Lord Gresford, a gentleman of three and seventy years who counted himself among my late father's closest friends. He lives very modestly in Wales and can ill afford to lose the money Otley has stolen, which is why, even if I didn't have a personal incentive for assisting him, I'd feel morally obligated. Gresford is not alone, as I've learned that the majority of Otley's victims were either old fools or callow youths. As you've already discovered, Mr. Skeffington and Lord Amersham are investors. They each lost two thousand pounds."

Despite the narrow confines of her life, Bea did not consider herself to be naïve or provincial. She read constantly—newspapers, journals, books—and had a strong grasp on the way the world functioned. But at the mention of this vast sum, her jaw dropped in astonishment. With coffers that deep, she could buy a small cottage in the country and supply it with books for the rest of her life.

"Their fathers do not know," Kesgrave added.

Although Bea had concluded that from the conversation she had overheard, she had not grasped it full meaning because she hadn't known how deep the well went. "From whence did they get such a large amount of money?"

"Money lenders," he said.

She scoffed in disgust and began to calculate the interest accrued on such a vast sum. Even using a conservative rate of twenty percent, she estimated the figure would increase by more than half by the time they reached their majorities. "Noodle-headed nodcocks."

"Indisputably," the duke agreed. "But in their defense, Mr. Otley was a longtime friend of Skeffington's parents and he had every reason to believe the investment was on the level. I don't think even the most fly cove or leery fox would suspect a family friend was out to fleece him. Naturally, one would assume he would be too honorable to behave in such a manner."

As judicious as he made the decision sound, Bea

could not believe that that was how all rational gentlemen behaved: Her uncle? Her father? The duke? Did they all really think it was wise to send massive quantities of money thousands of miles away to places they'd never seen and would never visit? It struck her at once as sheer madness and gross negligence.

Perhaps it was just as well her pockets were to let, for she would never have the courage for investing.

Correctly reading her appalled expression, Kesgrave said, "I understand your dismay, but it's not all just a roll of the dice. One typically researches an investment by checking previous successes and talking with associates who have had positive experiences. Every investment is a gamble, but there are many good and reliable ways to ensure that you've hedged your bets. The problem here is that these clodheads were so eager to double their blunt they let familiarity stand in for due diligence. If Otley had been an honorable man, he would never have accepted their money without first insisting they research the opportunity further or get the approval of their sires. But one cannot blame a scoundrel for behaving like a scoundrel."

Bea thought holding a scoundrel accountable for his actions was precisely the way you should deal with such a creature, but since this one had already been held to account by someone else, she decided there was no point in disagreeing. "Have you confirmed that Lord Skeffington knows nothing of this transaction? If the pair of them still owe thousands of pounds to the money lenders, then disposing of Mr. Otley would not further their cause at all. It seems exceedingly self-indulgent of them to fulfill their need for revenge when the outstanding debt is without question the more-pressing matter."

The duke laughed, and Bea, who had said the remark in all seriousness, stared at him in surprise, for the sound was far more melodic and joyful than she would have expected from one so didactic and assured.

His eyes still glimmering with delight, he shook his head

and said, "Your callous pragmatism is a thing of beauty."

It was truly impossible to know how to take such a comment, for it had the ring of sincerity and yet the words themselves were deeply unflattering. Nobody strove to be called either callous or pragmatic. Certainly, one didn't want to be overly sentimental, for clear thinking required rigor and prudence, but nor did one want to be considered hardheaded and coldly efficient.

"Your understanding of the situation, alas, does not take into account the fragility of a young man's ego," he said, seemingly unaware of her confusion. "Undoubtedly, they had a better chance of recouping their losses while Otley was alive. If Lord Skeffington was made aware of the whole debacle, he would only have to threaten to tell a few well-placed people in their social circle the truth and Otley would have returned the money. The success of his scheme and no doubt future ones depended on the solidness of his reputation. Young men, however, do not want to be rescued from their mistakes by their fathers, and they don't appreciate being played for dupes. Revenging himself against the man who took them for a fool would be enough for either one of these two gentlemen. The presence of my candlestick would seem to prove it."

"Or perhaps the candlestick is a trick meant to make you believe that," Bea said. "Don't let yourself be manipulated."

"And I would advise you not to let your imagination run away with you," Kesgrave said with a condescending smile. "It's easy for a young lady to imagine complex plots where only simple truths exist. Skeffington is a thoughtless young man who carried a candlestick back to his room and left it there."

Bea recognized his comment as yet another slight against poor Mrs. Radcliffe, and insulting as it was, she was grateful to realize that his respect for her extended only so far. In every way that mattered, he still considered her beneath his consideration.

It was an important lesson for her to remember.

Rather than respond defensively, Bea passed through the doorway into the dressing room and began to search for a receptacle for used shirts and underclothes.

Kesgrave followed her and explained that he had already explored the area for revealing pieces of information.

"Did you inspect the laundry?" Bea asked and was pleased to see by his expression that he did not. "If Skeffington is the thoughtless young murderer you think him to be, then he would have thrown his shirt from the other night in with his worn items. If it didn't occur to him to examine the candle for small splatters of blood, he wouldn't think to examine his clothes for evidence either."

Next to the imposing wardrobe, she found exactly what she was looking for and she stepped back with a gesture to Kesgrave. "Would you like to do the honors?"

His look of revulsion was priceless—brows shooting skyward, lips pressing together—and Bea laughed without restraint at the realization she was the first and only person in the world to suggest the Duke of Kesgrave examine another man's dirty laundry.

It was a badge of honor she would wear proudly.

While he stood there aghast, his dignity recovering by inches, Beatrice searched through Mr. Skeffington's used linens and found no evidence of blood on any of the items. It was not conclusive by any means, but it was another piece in an increasingly complicated puzzle.

"There was no blood in Amersham's laundry either," she said as she put the articles of clothing back into the large white sack.

"Of course you have already searched the earl's rooms," he said, his tone a mix of surprise and disapproval.

"Of course," she echoed. "Haven't you?"

From his annoyed expression she could see that he wanted to deny it, but he couldn't so instead he looked down at the letter in his hands and said, "Miss Otley?"

"She is worth considering," Bea said.

"Love is frequently a motivation for murder," he agreed, "and I do believe her parents hoped to arrange a match with Mr. Skeffington. I can see an argument getting out of hand. But how to account for the suicide ruling?"

Beatrice, who only minutes before had pronounced herself to be as clever as he, had no idea what he was referring to and resented the sensation of complete incomprehension. "Account for it in what way?"

"If the young lady actually killed her father, then she knows the ruling of suicide to be false," he explained. "Would she not try to dispute it in some way, for it deprived her and her mother of whatever monies Mr. Otley had left. The fact that she has meekly accepted the story would seem to remove her from suspicion."

Beatrice conceded the logic of his argument and was silent for a few moments as she thought through her theory. "If her intention was to clear the way for her marriage to Mr. Wilson, then maybe she's grateful for the ruling for it means she eluded suspicion."

"Ah, but the ruling might be a new obstacle," he pointed out. "Mr. Wilson could be more attracted to the lady's dowry than to the lady herself."

Given Emily's great beauty, Bea found this concept a difficult one to digest, for she naturally assumed that anyone who looked like she did was always wanted for herself. "Perhaps, but Mr. Wilson mentions making some money during his sojourn in India. He might not need her dowry."

Kesgrave nodded. "Very well. We will put Miss Otley on the list after Mr. Skeffington and Lord Amersham. Who else?"

Once again, she was confused. "Who else?"

"Who else should we consider as suspects," the duke said. "I have never investigated a murder before, so I don't know the established way to go about it, but I think a process in which we come up with theories and then identify their weak spots is the most practical method. It is how my colleagues and I in the House of Lords come up with solutions to policy issues."

Bea could not have been more startled if Mr. Otley's reanimated corpse had stepped out of the wardrobe to explain what Parliament was. Minutes ago Kesgrave had implied she was a ninnyhammer whose ability to think had been corrupted by Minerva Press novels and now he was treating her like a colleague.

It was an unprecedented display of respect and she felt herself flush with delight, a feeling immediately superseded by guilt at finding any pleasure in the brutal slaying of poor Mr. Otley.

And yet, she thought, he had hardly been a paragon of virtue. Unquestionably, she didn't believe he deserved to die in such a horrid way, but he did seem to be the architect of his own misfortune. If he hadn't fleeced the son of one of his oldest friends or pushed his own daughter into an undesirable match....

"Miss Hyde-Clare?" the duke said, pulling her out of her thoughts. "Would you like to propose another suspect?"

Called back to attention, Bea focused on the matter of additional suspects, which she hadn't considered before. Unlike Kesgrave, she hadn't participated in policy debates in the House of Lords, but she was a quick thinker and she relished the freedom to speculate wildly.

She closed her eyes and came up with the most outlandish idea possible. "What about Mr. Wilson? We do not know his current whereabouts. As there is no hibiscus crop, he had no cause to remain in a country he detested. For all we know, he's already returned to London. Perhaps he's even in the Lake District. Perhaps he discovered from Emily her parents' intention to rivet her to Skeffington and he came down here to make his objections known to her father. He might have even asked for her hand and been rebuffed."

Kesgrave conceded the possibility of a former opium smuggler responding violently to rejection by his employer, but he had a difficult time imagining Miss Otley allowing herself to marry someone so beneath her touch.

"I agree it seems unlikely," Bea said, "but it would just mean that she has hidden depth. I will try to find out more during our walk to the folly this after— Good gracious, the folly! Quickly, your grace, tell me the time."

Kesgrave checked his watch and announced it was a quarter to three.

"Do you realize how long we've been here?" she asked, horrified that she had been so engrossed in their discussion she had forgotten everything else—the time, where they were, who might come upon them at any moment and discover them. Her sense of urgency was sincere as she ordered him to leave immediately.

Kesgrave's lips twitched in amusement as he proceeded to the door at her direction. "I'm not sure why I'm the one leaving first when I don't have to be anywhere until dinner."

Bea growled impatiently, opened the door a crack, peered out to make sure nobody was there and gave him a healthy push. "Go," she whispered.

The duke complied with a laugh, which frustrated her even more, for how were they to be stealthy if he persisted in making noise. Nevertheless, he exited the room without being seen, and she leaned against the wall, closed her eyes, and counted to thirty. It wouldn't take him more than twenty seconds to return to his room, but she wanted to make absolutely sure he was gone before she stepped out into the hall. It would ruin everything if someone spotted them together.

Carefully, she opened the door again and confirmed it was safe for her to leave. She closed it softly, then ran down the hallway as quickly as she could, darting up the staircase and scurrying along the corridor until she reached her room. She'd planned to change into a more appropriate dress for the afternoon outing, but she'd lingered too long in Mr. Skeffington's room to do anything other than tidy her hair and slip on a pair of sturdy walking boots.

Seven minutes later, she presented herself to the group of women waiting on the patio and submitted docilely to her aunt's review of the punctuality section of her lecture while the housekeeper, Mrs. Langston, finished packing their picnic basket.

CHAPTER NINE

Bea gave Mr. Theodore Davies a scar on his face that ran from his right temple diagonally across his forehead and over his eye to his left nostril. In every other way he was classically handsome—six feet tall, bright blond hair, deep blue eyes, square jaw—but she couldn't resist adding a dashing mark that hinted at mystery and the encompassing sadness of his past.

She wasn't entirely sure that such a cut would not have gouged out his eye or significantly impaired his vision, but Emily, knowing less anatomy than Bea, did not question the detail. But even if her education had included an in-depth study on optical functionality, she would not have noticed the incongruence, for she was far too engrossed in the tragedy that shaped Bea's young life.

"And you never saw him again?" Emily asked, gasping at the cruelty.

Beatrice shook her head sadly and looked over her friend's shoulder, at the trees at the top of the hill they were climbing. "Never. His father sent him to visit his uncle in Yorkshire for a month, and when he returned, he told him I'd died of consumption in order to extinguish all hope of a reunion."

She brushed her cheek as if wiping away a tear as it slid down, but her eyes were in fact dry. She lacked Flora's ability to turn on the waterworks at will and had to content herself with hitching her breath dramatically every few minutes. It hardly mattered, for Emily was thoroughly persuaded by her tale of woe and star-crossed love.

"Oh, my dear, how my heart aches for you," Emily said passionately, taking her friend's hand.

Bea continued to look away, as if a display of sympathy for her pain was itself painful, and squeezed the hand that held hers. "Thank you, darling. Thank you. It's my sincerest wish that you never suffer a similar misfortune. I pray you fall in love with a man of equal standing, not a clerk in a solicitor's office who would never be accepted by your family," she said, darting her eyes to her companion to see the effect of her words. The young lady of her standing had to be familiar enough with the rules governing maidenly confidences to now share her own. "I tried to make the sensible choice, as I knew the difficulties that lay ahead, but, alas, it was love at first sight. The heart wants what the heart wants."

As Bea spouted banality after banality, she thought it would serve her right if Emily remained as silent as a clam. Putting oneself in the middle of a heartbreaking fiction to manipulate a young woman into telling her own sad tale felt contemptible to her. In the beginning, it had seemed like an amusing lark: their meeting at Hatchards when they both reached for *A History of Ships and Sailors* by Thomas Culver, her showing up every day at the same time for a week in hopes of seeing him again, his writing poems in celebration of her smile. But the more involved the story grew—as Mr. Davies progressed from Theodore to Ted to Teddy—the more unsettled she became, and by the time Teddy refused to accept marriage to the daughter of his father's oldest and dearest friend, she felt miserable about the deceit.

And yet she remained hopeful that the exhaustive lie

would bear fruit because murder was rather despicable too.

"It's true, about the heart," Emily said sadly, "for it does make very poor decisions indeed."

At last, Bea thought, relieved that her story of thwarted happiness had not been invented in vain. "Have you fallen in love with someone unsuitable as well?"

"Me?" Emily asked, her eyes wide with surprise as she started to laugh. "Miss Hyde-Clare...Beatrice, have you not looked at me recently? I'm an exquisite young lady with stunning features, magnificent hair and a figure of such pleasing proportions it cannot fail to appeal to all men. I'm what is commonly referred to as an Incomparable, and I do in fact defy you to find a woman who compares to me. I can aim as high as I please, and I intend to set my sights on a duke or a marquess. Can you believe my parents hoped to make a match with Mr. Skeffington? As if I'd settle for a lowly baron. It's almost as if they hadn't looked at me recently either."

Bea was grateful Emily relished talking about her perfection so much because it gave her time to recover from the shock. Despite evidence to the contrary, she was not besotted with her father's associate. Indeed, she'd revealed herself to be the type of woman who could not be besotted with any gentleman whose rank did not comply with her expectation.

How, then, to explain the letter from the young man swearing his eternal devotion? Had he created an entire romance out of thin air? Had Emily greeted him kindly the first time they met and he assumed it was mutual and enduring love?

"Naturally, Emily, I never doubted you would make a brilliant match," she said flatteringly. "In fact, the moment I first saw you, I actually thought to myself, *Now there is a beautiful woman who will make a brilliant match.* I was merely responding to the sympathy with which you spoke about the heart making poor decisions. It seemed as if you'd acquired that knowledge firsthand."

"I'm desolate to inform you that I have, for my suffering knows no bounds," she said, confusing Bea further. "But 'tis not my heart that has caused a great pain but my mother's, which, as you can imagine, is considerably worse because it demonstrates a weakness one does not wish to observe in a parent. She has always been forceful-minded and more passionate than kind, but her recent behavior indicates a total want of respect and decency. I only hope Papa remained ignorant of it to the end, but I fear the shame was more than he could bear."

Bea was so astonished by the information she could do nothing but say she was astonished by the information.

"Of course you are," Emily said sympathetically. "She's short, fat and wrinkly, and her lover is short, fat and wrinkly, with a hideous wart on his left cheek. He used to be Papa's steward, you know, until he was sent to supervise the India operation, as the previous agent had died because of some unpleasantness with the locals. I don't know the details because nobody tells me anything. It's maddening. The only reason I found out about Mama's scandalous relationship with Mr. Wilson was I discovered her correspondence while rifling through her things trying to find out information about Papa's business. I was so distraught to discover her true nature, I cried tears of rage as I read the letter," she said, drops forming again in the corner of her eyes as she recalled the moment. "You have no idea how lucky you are to have two parents who are deceased, for one cannot be mortified by the dead."

"Yes, being an orphan has many compensations," Bea said with more than a hint of sarcasm.

To Bea's surprise, the other girl recognized how horrible she sounded and was instantly contrite. She grabbed her hand again to offer another comforting squeeze. "What a wretched thing to say. My father has been dead for only two days and I already miss him more than I can bear. Please do accept my apology. Talking about my mother has made me all out of sorts, and you are a kind and thoughtful friend to listen to me rattle on. I knew you were kind and thoughtful the moment you brought me the mob cap. I realized then that you were a woman who valued my appearance as much as I did."

As appalled as Bea was by the girl's towering self-regard, she was more fascinated by the way beauty had corrupted her perspective. A lifetime of being appreciated only for her looks had taught her to appreciate only her looks. Were all Incomparables as vain as she, or was Emily particularly susceptible?

Bea rather suspected it was the former and wished the Duke of Kesgrave the best of luck with his tableau.

"Of course I forgive you," she said as they approached the top of the hill, which presented a clearing with the manufactured ruin of a medieval castle, its stone walls—half-fallen, half-standing—seemingly ravaged by the passage of time, though in fact the edifice had stood for less than twenty years. A Gothic tower, tall and topped with a crenellated turret with a half-moon carved out, as if it had survived a mortar attack centuries ago, brooded over the landscape, adding a soupçon of hopelessness to the otherwise jovial scene. "I would never hold a grieving woman's rash comment against her. I'm sorry for how much you have to suffer. Is there anything I can do to help?"

"Actually, there is, yes," Emily said gratefully. "A small thing. Your cousin Russell's infatuation with me, though understandable and in many ways inevitable, has grown tiresome. He follows me around like a puppy, offering to fetch and carry and asking almost constantly if I'm all right. It was sweet at first, but the charm has worn off. Would you mind hinting him away?"

The only thing that surprised Bea about her cousin making a pest of himself was how long it took for it to happen. "I will talk to him as soon as we get back," she promised.

"You are a darling," Emily insisted just as Mrs. Otley called her away to admire the folly. The young lady rolled her eyes to show either disgust for her mother or for her level of eagerness, then pasted a bright smile on her face as she turned around. "Yes, Mama, I'm coming."

While Lady Skeffington directed the servants to set up the picnic under a large willow tree and Flora took out a notebook to sketch the folly, Bea quietly observed Mrs. Otley and her daughter. Whatever the latter's true feelings for her parent were, she hid them skillfully behind a beautiful mask of polite interest. Nodding enthusiastically, she looped her arms through her mother's and strolled with her through a ruined archway.

As they disappeared from view, Bea marveled at the discovery that it was Mrs. Otley, not Miss Otley, to whom Charles Wilson had pledged his undying devotion. A revelation of that magnitude required a tremendous amount of thought, for it cast a new light on information previously assumed to be true. If Mrs. Otley had been conducting an affair with Mr. Otley's business associate, then her name must be added to the list of suspects. Her husband's premature death would provide her with the freedom to marry again while remaining in possession of his assets. The same motive applied to Mr. Wilson, who would stand to gain a wife and an estate in a single stroke—assuming the pesky barrier of Mr. Otley could be removed.

But Kesgrave had thrown up another obstacle to their success, as having the constable deem the event a suicide guaranteed that all monies would go to the Crown. If Mrs. Otley was in any way involved in the scheme, she would be desperate with anxiety and frantic to have the ruling overturned. As far as Bea could discern, she'd accepted the judgment without complaint and seemed no more distressed by the fact of suicide than she was by the death itself. If she was involved, she would be eager to get her hands on what was left of the estate, including all that lovely money her husband had swindled out of their friends.

Or was she simply happy to be free of the constraints of her marriage and confident that Mr. Wilson had saved enough money during his time in India to keep her in style?

"Appalling, isn't it?" Lady Skeffington said.

Startled, Bea turned to find her hostess standing beside her and staring at the gloomy ruin. For a moment, she'd thought the woman was talking about Mrs. Otley's behavior and found herself curiously at a loss for how to respond. But even when she realized she referred to the folly, she still could not think of an intelligent reply, for this was precisely the sort of facile conversation that had dulled her wits during her multiple seasons.

The silence stretched as Bea felt herself accosted by her old anxieties. How could she still be this person—this dullard who balked at a polite question? Had her verbal duels with the Duke of Kesgrave meant nothing?

Unsure of the answer, she responded with another question. "Is it?"

"I'm afraid I've never really understood the point of creating something new that looks old," her ladyship explained. "Skeffington and the architect spent months on the design, agonizing over every little detail and weighing its effect on the building's sensibility. Would one more window make it too desolate? Would one less make it too cheerful? Honestly, months and months of conversation over cheroots and brandy, which, to be fair, I actually found quite amusing, for they let me partake in all three. I always enjoy a vigorous debate, however trivial the subject. And now we have this grandiose edifice, like scenery in a play that is always just about to start."

Bea empathized with her point of view, for it could not have been inexpensive to build such a structure on the top of a hill, and decided the conversation was not facile at all. "I must admit it is strange to create something whose sole function is to decay," she said easily. "But I also must admit that I do like the feeling it evokes. Please tell your husband that he chose the perfect number of windows."

Lady Skeffington smiled and patted her gently on the shoulder. "You must tell him yourself, as he loves compliments on his folly. Now, refreshments are served. Do help yourself."

At the mention of food, Bea felt her stomach gurgle and realized she was quite hungry indeed. The strawberry jam tea cakes had been several hours ago.

The picnic spread, which was modest in its options but lavish in its quantity, consisted of cold meats, cheeses and fruit. Bea made herself a little plate of chicken, sliced ham and cheddar. The Otleys joined her soon after, while Flora continued to sketch and Aunt Vera stood at her shoulder commenting on how skillfully she'd rendered her subject. Her admiration was so effusive, Mrs. Otley felt compelled to appraise the work for herself and agreed that Flora's drawing was competent. Naturally, Aunt Vera, who had not now or ever used such faint praise to commend her daughter, took exception at the understatement, and the two old friends indulged in a vigorous exchange of increasingly underwhelming taunts about the other's off-spring. By the end, Miss Otley's appearance was "passable" and Miss Hyde-Clare could "draw a straight line if she put her full concentration into it."

"I think it will amuse you to know they were always like this," Lady Skeffington said. "At school, when we were younger. We all were, in fact. I fear competitiveness is essential to the nature of female friendship."

Bea thought it was incredibly gracious of their host to lump herself in with the two bickering women. "I find it very hard to believe that *you* were competitive."

Her ladyship laughed, pleased by the compliment. "Well, just between us, I will concede that I was never as bad as those two, but I did have my moments. I'm genu-inely delighted that despite all the dramatics—and I assure you, there were some monumental Cheltenham tragedies enacted in the study hall of Mrs. Crawford's School for Girls—we remained friends. It was touch and go for a while, especially after Amelia nabbed Thomas from me right under my nose."

Although Bea found this disclosure unexpected, re-cent revelations about Mrs. Otley's morals ensured that she wasn't entirely surprised. Nevertheless, she was taken aback by the betrayal of friendship.

"You are right to stare. It's quite shocking but mostly, I think, because it's clear all these years later how poorly Thomas and I would have suited each other. He and Amelia were a much better pair, peas in a pod, as they say. And I've done remarkably well for myself. Skeffington and I are ideally matched, folly and all," she said with a gentle sigh, her expression suddenly serious as she watched her friend lick the crumbs of a second pear tart off her fingers. "I'm grateful now for her interference, of course. But, oh, you should have seen Thomas then, freshly returned from India: handsome, confident, sophisticated, worldly. I was a little in awe of him, which is never good for a relationship. I'm not surprised he chose Amelia. Everyone said it was because she was the daughter of a baron and he wanted the noble bloodline, but I think that's too simplistic. Amelia had her own appeal. She sparkled back then the way her daughter sparkles now, and I'm sure it was irresistible. I was always a little more plodding."

Having heard the same description applied to herself by her own uncle, Bea strenuously objected. "Not plodding. Thoughtful."

Lady Skeffington smiled but shook her head at the distinction. "You are too kind," she said, sighing as a sad expression overtook her face. "I'm so sorry for Amelia's suffering. If I could have done anything to prevent it..."

The sentiment was expressed so simply and sincerely, Bea immediately recalled her ladyship's lone directive that morning during Aunt Vera's etiquette session: Consider the comfort of others to be of paramount importance, and everything else will fall into place.

She reminded Lady Skeffington of her advice now, for she thought it was tailor-made for a situation just like this. "You are offering comfort to a dear friend during a terrible time. I believe that's all you can do."

Lady Skeffington tilted her head and looked at Bea

with surprise. "You're not at all what your aunt described. You're quite insightful and very lovely indeed. Thank you, my dear, for considering *my* comfort. Now let's get you a pear tart before Amelia finishes them all. If nothing else, I owe it to her not to let her gorge herself in grief. In a few years, perhaps, she will look for another husband and she won't want to be saddled with a third chin."

Although Bea much preferred chocolate cake to pear tart, she happily ate the entire pastry because she didn't want to seem ungrateful to her hostess. She'd had little expectation when she discovered they were going to spend a week in the country with one of Aunt Vera's old school friends, for she did not consider her relative to be the best judge of character, but Lady Skeffington had turned out to be a true delight.

Bea was still marveling at the day's development a few hours later when she retired to her room to change for dinner. How fantastic that the kind Lady Skeffington had once been romantically linked with the venal Mr. Otley. That moment when she'd observed how poorly they would have suited each other, Bea wanted to grab her shoulders and say with heartfelt solemnity, "Good gracious, ma'am, you have no idea."

And Mrs. Otley!

It struck her as highly appropriate that a man who swindled money from elderly fools and callow youths would have a wife who dallied with his underling. It was a case of like attracting like.

Two peas in a pod, Lady Skeffington had said.

She couldn't wait to tell Kesgrave, for she knew he would be just as astonished. He'd read the letter, the same as she, and had drawn the identical conclusion. The truth changed the entire complexion of the situation, and she was eager to hear what he would make of it. More than ever, she was convinced Mr. Wilson was their chief suspect, for he had as strong a motive as Mrs. Otley and the strength, no doubt, to carry out the crime.

Dinner was an interminable ordeal, for she had to wade slowly and politely through four courses, including fish, when all she wanted to do was lean across Lord Amersham and Flora to the duke and say, "The letter was to the mother. The mother, your grace, can you believe it?"

Obviously, there could be no opportunity for such a communication during the meal or after, for when the women withdrew to the parlor, the men stayed in the dining room to drink their port. She hadn't expected to have a revealing conversation about one of their fellow dinner guests in the presence of all of them, but she had hoped to communicate the need for one. Her attempt at conveying urgency by blinking her eyelids several times in rapid succession in his general direction was thwarted by Flora, who intercepted the look and asked if she had sand in her eye.

"Would a cold compress help remove the grains?" she asked solicitously. "Here, let's ask one of the footmen to get you a cold compress."

Bea, slightly disconcerted by her cousin's thoughtfulness, thanked her for the offer and said her eye already felt better.

With no hope of conferring with Kesgrave, she had little interest in remaining in the drawing room and, as soon as it was appropriate, excused herself to go to sleep. Smothering a yawn, she explained that the walk to and from the folly had worn her out. "It must have been all that lovely fresh air."

Aunt Vera rose to her feet and announced that the day's exertions had fatigued her as well. She cheerfully bid the company good night and followed her niece out of the room. As they approached the staircase, she linked her arm through her niece's and said with sympathy she had never expressed before, not even on the death of Bea's parents, "You poor, poor dear. How you must have suffered. Come, you will tell me all about it and we will devise a solution that ensures a happy ending for all."

Although Aunt Vera's sudden interest in her long-term happiness intrigued Bea, she knew better than to ask questions, for that would only extend the conversation. The best way to handle the situation was to remain silent and let her aunt chatter herself out. No matter where the topic started, she was confident it would end with concern for Flora and Russell, as their happiness, followed by Aunt Vera's comfort, was the longstanding priority.

"I don't blame you for not confiding in me," her aunt said as they climbed the stairs to the second floor. "Based on our expectations for Flora, you naturally assumed your uncle and I would not have supported you. Please know that is not true. You are our niece, we hold you in some esteem, but our expectations for you are not the same as our expectations for our daughter. Naturally, it would never do for Flora to form an unsuitable alliance, but we would not object if you were satisfied."

As Aunt Vera found an opportunity to confirm her niece's secondary status in the household on a weekly or biweekly basis, Bea took no offense at her statement, which was, by all accounts, insulting and possibly hurtful. Rather, she thanked her aunt for her gracious concern. "You are far too kind to me."

"What can I do? You are my husband's brother's child," she said.

Bea bit her lip to keep from smiling at the confusion in her aunt's tone. Clearly, she'd intended the remark to stand as an earnest testament to the benevolence of the family bond, but she couldn't help injecting a note of curiosity—as if she would be delighted to take suggestions as to what else she could possibly do.

After they entered her niece's room, Aunt Vera beckoned to the chairs by the fireplace. "Come, let's sit and you can tell me all about your clerk. I understand he works in an office on Chancery Lane, which is…charming, I suppose. I'm sure he aspires to be a barrister, which your uncle can help him with as soon as he finds him and settles the arrangements. We'll have you married by the end of the month," she said matter-of-factly, then shook her head as if saddened by the circumstance. "Oh, you poor, poor dear. Tell me, how long ago was this affair? Was it last Michaelmas? It must have been last Michaelmas, for I did notice you looking inordinately wan in late September. Naturally, I just assumed the off-putting paleness was your normal complexion, but I realize now you must have been pining for your lost love. Honestly, Bea, it's so difficult to tell with you. I've never met anyone before who looks as if she's in a decline all the time."

The plaintive whine in Aunt Vera's voice, as if the ambiguity of her niece's appearance was her personal cross to bear, was too much for Bea, who had held on to her amusement with admirable control for the whole of this remarkable speech. Now, however, she broke into gales of unrestrained laughter, for it only seemed fitting that a lie calculated to elicit information from a grieving young lady would return to her tenfold. Unused to the demands of dishonesty and deceit, Bea hadn't thought to impress upon Miss Otley the importance of keeping her confidence. She suspected it wouldn't have mattered if she had, as the tale had been too salacious not to share far and wide.

Aunt Vera, fearful that the painful subject had un-hinged her niece entirely, regarded Bea with anxious concern and accused her of being hysterical.

Bea hugged her belly, for it hurt from the effort of laughing, and said, "Yes, yes, aunt, I think am."

"Oh, you poor, poor dear," she said sympathetically, lifting her hand as if to touch the girl consolingly but unsure where to place it. It hovered over her head for several seconds before landing on her shoulder. "It's all right. You get it all out, all the emotion you've kept contained for so long, and when you are calm again, we will come up with a plan. What is his name?"

This practical question was the very thing to quiet the gales, for it made Bea aware that she had a rather large problem on her hands. Her aunt was determined to marry her to a fictional law clerk. "He's dead," she said abruptly.

If Bea thought death could kill her aunt's ambitions, she was sadly mistaken. "Not necessarily. Consider, my dear, that it might have been a hoax perpetrated by his parents. Did they not use that very trick on their own son, devastating him with a report of your death while you were very much alive?"

Although Bea had forgotten that she'd already used that ruse in her original story, she was shocked to discover that Emily had recalled the detail. She'd assumed the other girl's egotism was so engrossing that she heard wind in her ears if the words being spoken did not specifically pertain to her.

"He's married," she amended quickly. "To a ginger-haired woman with rosy cheeks."

Aunt Vera stared at her. "But you just said he was dead."

"I did, yes, that was me," she muttered with a hint at annoyance—at herself, at her aunt, at Emily for having the unexpected ability to retain information. "I meant, dead to me. The moment he got married, he was dead to me. I cut him out of my heart as if he never existed, for I refuse to wear the willow for a man who found it so easy to throw me over."

"He thought you were dead," her aunt said logically, somehow sounding aggrieved on the imaginary suitor's behalf.

"But I wasn't. And yet he believed it. You didn't believe it," she pointed out. "A moment ago, when I said he was dead, you questioned it and advised me to allow for the possibility he might be alive. All this for a man you've never met. Do I not deserve the same courtesy you extended to a complete stranger?"

"Of course, my dear," her aunt said, her brow furrowed as she attempted to unravel the topsy-turvy reasoning at the heart of the statement. "I'm just not sure..."

"He has two children," Bea offered as a distraction.

"Twins. One boy, one girl, both ginger like their mother. They live in Cheapside now, next to a printshop."

Her aunt considered her silently for a moment and then said with a sad shake of her head, "I think you rather *are* wearing the willow. How else would you know so much about his life if you hadn't made a particular study of it?"

Bea opened her mouth to issue another impromptu explanation, but nothing came out. Her well of clever answers had run dry, and all she could do was stare stupidly at her aunt, trying to decide if there was any harm in agreeing with her statement. What ill could come from admitting she had spent days or weeks of her life observing a former lover who believed she was dead? It seemed a simple enough concession, and yet she couldn't quite smother the fissure of alarm. The bigger the lie, the greater possibility for fatal entanglement.

With no other option available to her, Bea took refuge in the tactic of cowards and changed the subject. The day had had so many startling revelations. Surely, she could come up with one to marvel about now.

And then she had it.

"Shall we talk about something truly shocking?" Bea asked in a conspiratorial tone. "How about the way Mrs. Otley stole Lady Skeffington's beau from right under her nose? Now that's a scandalous tale of love and betrayal. I cannot believe you did not mention this to me or Flora."

The brusque shift in conversation disconcerted Aunt Vera, who undoubtedly had more to the say about her niece's thwarted love affair, but the opportunity to gossip about her dear school friends was too much of a temptation to resist and she happily launched into a breezy retelling. "It was indeed scandalous, for Otley and Amelia eloped the night before he and Helen were to make the announcement. Her mother had already sent the notice into the *Times* and had to go to the office herself in order to make sure the item didn't run, which was no small feat, as the type had already been laid. Frankly, it was awful the way Helen found out. She saw them kissing on the terrace during the Erskine ball. Quite the passionate clinch, if the story is to be believed," she added with a sly smile. "Helen ran to the cloak room to cry and stayed there for the rest of the party, drenching the Duchess of Tetbury's spencer. Otley and Amelia, knowing it was only a matter of time before their parents found out, left for Scotland immediately. It sounds so dramatic and yet in the end it was but a tempest in a teacup. By the time the newly married couple returned from their wedding trip six months later, Helen was besotted with Skeffington and unable to remember what she had seen in Thomas Otley to begin with. She wished her friend well, and they've remained close ever since."

"Yes, that's very similar to what her ladyship said," Beatrice observed, wondering how far the acquisition of a title went in salving an ego—and immediately felt irritated with herself. Lady Skeffington did not deserve such an unkind thought, as she had been nothing but gracious to her. Bea had used exhaustion as a pretext to leave the drawing room, but her petulance made her realize she was more tired than she'd supposed.

"Would you mind excusing me, aunt? It's been a long day and I suddenly find that I'm eager to turn in."

At the mention of sleep, her aunt yawned hugely and professed to being quite weary herself. The day had been long indeed, but it was the intense disclosures of the past hour—the dizzying high of discovering Bea had a beau, the shattering low of learning he was unattainable—that had genuinely wiped her out. "I feel as though I could sleep for days."

Bea thought that was an excellent plan and urged her aunt to get as much rest as she needed.

"I will," she promised, then kissed her niece softly on the cheek. "Never fear. We will talk about this again."

Nothing the other woman could have said could

strike more terror into Bea's heart than the assurance that they would discuss the matter further, as she at once imagined her aunt orchestrating divorce proceedings for a man who did not exist.

For God's sake, he had two children!

They were fictional, of course, but Aunt Vera didn't know that.

Another woman might have been offended that her relative was so desperate to get rid of her she would resort to breaking up a happy family, but Bea took no affront at all. Indeed, it made her laugh.

And giggling lightly, she rang for Annie to help her change.

CHAPTER TEN

As Beatrice had had little interest in reading *The Vicar of Wakefield* in the first place, her patience had run dry by the time poor but kindly Mr. Burchell revealed himself to be rich and kindly Sir William Thornhill. The unmasking was a cheap and easy plot contrivance to save the Primroses from the excesses of misfortune the author had heaped upon their head. The fire that had burned down the family's home and destroyed all their possessions had already been one too many calamities for her, but for the wicked squire to then send the vicar to debtors' prison because he couldn't pay the rent on a house that no longer stood— 'twas a caricature of immorality.

Annoyed as always by a novel that told her how she was supposed to feel rather than allow her the pleasure of deciding for herself, she tossed the heavy tome onto the floor unfinished. This propensity in fiction was precisely why she preferred biographies, histories and travelogues.

The book landed with a thud that was shockingly loud for midnight in a country home, and as she worried about the clamor waking Flora, whose bedchamber was next door to hers, she heard a knock on the window.

Her heart almost leaped out of her chest at the unexpected sound, for it was late and she was alone and a murderer still wandered the floors of Lakeview Hall.

It could be anything, she told herself, such as a harmless branch blowing against the pane in the wind. It didn't *have* to be the killer himself conspiring to end her life while she slept.

Most likely, it wasn't.

The knock sounded again.

Persistent tree, she thought, annoyed that she'd been denied the luxury of pretending it had merely been her imagination.

Taking several deep, calming breaths, she climbed out of bed, picked up a candle and crept toward the window. Only an hour before she had been rolling her eyes at how easily the empty-headed Olivia had fallen in line with the squire's trick to ruin her, as if there hadn't been clear indications of his true intentions, and now here she was investigating a suspicious noise at her window with all the obtuseness of a Gothic heroine. She deserved whatever gruesome end came her way.

And yet what were her alternatives? Blowing out the candle and hiding under the covers hardly seemed like the optimal way to repel an intruder bent on her destruction, and running out of her room in a panic would only expose her to public condemnation. How would she explain her terror to her family? By telling them she was investigating the murder of a man who had committed suicide? Aunt Vera would cart her off to Bedlam at the first opportunity and consider herself lucky to have finally found a solution to her spinster niece problem. No need to break up a happy family when false imprisonment would do.

No, going to the window to confirm the source of the knock was the only reasonable response, and as she drew closer she could perceive the outline of a human form in the tree. Her heart racing, she stretched her arm to bring the candle near to the window, but the glass reflected the light, further obscuring the figure. She had no resource but to lower the candle and press her nose against the glass.

Reminding herself that the running and panicking option still remained, she stepped up to the window and peered through it. Blond curls glowed in the faint moonlight. Heaving a sigh that was equal parts relieved and impatient, she raised the sash and said, "I suppose tomorrow your valet will present a seminar to the young men on how to scale a tree with dexterity and grace."

Kesgrave climbed easily over the windowsill—additional fodder for his tutorial—and replied, "I continue to be confounded by your churlishness in the face of competence, Miss Hyde-Clare. As you appear to be quite capable yourself, I'd think you'd appreciate proficiency in others."

"That's because you've never sat across from you at the dinner table," she explained reasonably.

The duke chuckled and shook his head as if admitting to a great personal flaw. "No, for all my talents, I have yet to accomplish that feat, but I remain optimistic."

"And I look forward to the twenty-point lesson on how one masters the logistical challenges of being in two places at one time," she said, smiling as she closed the window. She gestured to the armchairs by the fireplace and asked if he was staying. "Or is this to be a brief visit? Leave your calling card on the salver and carry on to the next tree?"

"That is for you to decide," he said politely, "as I can only request a meeting. You have to grant it. We are, after all, in your bedchamber."

Beatrice required no reminder of the impropriety of the moment, for she was keenly aware of the hour and the silence of the house and her state of dishabille. She knew she was supposed to blush at the unseemliness of the situation—being discovered in her night rail by an unmarried gentleman with whom she had no familial connection—but she couldn't quite muster the embarrassment. Her dress was plain, the material was sturdy, and its cut was so modest a widow could wear it to church on Sunday without raising an eyebrow. Thick cotton ruffles extended all the way to her chin, as if in anticipation of one day having to rebuff the advances of an amorous suitor.

What *did* embarrass her was the impression that a display of modesty would make, as if she thought he thought she was young and attractive. At her age, she had no illusions or expectations, which the duke very well knew, for if he'd considered her an eligible female, he would never have invaded her bedchamber at midnight.

Kesgrave considered her a colleague, and acting missish now would undermine the entire project.

"Then do let us sit," Bea said in answer to his question. The fire, which had gentled to embers, glowed faintly, and she lit a pair of candles on the mantelpiece so she could see his face better. "Your visit is fortuitous, as I made a discovery today that will interest you."

"I know," he said with a confident grin as he took a seat.

She marveled how he could speak with such smug self-assurance and still wonder why anyone would take issue with his arrogance. "You know?"

"Yes, that's why I'm here," he explained. "Despite what you think of my climbing skills—and I appreciate the compliment, of course—I don't make a practice of scaling trees. The seminar, should Harris consent to host it, would last no more than five minutes."

Although Bea didn't want to give him yet another opportunity to show off, she couldn't resist asking how he knew she had something to tell him.

"Your performance during dinner. All that vigorous eye fluttering aimed at my end of the table. Naturally, I did not assume you were flirting with me," he said, a spark of humor lighting his eyes as he added, "You will note, I hope, the display of humility on my part. I don't think you credit me with enough modesty."

Beatrice raised an eyebrow as she considered him with amused skepticism. "Am I right in understanding, your grace, that you are now boasting about not boasting?"

He shrugged, displaying no hint of self-consciousness or unease. "It's the depth to which you've driven me, Miss Hyde-Clare."

"I must apologize if my attempt to find a decent human being under the preening lord has somehow forced you to preen more," she said quickly. "I do assure you that was never my intention."

Kesgrave laughed and claimed the moral high ground by insisting he would not debate the matter further. "I know how you love to distract me with trivialities, but the hour is late and we have much to discuss. Tell me, then, what you discovered."

At this unfair charge, a protest rose to Bea's lips, but she had to smother it, as countering with the fact that it was *he* who distracted *her* with trivial things would only prove his point. "We have the wrong Otley," she said.

Kesgrave furrowed his brow, not immediately grasping the distinction. "The wrong Otley?"

Bea nodded decisively as an ember crackled in the fireplace. She raised her eyes to meet his, so she could see his expression when he realized the truth. "The letter was not written to the daughter."

It took another brief moment more, and then understanding lit his whole face. "Well, that *is* quite a discovery," he said with thoughtful approval. "How did you ferret out that fascinating piece of information?"

She recalled the conversation with her aunt in all of its ridiculous splendor and decided to keep her response as simple as possible. "Just a little gossip among girls. Emily was not very delighted to have stumbled across her mother's proclivity. It was only a recent discovery, and I think she likes to reread the letter at regular intervals to remind herself of her mother's betrayal."

"Obviously, Mrs. Otley must move to the top of the list, as the relationship with the business associate is undeniable," Kesgrave said, resting his chin on his hand as he considered the news. "It provides additional incentive for her to remove her husband."

Bea, who'd been puzzling the matter for hours, immediately agreed with his reasoning but not with his conclusion. "I simply don't see how she could have done it. Her husband was a full head taller than she, and consider the placement of the wound in his skull. It was toward the top of his head. How could she overcome the height problem? And why do it at Lakeview Hall? As I've pointed out before, laudanum in his port at the privacy of their own home would make much more sense."

"Ah, you're assuming her actions were thought out and considered," he countered. "What I propose is a spontaneous act sparked by a flash of uncontrollable anger. If Mrs. Otley had found him here and they had gotten into an argument, then she might have been enraged enough to hit him over the head with the candlestick she happened to be holding at the time. Her fury would have given her strength."

"Strength, yes, but not height. I agree with your premise in theory," Bea said, for she knew from personal experience that bitterness carried its own force. There was a power in focusing your ire at the world's injustices on a single target and releasing your wrath. Too much power, she'd realized while she was still young. Resentment was a blunt instrument yielding wanton destruction, and she wanted no part in the wreckage. It was better, she'd decided, to find humor in the vagaries of fate, a resolution that had the added benefit of flattering her ego, for it required a certain amount of moral fortitude to laugh when most people would cry. "But I'm still not sure even the blackest rage would create enough strength for a woman who is barely five feet tall to overwhelm a man just shy of six."

"Fair enough. But I think you're making an erroneous assumption about the amount of damage that was done to the skull on the initial strike. Otley was hit several times. Perhaps the topmost blow came after he had fallen," Kesgrave proposed. "That said, I must admit that the other point I raised earlier is valid as well, which is that Mrs. Otley doesn't seem particularly troubled by the ruling of suicide. If she had murdered her husband to gain possession of his estate, she would be more agitated at the thought of losing it."

Although his remark bolstered Bea's argument, she was perverse enough to take up the other view. "But if the properties are mortgaged to the hilt and Otley was low in the water, she would have no reason to raise the issue and draw suspicion to herself."

"You are now making my case for me," the duke said with a laugh.

"Am I?" she said thoughtfully. "Or am I making *my* case for Mr. Wilson?"

Kesgrave tilted his head, curious but doubtful. "Ah, yes, the lover who may or may not be in England. Very well, make your case."

Although Bea had included Mr. Wilson on the list of possible murders only in an outlandish bid to consider every option, he struck her now as just as likely a suspect as Mrs. Otley. "I think he is. He had no reason to stay in India after the opium fields were seized, and if he booked passage on a ship that left in February, he could have arrived in London by the end of July. As you know, it's September now, so that would have given him plenty of time to renew his pledge to Mrs. Otley and begin plotting his scheme to remove his rival."

"I agree he has likely returned to the country," the duke said, "but I cannot conceive why he would attack Mr. Otley here, at the Skeffingtons' house in the Lake District. Would it not be easier to strike in the city?"

"Ah, but here nobody would ever suspect him, for nobody would even know he was in the district. It's the perfect cover for a nefarious deed," Bea said with relish.

Kesgrave did not dismiss it immediately, but after several moments of thought, he shook his head. "No, I cannot agree, for what you are proposing once again necessitates forethought. Consider the timing—in the house late at night. It had to have been done by someone who was at home here and merely took the opportunity when it offered itself. If an outsider such as Mr. Wilson had arrived in the village with this crime in mind, he would have acted when Otley was more exposed such as during an afternoon expedition to fish or hunt. His plan would not have hinged on his finding his victim in the library at two in the morning, for that is far too random an event."

"Not if he's working in tandem with Mrs. Otley," Bea said. "If he's hiding on the grounds or even in the house among the servants, then he would be near enough to respond as soon as Mrs. Otley signaled him."

"I fear the plot you are devising is too intricate to be credible," Kesgrave said. "In fiction, a complex plan might prosper, but in the world in which we live, the more components a scheme has, the more likely it is to fail."

As he had already made this charge against her, warning her with superb condescension about complicated plots when she'd suggested the candlestick had been placed in Mr. Skeffington's room to make him appear guilty, she was well-familiar with his opinion. "You will see, your grace when the second footman or the under-butler or the gamekeeper's assistant is unmasked as Mr. Wilson before the whole company in the drawing room."

His lips twitched. "You are imagining quite an elaborate scene."

"Naturally," she said, as if he had pointed out something simplistic and obvious. "Without the dramatics, how would we get Mrs. Otley to confess?"

Kesgrave praised her conviction even as he professed his doubt. "Nevertheless, I will consent to putting Mr. Wilson on the list."

Bea leaned forward as if to direct his hand. "Above Mrs. Otley."

The duke looked at her, his whole face gleaming with mischief. "You understand the list is figurative, do you not, Miss Hyde-Clare? The names aren't actually being compiled in order on a sheet of paper somewhere."

"Yes, your grace, I do understand that. But I see no harm in being as precise as possible. I'm surprised you object, as precision seems to be your raison d'être. HMS *Majestic,* HMS *Audacious,* HMS *Goliath,*" she said with a hoydenish grin.

"HMS *Goliath,* HMS *Audacious,* HMS *Majestic,*" he corrected.

He spoke without inflection and his expression remained blank, but Bea understood at once that he was making the joke this time at his own expense, not hers. Despite his many unappealing character traits, which she hadn't hesitated to point out—excessive pedantry, obnoxious competency, overweening arrogance—the Duke of Kesgrave wasn't above laughing at himself, and realizing that, Bea made a shocking discovery: She liked him. There, in her room, well past midnight, by the glowing embers of a dying fire, making a list of suspects in a murder, he was extremely likeable, and she could see for the first time how a woman could lose her heart to him.

Not her, of course. Never her. But a schoolroom miss having her first season or a beautiful young lady desiring only a good match and somehow getting a great deal more.

Bea found the revelation remarkably unsettling, not because she feared she would suddenly develop a tendre for the unattainable lord—for, no, she was far too sensible for that—but because it made her aware of something she hadn't known existed: amiable camaraderie. Although life with the Hyde-Clares had provided her with adequate if begrudging material comfort, it had provided no hint of the warmth to be found in convivial conversation among like-minded souls. Her aunt and uncle rubbed together tolerably well, but whatever amity they felt for each other did not extend to the unsought orphan in their midst.

Mortified by the turn her mind had taken—imagine, considering the Duke of Kesgrave to be a like-minded anything—she was grateful for the dim light, which hid the blush in her cheeks. The silence, which had already gone on too long, stretched as she tried to think of something to say. They had been discussing suspects, she recalled.

Yes, that would do. "Miss Otley," she said.

Kesgrave looked at her in surprise. "Miss Otley?"

"Yes, for the list," she explained. "Since we are making adjustments, I think Miss Otley should be shifted to the bottom. Without her thwarted love for Mr. Wilson providing a motive, I can see no reason why she would harm her father, even in a fit of anger. As far as I can tell, securing a rich and titled husband is her only goal in life, and she's far too sensible to do anything that would undermine her objective," she said. Then, unable to resist teasing him, she added, "You, of course, are good."

This seeming non sequitur disconcerted the duke. "I'm good?"

"In the event that you're worried your suit would not prosper with Miss Otley," she explained, "I wanted to assure you that you meet her requirements. She's entertaining offers from marquess-level peers and above, which, as you know, includes dukes. I trust you'll give the matter serious consideration, for she is, as Miss Otley herself helpfully pointed out this afternoon, an incredibly beautiful young woman. Incomparables of her stature do not come onto the market often. Do consider your cherubic children if not yourself."

A variety of expressions crossed the duke's face as she advised him of Miss Otley's availability—surprise, annoyance, anger, consideration—before settling into amusement. "You are far too kind, Miss Hyde-Clare, to worry about my happiness, but your efforts to ease my mind are entirely unnecessary. If there's one topic on which I'm qualified to lead a weeklong lecture series, it's the courtship of women."

The only thing Bea doubted about this assertion was the length of the series, which she imagined could extend fully into a month. "I hope you will give my cousin Russell a private session, then, for he seems bent on pestering Miss

Otley with his attentions. Following her request, I tried to point him in the right direction, but he assured me Miss Otley was only affecting indifference to encourage his interest."

"Ignorant puppy," Kesgrave said softly and promised to straighten out the young man's thinking at the earliest opportunity. Then, returning to the business at hand, he asked if there were other suspects to consider.

"Lord Skeffington?" Bea asked. "I know you believe he's unaware of the investment scheme, but is it possible he's learned of it? Discovering that one of his oldest friends had swindled his son would have made him very angry. Perhaps he confronted Otley and the two men had a violent argument. There was, you know, a cheroot among Otley's things when I searched his rooms. Otley himself did not smoke, as he claimed in his journal to find the smell repellent, but I know Skeffington does. Skeffington might have visited him in his room to discuss the matter originally, and unsatisfied with the conversation, arranged a second interview in the library. If the two men were in their cups, it could have gotten heated very quickly."

"It's an interesting theory," the duke said, "but I see a few problems with it."

Bea smiled faintly and assured him she'd expect nothing less from him than several dozen problems. She was needling him again about his love of finer points, but in this case she had to admit the issue he raised was fairly significant, as Skeffington had been the cause of his delay in following Otley to the library.

"If you recall, he congratulated me on catching the only fish of the day and by the time I extricated myself and arrived in the library, I was too late to witness the assault," he said. "Skeffington is an agile man for his age, but even he could not have raced from his study to the library quickly enough to dispatch Otley before I arrived."

"So you are ruling out entirely the possibility of a secret passage between rooms?" she asked in a tone that clearly implied such an assumption was foolish and shortsighted.

He did not rise to the provocation. "No, Miss Hyde-Clare, no. You will not get me to while away the next half hour discussing the likelihood that Lakeview Hall not only has hidden passageways between rooms but that it has one most suited to our particular need. You may try to distract me with your absurdity, but I will not fall in line. Your observation about the cheroot, however, is worthy of contemplation. Mr. Skeffington also smokes them, and he was no longer in the drawing room. He'd left about a half hour before."

"Burning with rage to revenge himself on the man who'd betrayed him, perhaps," she said darkly. "Where is he currently on the list? I can't remember."

"Before Mrs. Otley," he said.

Bea shook her head. "No, let's move him to after. The letter is still the most damning piece of evidence we have."

"More damning than a bloody candlestick?" he asked pointedly.

"That was planted in his room to make him look guilty," she said with firm insistence. "I'm sure of it. What of Amersham? Does he smoke cigars as well? I confess I haven't noticed."

"He prefers snuff. Collects snuff boxes, which isn't quite the fascinating hobby he thinks it is," he said with a hint of cantankerousness that delighted Bea, for she relished the idea of his having to sit through a seemingly endless lecture on an exceedingly dull topic. "Nuneaton smokes."

"Does he?" she asked thoughtfully. "Very well, let's put him on the list."

"Nuneaton?" Kesgrave said, furrowing his brow as he lifted his head to meet her gaze. "He has no reason to wish Otley ill. He was not among those who were fleeced. I made sure of it before accepting the invitation."

"I'm not doubting the accuracy of your research, your grace," she assured him calmly before doing just that, "but you cannot know everything about the gentleman. Perhaps he and Otley have a history that goes back farther than the hibiscus scheme. Perhaps he was involved in the opium venture. Don't you find it curious that his name hasn't come up a single time in our investigation? Is that not a cause for suspicion in and of itself? Why is he trying so hard to evade our notice? What is he hoping to hide? For all we know, he could be Mr. Wilson in the Bedford crop."

Bea knew the suggestion was preposterous for many reasons before she made it, for there was nothing about his appearance that aligned with Emily's description of him. She nevertheless still made it because she felt it spoke to a larger issue—namely, that they couldn't make any assumptions about anyone. When dealing with a growing list of suspects, they had to allow for all possibilities, even ones that seemed like plot devices from a Mrs. Radcliffe novel.

Kesgrave did not agree with her open-minded approach and shook his head firmly. "I would sooner grant the existence of a secret passageway from the study to the library before I entertain the notion that the gentleman calling himself Nuneaton isn't the gentleman I've known since our days at Oxford together. The fact that you would require me to even make such an absurd statement reflects the depths to which I've sunk in this investigation, and make no mistake, Miss Hyde-Clare, I resent it intensely."

Bea blinked at the duke innocently and said she was merely trying to be as thorough as possible. "Surely, that level of detail would appeal to you, you grace."

"I'll put Nuneaton on the list below Miss Otley," Kesgrave said, ignoring her taunt.

If she was a little disappointed the duke had taken the high road, she did not show it. "Very good. I trust we both know what we must do tomorrow," she said and paused to wait for the duke's agreement. When he gave it, she added, "Figure out where Mr. Wilson is hiding."

Kesgrave, speaking at the same time, said, "Discover Mrs. Otley's movements."

Irritated, Bea glared at the duke and discovered he was staring back at her with an equally annoyed expression.

"You are wasting your time," she insisted. "The murderer is Mr. Wilson in whatever form he is currently taking."

"The murderer is most likely the deceitful wife," he said, "as she had the most to gain from his death. Even if she does not inherit his property, she gets the freedom to marry the man she loves, who can offer a modicum of financial stability. Moreover, she had the opportunity to perform the deed, for she occupies Lakeview Hall and could have easily snuck into the library to kill him. Unlike Mr. Wilson, who not only isn't in the Lake District but also isn't a wizard in a child's fairy story to turn himself into a dragon to escape detection."

"Footman," Bea said, speaking through clenched teeth. "I said second footman, under butler or gamekeeper's assistant, not fantastic creature from a child's fairy tale. A dragon would hardly be a discreet disguise."

"Forgive me," he said without an ounce of contrition. "I'm afraid one fantastic theory is very much the same as another."

He sounded so arrogant and satirical, Bea wanted to scream, but she held on to her temper and accepted his apology with a placidity so calm it bordered on hostile. Then she advised him to work on injecting the proper amount of remorse into his apology to make it sound more convincing. "Oh, I'm sorry, I should define my terms so you understand. *Remorse* is when you feel distress for something you've done wrong. If the concept still escapes you, perhaps you can apply to your valet for a brief lesson. You're going to need it tomorrow."

"Tomorrow?" he asked, ignoring her condescension.

"Yes, tomorrow, when I unmask Mr. Wilson and you're forced to apologize for mocking my theory," she explained confidently.

Kesgrave laughed, not at all perturbed by the prospect. "What a delightful imagination you have, Miss Hyde-Clare. It's a wonder no man has seized the opportunity to take you to wife."

But it wasn't a great mystery at all, for she had none of the qualities men of their station considered necessary in a wife—beauty, wealth, position, poise—and she found as she replayed the statement in her head that she resented the ease with which he had been lulled into thoughtless cruelty.

Kesgrave immediately perceived the gravity of his misstep, and watching the expression of discomfort, then displeasure, overtake his face, she readily believed it had been an accident. His intention had not been to mock her unnatural state but to express sincere confusion over it.

Alas, it was not possible to do the latter without first calling attention to the former, and she simply wasn't deft enough to pretend she did not feel the slight. Before the entire sentence had been uttered, she had recoiled as if from a blow.

"You must forgive me. I spoke thoughtlessly, heedlessly. I never meant to imply there was any reason you should be married. I am sincerely sorry. Truly, I would never imply that you should be anything other than what you are. What you are is delightful," he said quickly, demonstrating that he was conversant not only with the concept of remorse but the notion of pity as well.

That would not do.

Oh, indeed not.

In agony over how she must appear to him—a lonely spinster still capable of feeling shame at her condition— Bea leaped to her feet, heading off whatever mortifying thing he planned to say next, and professed shock at noticing the lateness of the hour. It was just past two in the morning, she said with an almost comically exaggerated yawn, and she was exhausted from a long day of attaining information from unwitting houseguests. Furthermore, they were very fortunate nobody had discovered their wildly inappropriate meeting, but sleep was an unreliable enterprise and Flora or her aunt could awaken at any moment and decide to pay her a visit.

Naturally, she thanked him for dropping by, as she

felt the discussion had been quite constructive for both of them, and if the brusque primness of her tone struck him as oddly formal for the situation, he was too polite to say it. Rather, he thanked her in return and bid her good night.

They both reached for the window at the same time, turning an already awkward moment into an excruciating one. Their fingers met along the bottom, and Bea jumped back as if burned by the contact. Her overly dramatic response made everything worse, and she stood several feet away while the duke opened the window, cursing her stupidity and missishness. Neither one was like her and she could attribute them only to the strangeness of the situation: the late hour, the informal setting, the convivial fire. Briefly, she'd forgotten who he was. Even as she was mocking him for his pedantry, she'd forgotten he was the Duke of Kesgrave—above her touch and several yards over her head.

That would not happen again.

She waited as Kesgrave climbed over the sill and settled onto the thick branch that knocked against her window. He turned around as if to speak, then, thinking better of it, offered a tepid smile and half-hearted wave. She acknowledged both gestures with an equally hesitant nod and swiftly closed the window. Because she wanted to stand there and watch every moment of his descent, she instead purposefully strode away, walking over to the fireplace to blow out the pair of candles she had lit when he arrived. Guided by the glow of the remaining candle, she found *The Vicar of Wakefield* on the floor where she had thrown it, next to the dressing room door, its spine slightly bent from the force of impact, and carried it to the bed. She placed the candle down on the table and opened the book to the spot where she'd left off. As utterly ridiculous as Mr. Goldsmith's tale was, with its clandestine lords and extravagantly evil villains, it was somehow still more plausible than the story she had been unknowingly concocting in her head about the sad spinster and the handsome duke.

CHAPTER ELEVEN

Although the scrambled eggs served for breakfast the next morning were at once runny and thick, Beatrice gushed over how perfectly they were prepared. Her fork perched on the edge of her plate, she examined Thurman, the footman who attended the sideboard and appeared to be only a few years older than she. If she had to guess, she would place him on the verge of turning thirty. By all accounts, he was an impressive specimen, with broad shoulders, elegant calves and a thick crop of hair under the powdered wig he was obliged to assume. Despite the positive impression he made, Bea could not divine if he was the same man who had held her chair out for dinner last night or carried in the pot of tea during Aunt Vera's lecture yesterday. As fashionable as ever, the Skeffingtons had chosen their footmen on the basis of their appearance, ensuring they all presented as a matched set. Given that Thurman was six feet tall, Bea deduced that the other footmen were of equal height.

"Undoubtedly, they are a marvel, these eggs," she added as the footman refilled her aunt's teacup. "I don't know when I've ever had eggs that tasted so delicious before."

Aunt Vera, who had been picking at the unappetizing serving on her own plate, looked at her niece as if she had a screw loose and chastised her for speaking with inappropriate enthusiasm. "They're just eggs, my dear, and should be treated as such. Save your praise for suitable targets such as roast stubble goose and Oxford pudding."

Bea ignored her aunt. "I say, Thurman, have the eggs always been this scrumptious or is that a recent innovation?"

"Always, I believe, miss," he replied as Aunt Vera glared at her niece for conversing with a servant.

This was precisely the answer Bea was hoping for, and she smiled brightly. "Ah, so you've been in the Skeffingtons' employ for a long time, then?"

"Yes, miss."

"Have most of the staff been here for a long time as well?" she asked.

Her aunt, who had abandoned the runny eggs in favor of dry toast, choked on the bread. She coughed loudly in an attempt to clear her throat as she stared at her niece aghast at this sudden, bizarre turn in conversation. Concerned, Thurman topped off her teacup, which was nearly overflowing from the tea he'd added only a minute ago, while Bea waited for him to answer.

It was difficult to say if Aunt Vera or Thurman was more surprised by Bea's continued interest. The latter, however, was the only one who spoke, saying that, yes, most of the staff had been with the household for several years.

"No recent additions, then?" Bea said.

"I wouldn't say that, miss. One of the upper housemaids recently arrived and Lord Skeffington's valet has been here only since July, and there's a new assistant cook and a new groom just took up work in the stables this week."

"A new assistant cook *and* groom?" she asked sharply. "How old are they?"

Aunt Vera stood up abruptly, as if poked violently by a needle, and grabbed Bea by the upper arm. "A letter from your uncle. How could I have forgotten! We received a letter from your uncle in the morning post and he had a question for you about Daisy. It's vitally important that we answer it at once," she said, turning to Thurman and apologizing for their sudden departure. Then she pulled her niece down the hallway, muttering under her breath, "And now *I* am excusing myself to the servants. I don't know who was more embarrassed, me or the footman. No, that's absurd. Of course I'm more embarrassed. What if Lady Skeffington had been present or Mrs. Otley? They would have believed I'd raised you with common manners. I did not. I raised you to be unexceptional. But what if it is my fault? I did not take you to enough house parties. For certain, you've been acting strangely almost since we arrived, interrogating Kesgrave in the drawing room and asking a newly minted widow about the setbacks she has suffered. Being in the proximity of a self-murder has had a corrosive effect on your mental abilities. Maybe it's too much for you to bear. You always were such a wan child."

By the time they reached the second floor, her aunt's ramblings had descended into incoherence and her grip on Bea's arm had loosened enough that she could climb the stairs independently. They bumped into Flora, however, in the hallway, and when the young lady inquired after the health of her mother, she set off another round of recriminations. Flora's eyes widened in shock when she heard of her cousin's behavior, which she immediately attributed to her hitherto unknown thwarted love affair rather than the nabob's death.

"Think of all she has suffered in silence, Mama, the heartache and the loneliness, and now it has come pouring out in a great torrent," Flora said as Aunt Vera led them into her room. "How dreadful to be reminded of it all. We must be patient and understanding with her."

This display of compassion from her cousin was thoroughly without precedent and, shocked by the sympathy, Bea wrapped her arms around her in a hug, an act so out of character it convinced both her relatives that she had indeed been overcome by anguish and undone by grief.

As lovely as the moment between cousins was, Bea wished it to be over so she could find out more about the new groom and assistant cook. Aunt Vera, however, had no intention of letting her impaired niece walk around the manor alone, and she kept her by her side as she read the letter from Uncle Horace, who actually did want to know where the leash for Daisy was kept, as the terrier had lately taken to chasing birds regardless of the order to heel. Flora, who was not fond of pets, suggested the dog be sent to the country once and for all. Bea could not tell if she was using "the country" as a euphemism or not.

She finally managed to contrive an escape at noon, when Lady Skeffington sent a note inviting the ladies to have tea in the drawing room with the Otleys before the grieving pair took their departure. Bea announced that such a diversion sounded delightful and darted off to retrieve from her room a going-away present for Emily before her aunt could object. At once, she raced down the hall and the stairs, almost tripping over Mr. Skeffington in her haste to inspect the assistant cook.

"Oh, I'm sorry. So sorry," she said breathlessly, her movements slowing but not stopping as she stepped around the surprised young man. "Do excuse me. So clumsy."

As soon as she was out of his sight, her pace picked up again and before she knew it she found herself flying past the drawing room door to the dining room. Not surprisingly, Lady Skeffington hadn't included the kitchens in the tour she conducted when her guests had arrived, but Bea knew they had to be somewhere nearby, for the food always arrived hot.

In the dining room, she followed a curving corridor at the far end to a staircase that led down to the main cooking room, which was large and surprisingly modern, with its high ceiling and ventilation shaft. The once white walls showed years of use with nicks, stains and black soot that spread from the top of the hearth like a creeping rash. In the fire, four chickens rotated on a spit turned by one of the kitchen maids, a girl about Beatrice's age with blond hair and cheeks made flush from the heat. Another maid, younger and darker, sat at the large table in the middle of the floor chopping carrots. Both women jumped when Bea entered, the maid at the table rising so quickly to her feet that her chair toppled behind her.

Bea hastened over to help straighten the chair, then halted midstride for fear of embarrassing the girl further. Having already disturbed their peace with her sudden appearance in their private domain, she didn't want to exacerbate the transgression by being overly solicitous. Uncertain, she stood in the middle of the floor and cursed her imprudent behavior. She had been so determined to free herself from Aunt Vera's clutches, she hadn't devised a plan for when she finally obtained her goal.

"The eggs!" Bea announced.

A loud thump filled the room as the girl returned the heavy chair to its upright position.

"Yes, miss," the maid operating the spit said.

Although it was obvious the young woman had no idea what their sudden visitor was talking about, she knew enough to agree. It was, Bea thought with growing discomfort, always the safest thing to do when dealing with gentry. She was being humored by the kitchen staff, a treatment that was as humiliating as it was deserved.

Bea took a deep breath and ordered her thoughts. Then she calmly explained how much she'd enjoyed the eggs during breakfast. "Indeed, all the food has been wonderful."

"Thank you, miss," the girl said, sketching a curtsy as she grasped the back of the chair.

"I don't know when I've ever eaten so well or been treated so elegantly as I have at Lakeview. Because everything is so wonderful, I wanted to pay my compliments to the cook, if that is possible. Actually, I'm aware of how busy he is, what with a houseful of guests to feed and the dinner meal to be prepared, which I can see you are working on now. Perhaps I could express my appreciation to his assistant. As I said, I will be brief."

At that moment, a harried man as tall as he was wide entered the room wearing a splattered apron and waving a cleaver. "Chop, you miscreant, chop!" he said to the girl standing near the table. At once, the maid by the hearth resumed turning the spit, her arm moving twice as fast as if to make up for lost time. Growling with impatience, he turned his attention to Bea and opened his mouth as if to issue another order. Realizing she did not report to him or indeed anyone belowstairs, he abruptly shut his mouth and came to a halt. He was immediately jostled by another man, smaller and narrower, who had been following him, sight unseen, and had not anticipated the sudden stop. The cleaver slipped from the large man's hand and landed less than an inch from his shadow's foot.

Bea, her heart lurching from fear to relief, felt almost weak at the knees at the thought of her visit ending with the amputation of some poor servant's toes. Aunt Vera would never recover.

Determined not to extend her stay any longer than necessary, she immediately explained her purpose to the large man, who turned out to be the cook himself. At her first expression of admiration, his impatience disappeared entirely and he insisted Beatrice sit down and tell him exactly what she liked best. She started with the eggs, of course, as they had played such a pivotal part in the ruse and then painstakingly listed all the dishes she could remember eating. The ones she retained the clearest memory of were the plates she had imagined throwing at Kesgrave.

The cook delighted in her appreciation and sought her opinion on specific details such as the level of salt in the turtle soup. Was it not perhaps a pinch heavy on the hand? She promptly assured him it was not, a response that earned a satisfied harrumph from the fellow who had narrowly escaped a painful encounter with the cleaver. He, upon further investigation, turned out to be the new assistant cook, an apprentice whose grasp of the subtle advantages of salt still proved to be imperfect.

"You're the assistant cook?" Bea asked, unable to hide her disappointment.

Fortunately, he did not notice and proudly proclaimed himself to be a chef in training.

He was all wrong, of course: young, slim build, tall.

Having confirmed that Mr. Wilson had not infiltrated the house via the kitchens, she endeavored to excuse herself from the company, insisting that she had held up their meal preparation for far too long. Although the cook insisted otherwise, the two maids agreed with vigorous nods of their head, and Bea, seeing no other way to end the conversation, requested some recipes to give to her own cook at Welldale House. Perceiving now that the true purpose of her flattery was to hoodwink him out of his most-prized recipes, the cook rose stiffly from the table, bid her good day and stalked out of the room. His assistant grabbed the cleaver from where it still lay on the floor and dashed after him. The girl at the table smothered a smile as she redoubled her efforts with the carrots.

Eager to investigate her next suspect, Bea thanked the maids for their hospitality, and as she climbed the stairs back to the ground floor, she resolved to provide tips to all the staff even if it meant handing over every cent she had with her, a rather inconsiderable sum that would not stretch beyond mere gesture.

The dining room was deserted when she emerged from the corridor, and she walked cautiously through the house, dodging fellow guests and relatives by hiding in doorways. Despite a close call with her cousin Russell, whose pursuit of Emily continued unabated, she made it to the front door undetected and followed the walk to the right of the gardens. The path led to the stables, a pair of long brick buildings encircling a courtyard and neighboring coach house.

She could hear the gentle whinny of horses as she entered the first building, which had accommodations for six horses and currently housed two. She murmured softly to them as she walked briskly past to inspect the harness room, which was empty. In the second structure, she found three more horses and a trio of stalls well in need of mucking out. Shaking her head at the smell, she progressed to the washing box and then the feed room. Neither was occupied.

Outside again, she walked around the buildings to the

stable yard, where a groom was exercising a large black horse in the enclosure. Was it the new groom Thurman had mentioned? His build seemed about right, as he had a portly frame and stood only as tall as the horse's hind quarters. She could not see his face, as his back was to her, and his hair was covered by a cap. Nevertheless, she decided he could not be Mr. Wilson, as his control over the animal was impressive and he seemed quite familiar and comfortable with him. If he were new to the property and not truly a groom, he would display a less confident hand.

He would, however, be able to answer a few questions about the newly hired groom, but even as she considered gaining his attention, she realized it was not a wise idea. If she thought causing the assistant cook to lose most of his toes to a cleaver accident was untenable, then distracting the head groom into an accident in which he was trampled underfoot and possibly paralyzed for the rest of his life was intolerable.

Far better, she thought, to find a stableboy who could, at worst, injure his wrist in a shoveling mishap or something equally minor.

Now all she had to do was find one.

It was shocking, really, how quiet the courtyard was, for she knew the care and upkeep of horses required much effort on the part of many people. Perhaps the problem was the hour, for it was the middle of the day, when a busy underling might break briefly to consume a quick meal.

Over the stables were the living quarters for the grooms and other stable staff, and she wondered how one of the men would react if she knocked on his door requesting an interview. Recalling the awkwardness of the scene in the kitchen, she decided it would most probably not lead to the acquisition of useful information. Additionally, such scandalous behavior was sure to get back to her aunt, and she would have no satisfying answer. To explain to Aunt Vera that she was on the trail of a murderer would be to ensure her confinement to a mental institution.

Bea sighed and decided to keep looking for a stableboy or a groom not currently engaged in training a horse to question. Behind the stables was a trio of buildings that looked promising and she examined each one for occupants. She found shovels, rakes, harnesses, saddles, whips and boots but no people. Discouraged, she crossed the field to another shed, opened the door and looked around.

It, too, was—

Suddenly, Beatrice pitched forward and dropped to the ground, her knees slamming into a wooden plank and her head bashing against the side of a washbasin. Dumbfounded, she lay there, stunned by the pain that coursed through her and by the inexplicable force that had propelled her forward.

Was she pushed?

She had to have been pushed, for nothing else could explain how quickly her circumstance changed. One moment she had been standing at the entrance observing the empty room and the next she was lying with dirt on her chin and blood—she reached up to confirm that the substance was warm and sticky—trickling down her forehead.

It hurt to move, so she stopped moving and put her head down.

Only for a minute, she told herself.

Beatrice didn't know how long she stayed there, in the dirt of the shed, waiting for the pounding in her head to subside. It could have been a minute; it could have been an hour. Time felt like a small boat on the rough sea, bobbly and wobbly. She might have fallen asleep, although she rather thought she did not, for every moment she was aware of the pain in her head. When it became clear the throbbing would not abate no matter how long she waited, she forced herself to stand up. At first she was dizzy, but soon her body adjusted to the change in position and the world steadied.

"Very good," she said softly, surprised to discover she found the sound of her own voice comforting. "Now to assess the situation."

The assessment took almost no time at all, for the shed was small and it required very little effort to take its account. The most important aspect of the room was its door, which she promptly tried to open. It didn't move.

"It is merely stuck," she said and pressed her shoulder against it. She heaved with all her might, but the door remained stubbornly shut. She tried again and again, throwing her full weight behind each push. It made no difference.

Now she began to panic.

Fear intensified the ache in her head, which had already been made worse by the exertion of trying to force open the door. She rested her head in her hand and watched for a full minute as drops of blood appeared on her dress. She knew she had to bandage her wound, but she simply did not have the wherewithal.

Not yet, at least.

A few minutes more and she began to feel stronger. She ripped the hem of her grown to create a dressing and wrapped it around her injury to stem the bleeding. The absurdity of the act—like a heroine in a Gothic—made her laugh. Gallows humor, of course, but she was nevertheless grateful for it.

Once the bandage was in place, she turned her attention to the next pressing matter: her situation. That someone had pushed her into the shed was a fact readily understood even by a woman who had suffered a knock on the head. What baffled her was the question of who had done it.

An answer presented itself immediately, but she was determined to remain objective and not let prejudice tip the scales in favor of the obvious. Could it have been a random stranger who just happened to be walking around the Skeffington property when she crossed his path? Perhaps someone who was afraid of getting in trouble for trespassing and overreacted by attacking an unaccompanied woman? If he had performed another crime in the village, this reaction might make sense.

She considered the theory, which struck her as plausible but unlikely, as it relied too much on coincidence. It was too improbable that she would be assaulted by a random stranger on the same day she was hunting for a killer.

No, her captivity in the shed meant only one thing: Mr. Wilson was near and knew she was looking for him.

The groom, she thought with sudden fervor. The one in the enclosure training the horse. She had dismissed him as too familiar and competent to be Otley's associate from India, but that assumption seemed stupid now. How else would he have been able secure the position if not by demonstrating a sure hand with horses?

What a fool she was! Only a few yards from the killer and she walked in the opposite direction.

And now she was trapped in an abandoned shed well out in a field. If this was Mr. Wilson's plan to dispose of her too, she considered it rather inadequate, for it would take her days to die of thirst, which only increased her chances of being rescued. The dilapidated shack looked unused, yes, but it was still on the grounds in a busy area of the park. If the grooms didn't come out there to fetch tools, they certainly rode by on the horses. She imagined the Skeffingtons did as well, for the scenery was quite magnificent and the hill with the folly was over the next crest. If she wasn't discovered by chance, sooner or later her aunt or Flora would notice she was missing and mount a search. Every corner of the property would be scoured and eventually someone would remember the forlorn shed in the field.

Mr. Wilson would be as dumb as a rotted turnip to believe locking her in there would remove her and the threat she represented once and for all.

That meant he must have a more wicked plan in mind.

Having realized his true intention, she did not lack for possibilities, for in the small space her imagination worked overtime, coming up with different scenarios. He would light the shack on fire and let her burn to death like a heretic during the reign of Henry VIII. He would come back with a knife to stab her in the gut and watch her bleed to death. He would wait until the cover of darkness and drag her to the lake to drown her.

Well, she thought, looking around the neglected shed for something she could wield as a weapon, when he did come back, she would be ready.

The pickings were slim, with the largest item in the room—the basin for washing—also the least useful. If she grasped it by its handles, she could raise it up, but its size made lifting awkward and she doubted she could hurl it more than a few inches. It might afford her some protection as a shield if Mr. Wilson were to level a gun at her, but other than that, it had limited utility. Far better was the wooden plank she'd banged her knees against when she fell, for it had exposed nails at one end that could do a fair amount of damage when brought into direct contact with skin.

Yes, she thought, testing its weight. It would do quite nicely.

Having a plan made Bea feel steadier, and she flipped over the basin to use as a stool while she waited for Mr. Wilson's return. Her whole body stiff with anticipation, she clutched the plank in both hands, felt the ache in her head and stared at the door with every ounce of her focus. She held this pose for several minutes, her muscles clenched and ready, but the strain of staying still was oddly draining and the silence struck her as strangely menacing.

Why was it so quiet? Beatrice thought suddenly. More to the point: Why was *she* so quiet? She was trapped in a derelict shed on the edge of a field. Rather than docilely waiting for her opponent to make his next move, shouldn't she be screaming her head off until somebody heard? Why was she sitting on the metal basin instead of banging on it with her wooden plank? If she had any chance of being rescued before Mr. Wilson came back, then she had to create a racket. As Aunt Vera would be the first to observe, she excelled of late at making inappropriate noise.

Bea stood up, raised the wooden plank over her head and brought it down on the basin with all her strength.

The clang reverberated off the walls as she yelled, "Help! Help! Somebody help!"

She banged on the tub again and again, her energy suddenly returned as the clamor filled the small structure and, surely, hopefully, the countryside surrounding it. Swinging wildly, she hit the side of the shed with the plank, which made an unimpressive thud, but no matter, her screams remained thunderous. Raising the plank again, she noticed that her strike had splintered the weathered board that formed the wall.

"By all that is holy," she said in wondrous surprise, examining the crack through which she could see daylight and the stables off in the distance.

Of course! It was a dilapidated shack. A shack that was dilapidated.

How long had it stood in the field, battered by the elements—pummeled by rain, weakened by snow—and rotted by age, storing a washbasin nobody needed anymore? It looked like years, perhaps even decades. As the other structures were repaired and replaced, this shed had been allowed to crumble.

God bless the Skeffingtons' frugality.

With renewed vigor, she attacked the wall, aiming for the middle of the board that had already separated.

"Take that, Mr. Wilson," she said with each strike. "Take that, you miscreant of Satan. Take that, you wart on the face of decency. Take that, you insult to goodness and righteousness. Take that, you pus-filled carbuncle of veniality."

With each blow, a shard or a sliver or a chip broke off until the decrepit wooden board cracked entirely in half.

"Well done, Bea," she said in satisfaction. "Escape is imminent."

Escape, in fact, was still a full forty-five minutes away, but she was encouraged by her early success and didn't care how much time it took. For long stretches, she bashed the side of the shed with all her strength, and when her palms began to bleed from blisters and splinters, she tore off another portion of her dress and made a comfortable handle.

There, she thought, impressed with her own innovation, before redoubling her efforts to destroy the wall.

A second board split down the center, and, Beatrice, seeing the beginnings of a human-woman-sized hole, kicked the wood, which was hanging by a rusty nail. It fell to the ground, and sunlight, which had crept through the cracks, poured in through the opening. It was just big enough for her to stick her head through. Shoulders next!

By the time the third board fractured and fell, the fabric protecting her hands was almost entirely worn away and the long plank with which she'd begun the endeavor had been whittled to half its original size. The muscles in her arms throbbed, her throat longed for a cool refreshment, and the pain in her head continued to pound unabated. She was filthy, exhausted, achy and relieved.

Silently, she let the plank drop to the ground, clutched what remained of the wall with both hands, threw her right leg over the craggy wood and pulled her body through the opening. The fit was tight—there would be more splinters and scratches—but she was free. She was saved. She would walk away from the ramshackle shed. She would not be fodder for some murderous monster.

At least not today.

Grateful beyond measure, she sank to her knees for a moment, savoring her success and the cool air on her heated skin, but only for the briefest span. A moment later, she stood up straight and tall. Then she took a deep breath, tidied her dress—what was left of it anyway—and turned to walk back to the house. As soon as she did, her eyes met the angry gaze of Andrew Skeffington, who was walking toward her with a determined stride, the entire house party at his heels as he raised his right arm and pointed his finger directly at her.

"There," he said, his voice strong with conviction. "There's your murderer."

CHAPTER TWELVE

Mr. Skeffington's announcement was so astonishing, it was impossible to say who was more shocked: his mother, Aunt Vera, Miss Otley, the Duke of Kesgrave or Beatrice herself.

No, Bea thought with a quick shake of her head, as if trying to clear it of all distractions, it is I. I'm the most surprised one. Me. The person who just battered her way out of a death trap to find herself the target of a murder accusation.

I'm the victim here, she wanted to scream.

But screaming wasn't a viable option, for, despite all her outlandish behavior, which her aunt deemed insupportable, she rarely did anything more indecorous than speak out of turn. Raising her voice in mixed company, even to proclaim her innocence, was more outrageous than she could countenance.

It made no difference that Bea did not speak, for Lady Skeffington captured everyone's attention by gasping at her son in horror and shrieking, "Dear God, Andrew, have you become unbalanced? What murder?"

Mr. Skeffington paid his mother no heed and continued to advance on Beatrice. He stopped only when he was mere inches from her nose, "I caught you," he said triumphantly. "I caught you. You were trying to make it seem as if I were the villain, but you were the one who killed him and I have caught you in the act."

Despite the young man's intense focus on Bea, the company continued to stare at him as if he'd lost his mind. Nobody had yet to notice her wretched condition—the bloody field dressing on her forehead, the scrapes on her arms, the dirt and tears marring almost every inch of her gown.

The stunned silence stretched into seconds as Lady Skeffington stared at her son in horror. Her face pale, she turned to Bea and stammered out an apology for Andrew's inexplicable and despicable rudeness. "I cannot conceive of why he would do such a thing. To accuse an honored guest of something so wicked and depraved is beyond anything I've ever—" She broke her speech off abruptly and narrowed her eyes as if struck by something baffling. "I say, dear, why are you dressed like that?"

Now they noticed—all of them.

Eleven pairs of eyes looked at her at once and scrutinized her disheveled appearance, determined, it seemed, to comprehend why she would select such an unusual costume to wear at an elegant house party. Their response baffled Bea, for surely the hairstyle alone—strands everywhere, locks more down than up, the torn hem sweeping across her forehead—communicated some of the ordeal she'd suffered.

Kesgrave figured it out first, for when he saw the blood on her head, he blanched and took three aggressive steps toward her, stopping only when he seemed to realize how untoward it would look if he made physical contact. She and the duke had spent a fair amount of time together, yes, but none of the other guests knew that. As far as they were aware, the two had a passing acquaintance consisting of a few barbed exchanges for which the girl was immediately chastised by her aunt.

The strength of the duke's concern startled Bea, who looked up to find his eyes boring into hers and his mouth compressed into a hard line as if suppressing a very great rage. His gaze was intense—powerful and penetrating—and she felt herself at once sinking under its weight and rising with its force. In an afternoon of strange experiences, it was the strangest one yet, and as much as she wanted to turn away, she couldn't bring herself to move an inch.

How very strange indeed.

The moment might have stretched on indefinitely, with neither party breaking the contact, if her aunt, perceiving her niece's eccentric fashion choice to actually be the result of an injury, hadn't screeched. Aunt Vera rushed to her side and encapsulated her in a hug, an act that seemed to indicate genuine affection. Moved by the unexpected show of sincerity, Bea felt her throat clog up.

Shocked anew, she swallowed rapidly, determined to keep her emotions in check. After all she had gone through in the shed, she would not break down now.

While Aunt Vera tightened her embrace and murmured concern, Flora tugged on her sleeve and Russell admired her bravery.

"That cut on your head must be deep to have produced so much blood," he observed before adding with a touch of envy, "It will most likely leave a scar that will give your appearance an endearingly raffish look."

As far as she could remember, it was the first kind thing Russell had ever said to her.

Bea enjoyed the warmth of her family's concern and ignored the calls for an explanation, which grew more pressing as the moments passed. She expected Kesgrave to take command of the situation, as the uproar seemed particularly suited to his fondness for imposing order, but he remained silent. The cacophony grew louder and louder until finally Mr. Skeffington's petulance rose above the chaos.

"She's a murderess!" he yelled, stomping his foot in peevish displeasure. "Stop coddling her and listen to me!"

His sullen cry had the desired effect, for everyone stopped talking at once. His father, his face a mask of concern, stepped toward him and laid a reassuring hand on his shoulder. "Nobody was murdered, son," he explained gently.

Mr. Skeffington shrugged off his father and sneered, "Mr. Otley! Mr. Otley was murdered."

As concerned as his lordship was for his son's apparently fragile mental state, he had no patience for his recalcitrance. "Don't be absurd. He died by his own hand."

Mr. Skeffington laughed without humor. "The only absurd thing is that you believe such a blatant plumper," Mr. Skeffington insisted, his voice dripping with scorn. "It was obviously murder, for it's impossible for a man to kill himself by bashing his own head with a candlestick."

Bea's eyes swung to the duke to see if he was as surprised as she that the Skeffington heir had deciphered the truth, but his eyes were firmly fixed on the scene playing out before them. Their host opened his mouth several times, as if unsure how to respond, before saying, "But the constable. He himself declared it to be so."

"Because *he*"—now Mr. Skeffington glared balefully at the duke—"told him to. Kesgrave is protecting the girl. I don't know why, for she has nothing to recommend her and is not his regular style, but he is. She did it, and now she's trying to arrange matters so that it looks as if I did it."

Only moments ago, Bea could not imagine anything worse than fighting her way out of an abandoned shack with a splintery plank while enduring a throbbing headache and yet now she suffered a distress quite unlike anything that had come before. For him to link her name with Kesgrave's, for him to imply that the duke had behaved immorally to benefit her and to then plainly express the bafflement they must all be feeling, including his grace, was a mortification beyond bearing.

Aunt Vera called him a young fool, Miss Otley laughed with great amusement, and Lady Skeffington apologized to her guest, either Bea or the duke—it wasn't clear which one—for the outburst.

Lord Skeffington shook his head sadly, clearly worried that his son had developed a persecution disorder that perceived threats where none existed. "But why would she do that? What possible reason could she have?"

"Because she knows I have reason to desire revenge,"

he said, "as Otley swindled me out of two thousand pounds."

To say his father turned apoplectic at this communication would be to vastly understate his level of anger. The color in his face rose to an alarming shade of magenta, his eyes opened so wide they seemed to almost lurch outside his head, and he shrieked, *"What?"* with equal amounts of shock and disgust.

He was not alone in his distress, for Mrs. Otley also cried out in anguish and turned immediately to Lady Skeffington. "I had no idea," she said with vehement insistence, her hands reaching for her friend and, fearing rebuff, pulling away before they made contact. "I knew...that is, I *suspected* something wasn't entirely correct about the new venture. We had a setback, a quite devastating one. Otley had to respond quickly to save our family before we were exposed and ruined, and the need for a quick response might have undercut his usual scrupulousness. I cannot say as I did not consider it my place to question him about business. But after he lost his pop...ah, *crop* to misfortune, we had nothing. Nothing at all and there were all those bills to pay. The milliner, the modiste, the grocer. It never stopped. And the cost of candles! How could we run up such a large bill so quickly?"

"Mama!" Miss Otley said, either appalled that her mother's apology had devolved into a self-pitying tirade or mortified by the discovery of her father's perfidy.

Recollecting herself, Mrs. Otley reached again for Lady Skeffington's hands, and feeling more confident this time, grasped them. "However desperate our circumstances were, it was not an excuse for my husband to abuse the sacred trust of our relationship. Your friendship means the world to me, and I would never do anything to jeopardize it. I'm so very sorry," she said, and then, as if struck anew by the dreadfulness of the situation, she added, "Oh, wretched, wretched man, sullying our own nest to recoup our fortune. I always knew he wasn't particularly clever, but I assumed he was smarter than this."

"Mama!" Miss Otley's pitch rose as her mother continued to heap blame on her dead father's head.

Lady Skeffington, who had remained composed throughout the entire ordeal, not flinching at any of the revelations, seemed unsure whom she should comfort first: her husband or her friend or her son or even Miss Otley, whose self-control gave way to a torrent of tears. The young lady's weeping only served to make her fragile beauty more pronounced, and Russell presented himself at her side to offer comfort, which she was despondent enough to accept.

Russell's gallantry—or opportunism, Bea thought cynically—relieved their hostess of one problem and she freed her hands from Mrs. Otley's grasp to help calm her husband. In the minutes since he discovered the depths of his son's idiocy and his friend's villainy, Skeffington's rage had only grown hotter. He called both men several vile names, seemingly incapable of distinguishing between their crimes, as he paced about the field in a large circle.

"He fleeced me too, you know," Amersham said petulantly.

Bea wasn't sure if his intent was to defend his friend or declare his own victimhood. Mrs. Otley, claiming the latter for herself, whimpered and cursed her misfortune in marrying a scoundrel, which caused her daughter to cry even harder.

Mr. Skeffington, unable to bear how wildly things had gotten off course, whistled loudly and all activity stopped. "You are all missing the point," he said impatiently. "It doesn't matter what Otley did. All that matters is that this woman here murdered him in cold blood and is trying to blame me. I had no choice but to trap her in the shed while I fetched—"

"*You* trapped her in the shed?" Aunt Vera said, stepping forward with menace in her eyes. If she had a reticule in her hand, she would have bashed him on the head with it.

He stiffened at her tone, offended by the implication

that he had done anything wrong. "I had to. She murdered a man and was trying to set me up to take the blame. I had no choice but to shove her inside and lock the door."

Aunt Vera wasn't the only one who gasped in shock. Lord Skeffington's expression of anger was so acute, he looked as if had he had a reticule in his hand, he would do something far worse than merely hit his son on the head with it. He marched across the field until he stood nose to nose with his heir and said, "Shove her inside? You mean to say, you're the one who is responsible for the gaping wound on her forehead?"

Gaping wound? Bea thought in surprise. She reached up to feel her bandage and realized it had indeed slipped.

"I had no choice," he insisted. "Yesterday she broke into my room to leave evidence that pointed to my guilt. And today she has been quizzing the servants in a most suspicious manner. She is solidifying a case against me to hide her own guilt."

At this charge, Nuneaton stepped forward, while Beatrice looked at Kesgrave for some direction, as she had no idea what to do. Unaware of her attention, he kept his gaze on Mr. Skeffington. His expression was placid, which she took comfort in, as she knew there was little chance she would be condemned as a murderer while he stood by. As long as he was calm, she would remain so as well.

Nuneaton also considered Mr. Skeffington and said after a thoughtful pause, "That's a grave accusation. What is your proof in making it?"

The fact that someone was finally taking him seriously was enough to soothe the young man's agitation and he answered evenly. "If you recall, I spent yesterday morning practicing my ties with Harris—the duke's valet, you will note—who provided an interesting diversion in the form of a tutorial on how to improve one's flies. When I returned in the afternoon, I spotted Miss Hyde-Clare leaving my rooms. Looking around my bedchamber, I noticed immediately that the candle I had left on the night table had been moved to the clothespress. I carefully inspected the candlestick and observed it had blood on it. Naturally, I concluded that she had replaced my candlestick with a bloodied one to point to my guilt, as we all know Mr. Otley had been struck over the head with just such an instrument. Then, today, I saw her poking around where she didn't belong. She visited the kitchens and spoke with the staff there, then pried around the stables and the coach house. I observed her approaching this abandoned shed, which hasn't been used in years, and knew at once that she was using it for some nefarious reason. So I pushed her inside, locked the door and went to fetch my parents. As I found them having tea with Mrs. Otley and her daughter in the drawing room before they departed, I thought it prudent to invite everyone else along as well, so that we might dispense with the matter all at once."

Beatrice hadn't expected so much coherence from the man who had rambled feverishly about murderers and assaulted her at his whim. She realized now that his actions had been more considered than she'd credited. For two days, he'd been observing her carefully and slowly building a case against her. He'd even noted the growing association between her and Kesgrave, going so far as to imply that the duke's valet offered instruction only as a way to remove him from his rooms and provide her with an opportunity to place the incriminating candlestick within.

His catalogue sounded damning to Bea's ear, as did the extended silence that followed the narration. She longed to glance again at the duke to see how the list of charges affected him, but she was afraid such a move would only affirm her guilt to the others. Instead, she peeked at her aunt to see her response and was horrified to see her eyes were wide with shock.

She believes it, Bea thought.

And then Aunt Vera erupted into a gale of laughter so strong she had to steady herself on her son, lest she topple over from the force.

"Beatrice and the duke?" she said as she gasped for air. "Conspiring together? Are you mad?"

"Although she could put it a bit more delicately, my mother is right," Flora said to the Skeffington heir, whose cheeks had turned pink at the display of contempt. "The prospect that my cousin has formed an alliance with the Duke of Kesgrave is perhaps the most ardently ridiculous thing you could possibly propose. Beatrice is lovely enough, of course, but she's mousy and she's forever improving her mind with texts about farming and foreign countries. What interest would a duke have in that? Truly, sir, you appear to be under a great deal of stress at the moment, and I fear it might have addled your mind." She paused and turned to her hostess, who had been nothing but gracious to her, and apologized for speaking ill of her son. "I do not say it to be mean-spirited but out of concern. This interest he seems to have taken in my cousin is quite inexplicable. She couldn't possibly have murdered Mr. Otley, for she had no reason in the world to wish him ill."

"They were lovers!" Mr. Skeffington announced. "She is a woman of loose morals who dallied with a clerk in the Chancery. Everyone here knows it."

At this very grave charge, Aunt Vera's amusement overcame her to such an excessive degree, she had to sit down on the ground or risk falling.

Bea, however, felt her heart race in panic and fear that one of them, all of them, would recall the nonsensical story about Mr. Theodore Davies and find within it a kernel of truth to which to tether his claim about Mr. Otley. Her aunt, obviously, knew it to be pure fustian, and she didn't doubt her cousins were laughing quietly if not rolling on the ground like their mother, but the others were almost as strangers to her. They would be within their rights to believe it. Ultimately, it would not be any more bizarre than discovering the man they had all believed guilty of suicide had actually suffered a violent and unsought death.

She knew she had to say something, for she could not

continue to stand there stunned and mute as her name was sullied. Her mind could scarcely grasp the reality of what had happened—to escape from a makeshift prison, victorious and relieved, only to find oneself the target of a vile accusation. It seemed like a scene from a play. She ought to defend herself but what could she add to the conversation? All she could do was offer by-route denials, as anyone accused of such things would do. There was nothing particularly interesting about one's protestations of innocence. Indeed, was there anything more banal?

But silence had not served her well, for into the void had fallen another charge, and it was somehow worse to be thought Mr. Otley's lover than his killer.

She had to speak now.

Before Bea could say anything, Kesgrave moved a few steps closer to her, as if offering himself as a shield, and smiled at Mr. Skeffington with mild amusement. "Is your imagination so limited that a torrid affair is really the best you can do? You're young, of course, and your experience with women is quite limited, but I assure you they are complex and fascinating creatures and could be spurred to do harm for a variety of reasons that have nothing to do with carnal pleasure. Your inability to come up with one demonstrates your level of desperation to ascribe a motive to Miss Hyde-Clare."

Kesgrave's comment had the intended effect, and the Skeffington heir bristled at the mockery. "Your protests mean nothing, as you are conspiring with her. I cannot begin to fathom what your motives are, other than you are simply bored in the country and looking for some freakish novelty to divert you."

Although Bea knew the duke was quite capable of defending himself, she decided to step in before he ripped Mr. Skeffington to shreds. Yes, the dreadful young man had assaulted her both in spirit and in fact, but he had arrived at his abhorrent conclusions honestly. If she had discovered the bloodied candlestick by her own bedside after watching him sneak out of her room, she would have drawn the exact same conclusion.

"Mr. Skeffington is correct," Bea said, her voice firm as she held herself stiff to control the sudden shaking of her limbs. "Mr. Otley was indeed murdered. As he has explained, the manner of death would have been impossible for a lone man to contrive. And, yes, I stole into his room to search for information because I knew about his treatment at Mr. Otley's hand, and I did spend much of the morning talking to the staff in order to find out more information about newcomers to the estate. But he is also wrong because I did not kill Mr. Otley." She paused to let the statement sink in with her audience. "I'm not a murderer. Now, I know we are all upset..."

Bea faltered as something fluttered on the edge of her consciousness. She batted it away and tried again. "I know we are all..." But it persisted and persisted until at once she knew exactly what her mind had intuitively grasped.

Unconcerned about who might witness the moment, she turned to the duke with apprehension and excitement flickering in her eyes. "I know," she said simply.

She didn't have to elaborate, for Kesgrave grasped at once her meaning and announced to the party that the poor girl was so tired she could no longer finish her sentences.

"Added to that," he said, "she looks as if she just emerged from a coal mine. She could use a bath and a rest and someone must tend to those wounds before they become worse. I propose we adjourn for the moment and pick up this fascinating conversation in a few hours in the drawing room. We can have tea and some cakes while we talk it over."

At the mention of food Bea realized she was desperately hungry—how many hours had it been since those eggs?—and just the thought of soaking in a hot tub made her aching body melt. Yet she still opened her mouth to protest this proposal, for, like Mr. Skeffington, she believed it was prudent to unmask a killer as soon as you deciphered his identity. Unlike that thoughtless young man, she had constructed an unassailable case against her suspect.

Kesgrave silenced her with a look, which was hardly surprising. Naturally, he wanted to hear her theory and confirm its accuracy before she leveled the charge. As the target of an erroneous accusation, she could understand his caution and complied with his unspoken request.

Nevertheless, it rankled, for she knew her deductions were correct.

She wasn't the only one who objected.

"He's trying to distract us," Mr. Skeffington said. "He's postponing the inevitable to give her time to devise an alternate plan. I told you, they are working together."

"I am trying to be respectful of your imbecility," Kesgrave said, his voice bathed in mild scorn, "but you're making it very difficult. Miss Hyde-Clare is clearly exhausted, and I can perceive no harm in letting her return to the hall and rest before we resume this discussion. Pray, Mr. Skeffington, what do you think is going to happen in the interim? Do you imagine she will take to the open road with her belongings in a carpet bag? Perhaps she will liberate one of the horses from the stable and steal away while Mrs. Langston is brewing tea? I know it's hard for you to be sensible, young man, with your flights of fancy, but do apply yourself a little."

As furious as Lord Skeffington was with his son for handing over several thousand pounds to a charlatan, he could not let such scathing contempt for his offspring stand. "I say, Kesgrave, ease back. The boy merely misjudged the situation and will apologize accordingly. That said, I do believe he was both well-justified and persuasive in his conclusions. I myself am not convinced he is entirely off the mark."

Aunt Vera rose to her feet to defend her niece, but the duke forestalled her angry comment with a cutting remark of his own. "I would never deny a father the opportunity to draw the same asinine conclusion as his son, as

intelligence is known to be a thing that runs in a family—
or not, as the case may be. However, I trust you are astute
enough to recognize that having obtained his suspicions
about Miss Hyde-Clare, Mr. Skeffington should have han-
dled the matter in a way that did not include assaulting and
terrifying her. Surely, we can all agree that such behavior is
beyond the pale, and having suffered it with what seems to
be remarkable grace, the young lady has earned the right to
clean herself up and settle herself down before having to
defend herself further against a murder charge."

"Bravo," Russell said, approval ringing loudly in his
voice as he stepped away from Miss Otley to draw closer
to Kesgrave. An Incomparable with delicate tears in her
eyes was a sight to behold, of course, but a stinging setdown was a thing of beauty. His admiration for the duke
shot up tenfold.

"I think we could all benefit from a little rest," Lady
Skeffington said with a soothing smile. "Let's return to the
hall and retire to our rooms to clear our thinking. The Otleys, of course, will delay their departure until this matter
has been sorted out."

Mr. Skeffington took umbrage at the suggestion that
his thinking required clearing, but one look from his father
quelled him. Surly and thwarted, he walked across the field
in the company of Amersham, who couldn't help sharing
his concern that Miss Hyde-Clare had tried to make him
look guilty as well.

"I didn't find anything as startling as a bloody candlestick in my bedchamber, but I did notice my clothing
wasn't as neatly folded as it should have been," he explained. "I assumed my valet was at fault, as his attention
to detail is not as finely honed as I would like. And, to be
entirely candid, I'm not quite sure he knows the difference
between a Waterfall knot and the Stagecoach. Perhaps I
should let him go? He is the nephew of my father's butler,
so there might be some trickiness there, but ultimately the
only concern should be my comfort, as I am the employer,

am I not? And yet I'm uncertain how to proceed. I assure you, it weighs on my mind quite a bit."

His friend responded with a heavy sigh and drooped his shoulders even more.

Lady Skeffington, seeming to bear Mrs. Otley no ill will for her husband's crimes, offered her old school friend her arm. "Do not think I have forgotten that you have suffered a grave shock as well," she said comfortingly. "Come, you must rest before we reconvene. Emily, you as well. I must apologize to you both for the unfortunate setting of such an unhappy scene. If one must discover one's husband is a cheat and a liar as well as the victim of a violent murder, one should do so close to one's bed, so one can take to it swiftly."

"How very wise," Nuneaton murmured.

Mrs. Otley managed only a nod of consent, and Nuneaton watched as the three women strolled off toward the house. Then he approached the ramshackle structure and, unconcerned about the possible damage to his exquisite silks, examined the hole from which Bea had emerged. He noted the sharp and jagged edges of the wood as a splinter pricked his thumb and peered inside the small space. Straightening his shoulders, he regarded Bea with the light of respect gleaming in his eyes. "Although your ordeal has only been hinted at and not explicitly stated, I can infer from the evidence what you have been through and would like to tell you how impressed I am with your resourcefulness and determination."

The cognitive leaps he had to make to arrive at that deduction presented the first genuine sign of intelligence Bea had observed in the viscount, and she took the effort as the real compliment. She imagined the dandy did not exert his brain power for many people.

"Thank you," she said before dismissing her efforts as merely a function of boredom, as she had nothing else to do while waiting for her attacker to return. "I didn't know the circumstance of my captivity, you see, and thought my life was being threatened. If I had known Mr.

Skeffington would return with the entire house party in tow, I would have of course waited patiently."

"Ordinarily, I would counsel patience in all things," Aunt Vera said, inspecting the rundown building for herself, "as there can be nothing more feminine than forbearance. But in this case, I must applaud your initiative, for you were provided with no amenities, not even a cushion to make that washbasin more comfortable. It's barbaric. Now, let's do follow the others so that we may clean that wound on your head and get a better look at it. I think it's an indication of Helen's distress at her son's behavior that she didn't offer to send for the doctor to examine you."

The gash in her forehead did indeed throb, but it was all the little cuts and scratches stinging in concert that caused her more pain. She thought again of the tub of hot water and decided the moment could not come quickly enough. She straightened her bandage and began walking toward the house.

Aunt Vera, determined to keep up with her niece's wide stride, all but trotted alongside. "You must not despair, my dear. We will offer a vigorous defense of you," she said to the approval of her children. "You are not altogether blameless, as you have admitted to searching Mr. Skeffington's room when he wasn't there, which I do wish you hadn't done. My lecture did not specifically address the impropriety of stealing into a man's bedchamber when he isn't present because I assumed no such provision was necessary." She turned bright pink as she heard the words replay in her head and promptly amended her statement. "It's just as improper to steal into a man's bedchamber when he *is* present. Actually, no," she said, shaking her head, "it's more improper. Indeed, a great deal more. It is perhaps the most improper thing a lady can do."

Naturally, her son felt compelled to challenge this declaration with other inappropriate situations, and Aunt Vera, not at all aware she was being teased, answered each one solemnly and pointedly. Bea, who was still touched by her family's sincere concern for her well-being, paid her aunt the respect of looking chastened.

Kesgrave stayed several feet behind them during the walk back to the house, conversing quietly with Nuneaton. She wondered if they were discussing the shocking events of the afternoon or if the duke was distracting his friend with nonsensical banter. Perhaps he was cataloging all the different types of timber one could use in a garden shed organized from the most durable to the least. She didn't think his grace would tell the viscount anything important, for until the moment when they revealed the name of the killer, the investigation was ongoing and she rather thought he'd honor the sanctity of that. He'd also welcome any opportunity to show off his knowledge.

At last they arrived back at the hall and Bea went straight up to her room, where, as the housekeeper had attested, the bath was already being filled. While she waited, she inspected her appearance in the mirror and discovered that comparing her with a coal miner had been wildly optimistic. With the streaks of blood on her face, tufts of hair pointing in a multitude of directions and smudges of dirt everywhere, even on her eyelids, she looked like a chimney sweep who had lost a street brawl with a tiger.

What a picture she must have presented when she stepped clear of the building—a wild thing capable of any sort of depravity. It was a wonder they hadn't strung her up for murder right then and there.

They still might, she reminded herself, for Mr. Skeffington was hardly done making his case. His evidence was insubstantial and his reasoning deeply flawed, but he had managed to convince his father and might yet win over others.

Well, she thought as her maid entered to help her out of her gown, I'm not done making my case either.

But the thought of the impending scene in the drawing room—dueling versions of the same horrific event—caused butterflies to take flight in her stomach, so she cleared her mind of everything for a little while and sunk into the warm oblivion of the tub.

CHAPTER THIRTEEN

Mr. Skeffington, who entered the room with a stormy expression on his face as he grumbled heatedly to his friend Amersham about the farce they were about to witness, broke into a wide grin as he spied the imposing stranger in a red waistcoat standing near the window. His reaction surprised Bea, who had felt nothing but an increase in her unease in knowing a Bow Street Runner would be present for the revelation of the murderer. It gave the proceedings a gravitas that unsettled her, which, she knew, was an absurd response, as the matter was already as grave as possible.

Assuming the Runner was there at his father's contrivance, Mr. Skeffington thanked his sire for taking the matter seriously. "As outlandish as it appears, I know I'm right and by the time this ludicrous meeting is concluded, everyone will know it too and offer their apologies for ever doubting me."

His lordship harrumphed loudly and declared he had nothing to do with the Bow Street Runner currently occupying his drawing room. "Kesgrave brought him here—sent to London for him days ago and lodged him in the village—without consulting me, which is, I think, a rather poor way to repay one's host for his hospitality. If I wanted an enforcement officer to darken my doorstep, I would have arranged for one myself."

Mr. Skeffington greeted this information with a skeptical expression and then announced that he for one would not be fooled by the duke's attempt to change directions midstream. "Others might take the hard stance the Runner represents as proof he had nothing to do with Miss Hyde-Clare's crime, but I know he has been conspiring with her to hide the truth. Now he's trying to hide the fact that he's been trying to hide the truth. It's all a ruse, a rather incompetent one, I might add."

"On the contrary," Kesgrave said as he entered the room, "I fully own that I've been working with Miss Hyde-Clare to solve the mystery of Mr. Otley's death."

Aunt Vera gasped, Viscount Nuneaton laughed, and Mr. Skeffington furrowed his brow as if trying to see the trick before it felled him. Bea imagined her own expression was not very different from her accuser's, for she could not decipher what the duke's game was in bringing a Bow Street Runner there. It spoke, she thought, of a disconcertingly deep faith in her judgment, as he had taken the rather extreme action based solely on her insistence that she had figured it out. He had not sought out the details of her theory to confirm it was sound, and for all he knew she would present the flimsiest of cases to the room. Mere hours before she had been sure beyond all doubt that Mrs. Otley's lover was secreted somewhere on the estate. She had even interviewed the kitchen staff, for God's sake!

How wrong she had been.

Bea knew this time she had her facts right, but since that certitude lent her no confidence, she was baffled by the duke's conviction.

"Are we all here?" Kesgrave asked, surveying the room to make sure all members of the house party were present.

Indeed they were.

The Otleys sat huddled together on the love seat across from the fire, their faces twisted into twin expressions of caution as they waited to hear more unpleasant things about the man whom they had both trusted. On the armchair adjacent to them was Lady Skeffington, as composed as ever and determined to make the proceedings as relaxed as a morning call between intimates, as she offered tea to her guests and talked about the lovely weather. ("Such a delightful relief given the soggy start of the week.") In the chair next to her, Aunt Vera accepted the cup of steaming brew as well as a teacake from the tray offered. Flora perched on the edge of the settee across from her mother, as if afraid she might miss something if she leaned back too far. More comfortably situated beside her was Russell, who was staring at the duke as if worshipping an idol. Amused by the young man's adoration of his friend, Nuneaton stood behind the settee next to Amersham, whose expression was at once sulky and intrigued. His lordship sat next to his wife in a wooden chair borrowed from the writing table, while his son impatiently paced the length of the floor.

Flanked by her cousins on the settee, Beatrice watched Kesgrave stride to the front of the room and position himself before the fire. He rested one arm on the mantelpiece as if posing for a Gainsborough portrait, and watching his blond curls gleam in the soft light, she was struck by how handsome he was. It was nothing new, for one had only to look at him to see his attractiveness, but in the days since she had gotten to know him, his appearance had faded into the background. In the foreground was his character, which was far more irreverent and appealing than one would expect for a pedant. Discovering he was a likable human being should not have made her sad, and yet it did, for it served only to emphasize the yawning gap between them. In any other circumstance save a gruesome murder, he would never have noticed she existed.

Bea had known it all along and called herself a fool for regretting it now.

Fortunately, she had more-pressing matters to worry about.

"Another trick," Mr. Skeffington said of the duke's ready admission that he was working with Beatrice. "He's trying to confuse the situation."

"On the contrary, I'm determined to simplify it," Kesgrave said smoothly. "With your permission"—he looked at the father, not the son—"I would like to take a moment to review the events so that we may all start from the same place."

"You may do whatever you like, as long as you do it quickly," Lord Skeffington replied, darting his eyes again to the Runner by the window. Bea appreciated his anxiety, for it was indeed unnerving to have a man present who sported a pair of handcuffs.

The duke dipped his head in gratitude or acquiescence, while Mr. Skeffington muttered, "For God's sake."

"We will begin," Kesgrave said, "at the beginning— that is, the night of the murder. As you all know, I discovered the body in the library a little after two o'clock in the morning. What you do not know is Miss Hyde-Clare discovered me discovering the body."

Several people in the room gasped, including Emily and Flora. Aunt Vera, immediately thwarting his lordship's desire to move the process along as swiftly as possible, cried out in alarm at the idea of her niece bearing witness to such a ghastly scene—no wonder the girl had been acting so strangely this week!—and required a full three minutes of soothing before she was calm enough to allow the duke to proceed.

"Although Miss Hyde-Clare was a witness to the events, I convinced her to return to bed and allow me to handle the matter on my own. I woke up his lordship, who sent for the constable. As Mr. Skeffington has observed, the gentleman's death was without question a murder, but I found it very easy to convince the constable that Mr. Otley had suffered of his own hand. He was easy to persuade,

I believe, because it was what he wanted to believe, as it would require nothing more of him. He was, by all indications, grateful for my insistence on ruling it a suicide. Would he have been less vulnerable to my argument if I were not a duke, I cannot say. I suspect the answer to that is yes."

Although the butterflies in her stomach lurched with increasing menace the longer Kesgrave drew out his presentation, she was amused by his pompous performance. Clearly, even in this dire situation, he could not resist pontificating.

"Now, why did I insist on deeming a murder a suicide?" the duke asked. "That is a very good question. I had several reasons. First, if the constable declared Mr. Otley's death to be murder, the perpetrator would be on his or her guard. But if he or she believed they had gotten away with their crime, they would be more relaxed and therefore more likely to make a mistake. Second, if such a ruling was made, the house party would break up at once and all the suspects would disperse to their various residences. I knew that if I were to stand any chance at discovering the villain, that must not happen."

"I say, Kesgrave, that was damned presumptuous of you!" Lord Skeffington growled. "This is my house and thus my decision to make."

The duke was unperturbed by his display of anger. "As loath as I am to disagree with my host, I must insist that you are incorrect. As the one who discovered the body, the decision fell under my purview. Naturally, you are welcome to decide differently when you are the first person to discover a corpse."

Skeffington sputtered at the treatment, flapped his lips without producing a coherent response and settled on calling his guest impertinent.

Kesgrave accepted the comment with a gracious bow and then continued, "I assumed this decision to call the death a suicide would be uncontroversial, but Miss Hyde-

Clare, who, you will recall, also witnessed the evidence of a brutal murder"—here, Aunt Vera wailed again at the atrocity—"was quite disturbed by the misclassification. She resolved to find justice for Mr. Otley, an admirable impulse, to be sure."

"I had the same one!" Mr. Skeffington called from the other side of the room. He was ignored by everyone, except his mother, who assured him he had always been a diligent child.

"In the course of her investigation, Miss Hyde-Clare did indeed search Mr. Skeffington's rooms, as did I myself. That is how I know for a fact that she did not plant the candlestick in his rooms, for I was the one who discovered it and I was the one who put it back in the wrong place. It was an egregious oversight on my part and one I can only attribute to my shock at finding it there in the first place. Why was I so surprised? Let me explain: When I ventured to the library that night at two in the morning, I had brought a candle to guide my way, a candle that I had placed on a bookshelf while I was examining the body. This same candle disappeared during my examination, taken, presumably, by the perpetrator, whose own candle had been used as the murder weapon. And now that candlestick had appeared in Mr. Skeffington's room with blood on it. How did it get there? Why was it there?"

Kesgrave paused to let his audience consider the questions on their own. Mrs. Otley murmured, "How very strange," while Nuneaton rubbed his chin thoughtfully and his lordship grumbled about unnecessary theatrics.

"It is a puzzle indeed. Miss Hyde-Clare, however, has some thoughts on the answer and I will now cede the floor to allow her to share them with us. Miss Hyde-Clare?" he said with a look in her direction. "I think it would be best if you came up here to speak. I would urge the other gentlemen to remain seated, as the unconventionality of the situation is enough to justify the minor break with custom."

Beatrice wanted to say, "No, thank you, I'm fine where I am," as the thought of standing before the company like a lecturer at a university seemed needlessly portentous. It had worked for Kesgrave because he *was* needlessly portentous. Seeing no way to avoid it, for to demur would be to draw even more attention to herself, she rose cautiously and walked over to the fireplace.

If only she and the duke had discussed the meeting beforehand! Then she would have known what to expect and would not have this vaguely terrified look on her face as she turned to address the company—half of whom were convinced she was a coldhearted murderess.

Truly, if Kesgrave had told her what he intended to do, she would have politely but ardently declined the honor. It was one thing to poke around in empty rooms and ask the servants intrusive questions and another entirely to boldly announce you had solved the mysterious death of a fellow guest.

Even the prime minister would balk at such an assignment.

The only person she could imagine who would relish exposing a vicious killer to a roomful of curious and suspicious onlookers was the duke himself. Indeed, with his fondness for explication, his penchant for excessive detail and his love of hearing himself talk, he was particularly well-suited for the task. That he was willing to entrust the matter to her indicated a level of respect in her abilities she'd never expected to earn.

Or he was simply throwing her to the wolves.

Both prospects seemed equally plausible.

Kesgrave greeted her with a brusque nod before yielding his position in front of the fireplace. He went and stood next to his friend Nuneaton, whose interest in the proceedings seemed as keen as everyone else's, and she flinched at her argument only the day before that even he may be Mr. Wilson in disguise.

Her expression must have conveyed some of her apprehension because Aunt Vera drew her attention with a discreet flicker of her hand and grinned broadly at her, signaling that she should do the same. Bea wanted to roll her eyes at her aunt's advice, but she realized there was nothing to be gained by standing there looking thunderous and scared. She smiled.

"Um...g-good afternoon," she said, stumbling over a greeting because she wasn't sure if a greeting was necessary. But she had to start with something, for she couldn't just announce without preamble, "And the murderer is..."

If she didn't want to seem as wildly speculative as Mr. Skeffington had only hours before, she needed to first provide context for her conclusions. "As his grace explained, I was very surprised and troubled by the ruling of suicide in the matter of Mr. Otley's death. It had grave implications for not only his soul but also his family's future and that seemed deeply unfair to me. Not aware of the duke's reasons, I began to look into the matter myself in hopes of proving the truth in order to attain justice for the dead man and his wife and daughter."

Did she sound sanctimonious?

She didn't want to sound sanctimonious. She wanted to sound sincere and concerned.

"Naturally," she continued, "to discover what really happened, I had to remain open to all possibilities, and that included the prospect that the guilty party was one of the guests at Lakeview Hall."

Now *that* did sound sanctimonious.

And it made it startlingly clear that she considered herself above suspicion.

"Kesgrave seemed at first to be the most likely culprit, as he was on the scene and he lied about the cause of death," she explained.

"For goodness' sake, Beatrice," Aunt Vera said impatiently, "he couldn't have done it. He's a duke."

"Yes," Beatrice said, recalling the early interaction with Kesgrave, "that's precisely the argument he made."

Her aunt wasn't amused by this continued abuse of such an esteemed personage, but Nuneaton chuckled and the duke himself smiled.

Now Bea worried she didn't sound sanctimonious enough.

"Mr. Skeffington also required investigation, as did Lord Amersham, since both had been swindled out of a great deal of money by the deceased. That provided them both with a reason to wish him dead, which I couldn't in all good conscience ignore," she explained.

Amersham's cheeks reddened at further discussion of his credulity, and Mr. Skeffington abruptly ceased his pacing to defame the absurdity of a proceeding that allowed the guilty party to stand in front of the company and point her finger at everyone else.

Kesgrave, his tone slightly bored, assured the young man that he would get the opportunity to present his case next.

Mr. Skeffington glared at him balefully and asked, "Why do you get to decide? Who put you in charge?"

With a rueful smile at Aunt Vera, he said, "I'm a duke. As it has been suggested, these things generally go in order of precedence." Then he turned to Bea and advised her to continue.

She looked warily at Mr. Skeffington, then at the Runner, whose interest was impossible to gauge at a glance. "Because of their history with Mr. Otley, I felt compelled to discover more about the two men. My foray into Mr. Skeffington's rooms has already been detailed by Mr. Skeffington himself as well as the duke. It's true Kesgrave and I found the candlestick in his rooms. Kesgrave recognized it at once as the one he had carried to the library and observed the blood. It did seem pretty damning evidence against Mr. Skeffington, but it was hardly conclu-

sive and I had no intention of rushing to judgment—
especially when there were other people to consider."

Bea darted a glance at Mrs. Otley and her daughter
and wondered how to proceed. It did not seem right to
reveal private information about their relationships, and
yet the murder itself had already exposed so much. "His
family, which was not immune from suspicion, was also in
need of a careful look," she said cautiously.

This revelation did not surprise Emily, who always
considered herself in need of a careful look, but her mother
paled at once, visibly unsettled at the thought of someone
discovering her secret liaison with her husband's business
associate. Seeing her discomfort, Bea could only conclude
that the poor woman had no idea her daughter had discovered the revealing letter.

"That careful look turned up some interesting information that necessitated further examination and most
certainly required me to add Mrs. Otley's name to the list
of suspects," Beatrice announced.

Mrs. Otley let out a strangled cry as her daughter
looked at her with a mix of trepidation and complacency,
as if at once worried for her mother's future and gratified
at how quickly the chickens had come home to roost.

"Really, Beatrice," her aunt said crossly, "there's no
need to be so impolite to a fellow guest, particularly one
who just discovered her husband has been murdered."

"Of course not," Bea agreed calmly, as if the proceedings were not about to grow significantly more indecorous.
As they had all learned earlier that afternoon in the field by
the shed, one could not accuse a person of murder without
creating a great deal of awkwardness. "Although Mrs. Otley was on the list, I did not consider her very seriously for
her frame is too small to overcome a man of her husband's
height and girth. It seemed highly unlikely she would be
able to bash him over the head with a candlestick until he
was dead."

"Beatrice!" Aunt Vera said in dismay. "A lady doesn't say *bash*."

"After the Otleys, I considered the possibility that Lord Skeffington was responsible," Bea continued as if her aunt hadn't spoken. "If he had learned about the two thousand pounds, he and Otley might have had words about it. This seemed like a distinct possibility, as I'd found a cheroot in Otley's dresser when I searched his rooms. The deceased did not like the smell or taste of cigars, so it couldn't be his. Perhaps it was his lordship's, brought with him when he went to confront Otley about cheating his son. If he knew the truth, it would provide motivation for harming Mr. Otley, as it must be particularly stinging to discover an old friend has swindled your child."

"He didn't know," Mr. Skeffington called from the other end of the room.

"No, I did not," his father said calmly. "Your speculation about me, like your speculation about everyone else in the room, is worthless. How much more do we have to endure? I've already told the cook to push dinner back by an hour so that we'll still have time to change." He turned to Kesgrave and said with aggressive humility, "I assume, of course, that's all right with you."

The duke nodded and congratulated him on his foresight. "I'd been about to suggest that very thing."

"I apologize, my lord, if it seems as though I have drawn the matter out," Bea said, wondering at her own need for courtesy when things had already strayed so far from conventional etiquette. For goodness' sake, there was a Bow Street Runner in the room waiting to take someone into custody. When that happened, she imagined dinner would be the last thing on any of their minds. "I assure you, I'm very nearly done. Your name was promptly removed from the list by the duke himself, who said he'd left you in your study when he followed Otley to the library. Obviously, there was no way for you to travel so quickly between the rooms unless you had a secret passageway connecting the two." She looked at him out of the corner of her eye and said, "You don't, do you?"

"For God's sake!" Skeffington said.

"Of course," Bea added quickly. "Your removal from the list left one last name, a gentleman whom I shall call Mr. X, as it's not my place to divulge private information about other parties present. Having considered and found wanting all the other suspects, I could see only one remaining possibility: an accomplice, who, in order to have committed the crime, must be at large on the property. This assumption is why I was interviewing the staff this morning. I deduced that the easiest way for Mr. X to infiltrate the house was to hide among the servants. Thurman mentioned a new groom, and I was seeking him out to confirm he wasn't this mysterious Mr. X when Mr. Skeffington assaulted me and locked me in the shed this afternoon."

"Harker?" Skeffington said churlishly. "Harker the groom, whose father is the village blacksmith. My dear girl, you are perfectly ridiculous and I don't know what Kesgrave is thinking to subject us to your feeble reasoning."

Before the duke could defend her—if he planned to defend her—Beatrice enthusiastically agreed with him. "You're right, my lord. My reasoning was feeble. I had become so attached to my own theory about an unknown accomplice that my hypothesis had grown increasingly and more implausibly elaborate, which, to his credit, the duke had tried to warn me about. But when we were standing in the field in front of the shack that was my prison this afternoon, it all suddenly became startlingly clear. All the various pieces of information I'd gathered coalesced into a single, simple solution."

"Curious how the moment I reveal the truth is the moment you discover it," Mr. Skeffington said jeeringly.

Nobody paid him any heed, not even his mother.

"I will tell you now who the murderer is. But first let me review the information," Bea said to grunts and exhales of impatience from everyone save Kesgrave and the Bow

Street Runner he had fetched from London. She wondered if her unprecedented reluctance to say something without providing the proper context was how the duke felt all the time. All of a sudden, knowledge felt like a responsibility. "We know someone left the candlestick in Mr. Skeffington's room, and by all indications it was the murderer. Mr. Skeffington believes the candle was placed there to make him look guilty. And yet nobody has produced the candlestick in question as evidence of his guilt. In fact, he's the only one who has drawn our attention to it. We know someone visited Mr. Otley in his rooms and left the cheroot behind, which indicates whoever killed him enjoys taking a smoke and felt comfortable enough to visit him in his private chamber. We also know that Mr. Otley's size means his assailant had to be of a certain height in order for the candlestick to be an effective weapon. And last, the killer had to have known that Otley had fleeced his hibiscus investors, for the swindle itself was the main motivation for the attack. It was, however, not the only motivation. The murderer also acted out of a great deal of rage, revealing the murder to be a crime of passion, as—"

"Good God, Beatrice," her aunt squealed, "what a ghastly description."

"—spontaneous as it was brutal," Bea continued, once again ignoring her aunt's objection. Now that the moment had finally arrived, she discovered her heart was beating with almost unbearable apprehension and dread. She had no idea what would happen when she finally said the words. As someone who had stood accused hours ago, she could only imagine the new defendant issuing an equally vigorous denial while the Bow Street Runner stepped forward with handcuffs. "Only one person meets these criteria, only one person would possibly leave the candlestick in Mr. Skeffington's room and the cheroot in Mr. Otley's, and only one person showed not the least bit of surprise when it was revealed that Mr. Skeffington had invested in the India hibiscus scheme. To be clear, this person also—"

Lady Skeffington stood up, her hands raised as if unable to take yet another review of the evidence. "For goodness' sake, dear, I confess," she said irritably. "I did it. I killed Thomas. Really, young lady, has nobody ever taught you that brevity is the soul of wit? I begin to see now why you remain unmarried. I'd naturally assumed it was because you were a plain-faced girl with a meager portion, but now I see it's because you're deadly dull. You are quite the dullest girl in Dullminster."

"Mother!" Mr. Skeffington shrieked, so stunned by her admission, he had to hold on to the back of the settee to steady his balance.

"I'm sorry, darling, about the candlestick," she said comfortingly as she walked around the sofa. "There must have been some blood still on my hands when I picked it up. I'd thought I'd wiped it all on my dress. If I'd known, I would never have left it in your room when Mrs. Langston and I visited to discuss repainting. As you know, it's been several years since we redecorated the upstairs and I think the entire floor could do with a little brightening. But I didn't mean for you to think I was trying to make you appear guilty. I would never do something so atrocious to anyone, let alone my own son."

Although her apology was both earnest and heartfelt, it merely agitated Mr. Skeffington further, and he looked to his sire for help in comprehending what was happening. "Father!"

His lordship was also struggling to understand and looked at his wife with a sort of curious disinterest. "I suppose this was about your affair."

Mrs. Otley, who had been staring at her old school friend with horror and confusion, for the declaration of guilt had been so blandly stated it seemed like a prank, convulsed with shock at this comment. "*What?*"

Bea thought it was a little hypocritical for a woman who had been conducting a love affair with her husband's former steward to be surprised or appalled that he in turn had been trysting with her friend.

Her daughter thought so too, for Emily immediately rose to her feet, pointed a finger at her mother and said with ringing condemnation, "You drove him into her arms with your liaison with Mr. Wilson."

Aunt Vera gasped to discover how much salacious behavior had been going on under her nose, while Nuneaton murmured, "Mr. X."

With her son taking no comfort in her presence, her ladyship walked around the couch to console Emily. "Oh, you poor dear," she said softly, wrapping her arms around the girl. "What a burden you have been carrying. No, don't think that. Never think that. Indeed, your mama did everything she could to keep him out of them. To his credit, your father resisted my overtures for a good many weeks, preferring to keep his birds-of-paradise a little farther from his own nest."

Miss Otley, shrugging free of her hostess, stared aghast. "You seduced him?"

"I had to. 'Twas almost a moral imperative. He was engaged to me before he threw me over for your mama, and I could not let that stand without reprisal. It was merely a matter of finding the right moment to strike, and it finally arrived when East India Company took over his poppy fields and bankrupted him. Yes, Amelia," she said to her friend, who'd gasped in surprise, "I know your husband's so-called spice-trading business was really a disreputable opium-smuggling venture. I've known it since the very beginning, first because I would never consent to marry a man I hadn't investigated thoroughly and then because I made it a particular hobby of mine to stay abreast of all the dealings of the cad who threw me over. That is how I knew Thomas had swindled my son. I waited until he'd lost everything before showing my interest because it would allow me to brandish my very great fortune most effectively. It had come down to dowries, you see, all those years ago. Despite the vast buckets of money he had made in India, he still wanted more, and your mother had the larger one. She knew precisely how to sway him with it."

"I did not sway him," Mrs. Otley said. "He chose me out of love."

As far as protests went, it was not the most convincing one, certainly not to her daughter, who shuddered with tears at the chilling indifference her parents seemed to feel for each other and dashed out of the room. Her misery felt so acute, Bea had to smother the compulsion to run after her and resolved to seek her out later. Perhaps witnessing firsthand the destruction superficiality could work would persuade her to cultivate a little depth and aspire to more than merely relying on her beauty to achieve things in life.

Aunt Vera watched Lady Skeffington air ancient grievances with astonished wonder, her eyes wide, her mouth agape, her head darting from one old school friend to the other. Every so often she turned to Beatrice and glared at her with unarticulated urgency, as if expecting her niece to somehow bring the ugly scene to an end. You're the one who started it, her expression seemed to say.

Beatrice, who wanted to be flattered by her aunt's apparent belief in her preternatural abilities, stared back helplessly, while Mrs. Otley contemplated the door through which her daughter had just run. Her brow knit as she debated the wisdom of following her distraught progeny.

Lady Skeffington, caring nothing for the demands of motherhood, commanded her full attention. "What I find particularly interesting is that Thomas's qualms about sullying his own nest did not extend to my son. He had no compunction about fleecing a boy who had been like a nephew to him for thousands of pounds."

Although affecting outrage over his wife's scandalous behavior to comfort his son was beyond Lord Skeffington's ability and interest, he glowered at her now, disgusted that she could be intimate with a man so blatantly bereft of morals. "You were always an appalling judge of character."

Rather than angrily defend herself against the charge, she conceded its validity and apologized for not grasping how thoroughly unscrupulous Mr. Otley was before engaging in the affair. "You understand my fury, then, when I discovered the truth. At first I assumed it was an oversight, that he hadn't intended to cheat my son with his fraudulent scheme. I assumed there were two funds—one legitimate, one fraudulent—and he simply put Andrew's contribution in the wrong envelope or column in his ledger. I confronted him on the matter in the library, where we had arranged for an intimate rendezvous away from the prying eyes of my guests, and he freely admitted that there had been no mistake. Skeffington had plenty of blunt, he said, and would hardly miss such a trivial amount. He resisted all attempts to convince him to return the money, and then he walked away, laughing at my foolishness for thinking my son deserved special consideration because of the nature of our relationship. I could not let that stand, either, without reprisal."

Despite the many explanations his mother had given for her behavior, Mr. Skeffington's understanding of events was no more keen than before. "But killing him?"

Perceiving her son's distress, Lady Skeffington immediately assured him it was an accident. "You know I would never intentionally harm anyone. I merely struck him in the back of the head with the candlestick to get his attention, for I couldn't believe he would have the audacity to walk away from me in the middle of an argument, and so blithely too, as if I were a bird chirping outside his window. I must have misjudged the force I used, although, to be completely candid, I suspect the problem was with his skull, which was unexpectedly soft. Are all skulls such fragile things? Once I heard the crack, I knew the damage had been quite grievous, and it seemed kinder to stay the course than to let him live with a hideous debility. I suspect the damage would have diminished his ability to think effectively."

Although her ladyship described these events calmly, her depiction agitated her listeners, who all reacted with various degrees of horror. Aunt Vera let out a strangled cry and rushed to embrace her daughter, whom she considered too delicate to be subjected to such depictions of vicious brutality. Flora was pale but composed and directed her mother's attention to Russell, whose face had turned startlingly white at the use of the word *crack*. Amersham seemed similarly unsettled by his hostess's dispassionate account of ending a man's life, and he leaned forward, resting his hip against the settee as if determined to hold himself upright. Even Nuneaton blanched at the depravity.

Only Skeffington greeted the report with equanimity, dipping his head in a nod of understanding at the predicament in which his wife had unexpectedly found herself. His lordship's easy acceptance of the wildly dismaying situation horrified his son, who, finding no indication of humanity in either parent, began to cry in earnest.

Kesgrave, who had stood by so silently during the unfolding horror Bea had actually forgotten about him, now stepped forward with a speaking glance to Nuneaton. Comprehending at once, his friend walked over to the devastated young man, laid a hand on his shoulder and murmured softly in his ear. Mr. Skeffington nodded and allowed his cousin to lead him out of the room. Next, the duke looked at the Runner, who, also responding to an unspoken cue, came forward from the shadowy corner to escort Lady Skeffington to the local magistrate.

When the officer from London took out the handcuffs, Skeffington swore and said, "Damn your impertinence, Kesgrave! Not in my house."

The duke shook his head slightly and the shackles went away. But he could not be convinced, despite his lordship's threats, pleas and curses, to dispense with the Runner altogether.

"Mr. Otley's life, however repellant it might have been, is not a trivial matter," Kesgrave said soberly.

Skeffington, who had seemed indifferent to his wife's fate only a little while ago, bristled at the idea of Kesgrave deciding it and immediately rang for the butler to get his coat. His wife would not see the magistrate without him!

"Do not worry, my dear, we'll have this mess sorted out before dinner," he said with a cool look at the duke, as if challenging him to disagree. "Gosport won't refer your case to the Crown courts. I know him well and am confident he will be reasonable. If you recall, he accompanies me to my hunting box every first of October to shoot pheasant."

Kesgrave refrained from comment and watched quietly as the Bow Street Runner escorted Lady Skeffington out of the room in the company of her husband, who was so unconcerned about their errand he was reminiscing fondly about the previous year's triumph.

"It was four pounds," he said proudly, "and at least forty-two inches long. I say 'at least' because I believe Gosport plucked a few feathers from its tail to make my accomplishment seem less impressive."

As they turned left into the hallway, Lady Skeffington could be heard advising her husband not to mention the bird until after they had secured her release.

Long after the sound of their voices faded, the room remained silent, for nobody knew what to say. The scene they had just witnessed had the stark unreality of a play, and to discuss it at all felt too much like reviewing a theatrical performance, a prospect that seemed hideously frivolous to Bea and, presumably, the rest of the company.

But someone had to say something or they would still be sitting in the drawing room when Lord Skeffington returned with or without his wife.

The unpleasant thought occurred to Bea as her whole body ached—head pounding, cuts stinging, muscles throbbing, stomach growling—now that the pressure of identifying Mr. Otley's murderer had passed. It seemed

excessively mundane to desire food after so many unpleasant revelations, and yet there was nothing she could do
about it.

And, indeed, there really *was* nothing she could do
about it. She was a guest of the Skeffingtons, and her hosts
had just left the hall to explain to the county's magistrate
why Mr. Otley's ruthless slaying at the hands of her ladyship didn't quite rise to the level of murder.

How very ironic, Beatrice thought without humor,
that the woman who had only the day before advised her
young guests to consider the comfort of others to be of
paramount importance had managed to create the single
most uncomfortable experience possible for her visitors.
Her definition of *comfort* veered wildly from the standard
one generally agreed upon by the populace.

"We will eat in the breakfast room," Kesgrave announced, "something informal and simple."

Although the duke spoke to the room in general, Bea
realized when she looked up that he was talking directly to
her. She nodded in gratitude.

Aunt Vera sighed, as if too tired to contemplate food,
then straightened her shoulders and stood up. "An admirable plan. I will arrange it with the housekeeper right now."

Mrs. Otley opened her mouth to volunteer as well,
and immediately shut it when she saw the venomous look
her friend sent her. With as much dignity as she could
muster, she excused herself to go comfort her daughter.

One by one, the remaining occupants of the drawing
room dispersed, eager to leave the site of so much misery.
Amersham claimed he had a letter to write, and Russell,
lacking the imagination of the slightly older gentleman,
said the same thing a few minutes later.

"To my father," he added. "He invited me to a prize
fight in Guilford. I have been remiss in responding."

Kesgrave excused himself next, dashing Beatrice's
hopes of getting a moment alone with him. She didn't
know what she wished to gain from such an encounter, as,

with Lady Skeffington's surprising confession, their business had officially concluded.

Their association was at an end.

And still Bea waited with unbearable anticipation for a sign that he, too, desired an opportunity to talk. She thought it might happen at dinner when she found herself sitting next to him for the simple collation of mutton and meat pies. But the conversation at the table was subdued, with Aunt Vera singlehandedly keeping up the chatter with insipid observations about the weather and the meal and the enduring popularity of pomona green.

Kesgrave, however, did not talk to her during dinner. Indeed, he spoke few words to anyone, and watching him sullenly examine his fellow guests, Bea found herself wanting to hurl a dinner roll at him just to elicit a lecture on the throwing arch of flour-based projectiles.

It was an unpleasantly familiar sensation, and she wondered if she would always be plagued by a compulsion to assault him with food.

Thurman offered the men port, but nobody was inclined to linger after the meal and by nine o'clock, the members of the sad, strange little party had retired to their rooms. A few minutes later, a knock sounded at her door, and although she knew it was impossible for her visitor to be Kesgrave, she was deeply disappointed when she opened the door and saw her cousin.

Flora, who had shown very little interest in Bea for her previous nineteen years, was suddenly full of admiration for her skills and deductive powers and ability to escape ramshackle sheds in the middle of fields.

"You are remarkable," Flora said.

Bea had never expected to hear such words pass her cousin's lips in reference to herself—to describe a French ruffle, yes, to be sure—and simpered at the praise. She felt genuinely torn over what to do, for as much as she wanted her cousin to stay and compliment her, she also wanted her to go and leave her in solitude to wait for Kesgrave.

What if he was at that very moment peering into her room from the tree outside her window?

She glanced at the window and saw nothing but branches blowing gently in the light wind.

Flora stayed for almost half an hour, helping to change the bandages on Bea's hands with surprising gentleness and asking all sorts of questions about the investigation with thoughtful astuteness. She expressed amazement at her cousin's ability to keep a cool head when trapped inside the dilapidated shed and marveled at her boldness in accusing their host right there in her own drawing room.

Bea appreciated her enthusiasm but laughed uncomfortably, for she never did get around to making the accusation. Her ladyship had taken care of that part for her.

After Flora left, Bea picked up *The Vicar of Wakefield* and tried to finish the last few chapters. She kept turning the page as if she was making progress, but she was paying little attention to the ridiculous trials of the Primrose family. Rather, she was darting her eyes every few minutes at the window to see if the duke had appeared.

An hour later, she gave up on the book, blew out the candle and laid her head down on the pillow to go to sleep. Worn out from the day's exertions, she tucked the blanket around her, rolled onto her side and watched the window.

Beatrice fell asleep waiting for the duke.

CHAPTER FOURTEEN

Typically, when Bea's aunt announced they were leaving on a journey at an appointed time—say, nine o'clock or half past noon—her party didn't actually depart until an hour or two later. This morning, however, she was at the door promptly at ten and impatiently tapping her foot while Bea dawdled over her luggage.

"Just another moment, please, to make sure I have everything," she said, opening her small case and moving items around as if looking for something. "I can't find my book about Viscount Townshend. Ordinarily I would consider it a donation to the house, but it's from the lending library and must be returned."

Bea shifted the same shawl from one side to the other three times without even looking. Rather, her gaze was focused on the door to his lordship's study, behind which Kesgrave conferred with Skeffington. The pair had been in there for almost an hour, and she refused to leave until they emerged. Her aunt's goal was in fact the opposite. She wanted to be in her coach and on the way to Welldale House before Skeffington appeared to make an awkward situation even more uncomfortable. As it was, he had lingered over a cup of coffee at breakfast while his guests stared silently at their eggs. Either indifferent to their discomfort or oblivious to it, he rattled on about how the matter would be cleared up just as soon as his friend Gosport could be made to understand the actual events. The magistrate had been confused by the story Lady Skeffington had told and had asked her to remain behind—under his aegis, of course, not in the county goal—while he deciphered the report.

A proper gentleman with a sense of decency would have sequestered himself in his study until after everyone left, Aunt Vera said. If someone must be inconsiderate in this situation, let it be the guests, who would depart without politely thanking their host for his hospitality. Should any of them feel so inclined, they could always send missives expressing their effusive appreciation later.

Speaking of discourteous behavior, Bea thought as she glared at the closed door, it was beyond rude of Kesgrave to keep his own servants waiting. His valet and his coachman had been ready to leave for more than an hour.

"Isn't it that there?" Flora asked.

Bea, reluctantly pulling her eyes from their target, glanced at her cousin with confusion. "Excuse me?"

"The book you're looking for," Flora said helpfully. "Isn't it right there?"

Sure enough, the corner of *Viscount Townshend: A Life* was peeking out from under her shawl. Darn it. She had moved the silk shawl around one too many times.

"Is it?" she asked, squinting her eyes as if to see it more clearly. "You're right. It is. Thank you."

"Very good, Flora," her aunt said with a relieved smile. "I can see no reason to remain any longer."

Bea thought quickly and reacted with haste. "My earrings! The pearls left to me by my mother. I think they're on the night table."

"They're in your ears, silly," Flora said.

Aunt Vera shook her head with concern. "There's little wonder why you are so discombobulated, my dear. The ordeal you have been through in the past few days has been so overwhelming, it's a marvel that you are even still standing. We will, of course, discuss your penchant for investigating things that should be of no concern of yours when we get into the coach. My, how lucky we are to have an entire day's drive ahead of us to properly address the matter."

Flora made a face and announced she'd rather read Bea's book on crop rotation than participate in such a discussion.

"Nevertheless, it's a lesson we could all benefit from," her mother said.

Realizing she could procrastinate no longer, Bea sighed heavily and picked up her bag. She didn't know what she hoped to accomplish in seeing Kesgrave one last time, anyway. The opportunity for a private conversation had long since passed. Even if he had appeared at breakfast and sat down in the chair directly next to her, he would have talked of innocuous things. He would not have praised her cleverness in figuring out Lady Skeffington was the killer or complimented her on how well she had revealed her discovery. He certainly wouldn't have suggested they renew their acquaintance when they both returned to London for the season.

Accepting the futility, Bea sighed heavily and resolved to stop putting off the inevitable. If she was to be subjected to a multihour lecture on how to respond to a bloody corpse, she might as well embrace it as her fate. Fighting it would only make it worse in the end.

Bea bravely stood up and lifted her small suitcase. "Very well, I'm ready."

At that moment, the door to Skeffington's study opened.

Aunt Vera tensed and looked down the corridor toward the hall's entrance, trying to decide, it seemed to her niece, if she could run out to the driveway before her host noticed her.

She was not so fortunate.

"Mrs. Hyde-Clare," his lordship called as he walked toward her, "I was afraid you had left without a proper goodbye. Lady Skeffington will be desolate she missed you. Allow me to wish you a safe journey in her stead."

"Yes, of course, thank you," she said, coloring slightly at the mention of her friend's name. It seemed strange to accept the glad tiding of a murderess, even in absentia. Immediately, she turned to the duke. "Thank you, your grace, for taking charge last night when everything—" Realizing she had been about to make reference to the evening's dreadfulness, she broke off abruptly and changed course. "That is, thank you for your attentions to my niece. She is very grateful."

Although Beatrice did not appreciate the way her aunt reached for her like a prop in a melodrama, she stepped forward with an agreeable smile and said, "Indeed, your grace, I'm especially grateful for your attention to detail. HMS *Audacious*, HMS *Majestic*, HMS *Goliath*."

Taking her niece's seemingly nonsensical answer as further proof her wits had been undermined by the taxing events of the past few days, Aunt Vera giggled nervously and apologized to the duke. "I worry that exposure to Mr. Otley's corpse as well as the terror of escaping from the shack and the pressure of exposing a murder has permanently damaged her brain," she said, then turned an intolerable shade of red as she realized Lord Skeffington was standing only a few feet away. "I mean, exposing a dreadful accident."

Kesgrave's serious expression lightened, and although Bea couldn't tell for sure which had amused him more—her aunt's antics or her own provocation—she was fairly certain it was the latter when he said, "HMS *Goliath*, HMS *Audacious*, HMS *Majestic*."

Skeffington nodded in approval and tried to reprise their earlier discussion about the Battle of the Nile, this time overestimating the number of British ships involved by six rather than underestimating it by three. It was many days, however, and one dead body since their first discussion of the topic, and the duke had no interest in making convivial small talk with his host, a fact revealed by his insistence that the famous naval encounter was actually called the Battle of Rosetta.

His lordship, surprised and perplexed by the duke's sudden ignorance, scampered off to get a book from the library to prove the correct name.

As soon as Skeffington was gone, Kesgrave said, "It is I who must thank Miss Hyde-Clare for allowing me to assist in her investigation of Mr. Otley's death. I would never go so far as to say it was a pleasure, as much of the experience was horrendous, but I will not pretend there weren't moments I enjoyed."

Aunt Vera could not have been more delighted if the Duke of Kesgrave had led her niece out onto the dance floor at Almack's. She blushed and stammered and simpered and finally said, "Oh, your grace, you are so very kind. I do hope when we return to London you will show Beatrice more of that kindness as I'm sure her popularity would increase with just a small show of interest on your part."

And with that one horrifying statement, Aunt Vera managed to accomplish what a bloody corpse, a ramshackle shed and a delusional peeress could not: break Bea's spirit.

Obviously, Bea harbored no illusions about her position in society, and she certainly understood her lowly status in relation to Kesgrave's exalted one. And yet there was something breathtakingly brutal about the way her aunt reminded them both of her inferiority.

Bea had not forgotten it, of course, for her unimportance had been impressed upon her by providence at the tender age of five and reinforced at regular intervals by her family. But the camaraderie that had sprung up between her and the duke during their investigation had felt so genuine and sincere, she'd almost believed they were equals.

Fortunately, Aunt Vera was there to keep her in line with a simple request delivered with just the right mix of hope and supplication, as if her niece was so beneath a duke's touch she had to beg him to show interest.

Bea did not want his charity.

To say that, of course, would be to sound churlish, and it would only draw stark attention to what they all knew to be true: She actually did need his charity if she was ever going to be anything more than an overlooked mouse on the farthest fringe of society. To agree with her aunt would only expose her to further humiliation. To walk away without responding at all would make it appear as if she could not cope with the situation.

With no good options, Bea stood there silently and listened as Kesgrave graciously promised to call on them when they were all in town, a pledge that delighted Russell, who hesitantly suggested a morning ride in Hyde Park. The duke, evidently in a benign mood, also agreed to that, and Bea waited irritably for Flora to make a request of him as well. Her cousin, however, said goodbye to his grace without seeking a favor.

Next it was Beatrice's turn to bid Kesgrave farewell, but her mind was curiously blank of all useful thought. Although she was the same person who had greeted him with aplomb as he stepped from a tree branch into her bedchamber, she felt ineffably altered by her aunt's comment, as if something inside her had been dulled.

'Twas almost as though, standing on the threshold of Lakeview Hall about to return to her family's home in Sussex, she had reverted to the person she had been when they'd arrived. How clearly she could remember that Bea—the Bea who sputtered, the Bea who stammered, the Bea who faltered and stumbled and tripped over her own words and lapsed into silence rather than misspeak.

A pitiable creature, to be sure.

No, Bea thought, rejecting that abject being, that earlier version of herself, as her shoulders stiffened with rage at the years she had passed almost cowering from her own shadow. She would not go back.

This house was not a magical castle in a child's fairy story with fire-breathing dragons and hidden secret passageways. She did not have to be within its confines to be the new Bea, the better Bea, the Bea who spoke up for herself and defended her point of view and identified a murderess and clawed her way out of a dilapidated shed in the middle of a field.

Determinedly, she lifted her head and raised her eyes to meet the duke's, which were curiously bright and astoundingly blue. "Until next time, your grace. You bring the pedantry. I'll bring the dinner rolls," she said provokingly, and her aunt gasped in horror.

Kesgrave's lips twitched, making it clear that he didn't have to understand her words to comprehend their meaning. "Until next time, Miss Hyde-Clare."

"She meant pleasantries, your grace. Pleasantry, not pedantry," Aunt Vera insisted on an awkward laugh that quickly became a cough of concern when she heard Skeffington call out to Kesgrave from the staircase. Hastily, she added, "We must go at once, while the weather is still good. I believe there's concern it might rain, as the clouds are thick. Do make our apologies to our host."

The swiftness of their departure contrasted sharply with the slowness of their progress, as the sky did indeed open up soon after and make the road muddy and difficult to cross. Aunt Vera didn't mind, for the extra travel time provided her with the opportunity she needed to educate her niece on proper behavior. Young ladies did not stare openly at the shattered skulls of fellow guests, and they most certainly did not provoke their hostesses into confessing to vile murders.

On and on she went, specifying the many ways her niece's conduct had fallen short of accepted standards during their stay at Lakeview Hall. She fussed over minor mistakes, lingered over small peccadilloes and heaped generous disapproval on her niece's head. She was meticulous, particular, schoolmarmish, and mean.

Despite it all, Bea smiled the whole way home.

ABOUT THE AUTHOR

Lynn Messina is the author of more than a dozen novels, including the best-selling *Fashionistas,* which has been translated into 16 languages. Her essays have appeared in *Self, American Baby* and the Modern Love column in the *New York Times,* and she's a regular contributor to the *Times* Motherlode blog. She lives in New York City with her sons.